TH SILENT VILLAGE

THE SILENT VILLAGE

Merryn Corcoran

UMBRIA PRESS

Published by Umbria Press
SW15 5DP
www.umbriapress.co.uk

UK edition ISBN 978 0 9573641 2 7
New Zealand edition ISBN 978 0 473 26437 6
eBook ISBN 978 0 9927556 0 7

www.merryncorcoran.com
Find Merryn Corcoran on Facebook at
www.facebook.com/merryncorcoranauthor

This book is dedicated to the memory of the following families from Castel Vittorio in Nervia Valley, Liguria, Italy. 30 innocent civilians ranging in age from 2 to 72 years old were needlessly massacred by German soldiers in 1944 while they gardened at their allotment at Gordale:

ALLAUMA

BALBIS

FAISSOLA

MILLO

MORO

ORENGO

PASTORE

PEVERELLO

PICCONE

REBARDO

TORRE

Acknowledgments

My heartfelt gratitude and thanks to the special friends who supported me in my research and read for me during the writing of my novel: Michelle Amass, Dame Pieter Stewart, Mary Ciurlionis, Pam Lindsay, Felicity Price, Marilyn Morse, Robyn Opie, Amelia and Tom Stafford, Jeannine Verrando, Sally Coleman and Mark Rennie.

To the professionals who tolerated and guided me to the path of publishing: Anna Rogers, Zoe King, Joanna Swainson and Louise Millar.

My sincere thanks to Alan Gordon Walker for believing in me.

To Malcolm Lakin and Sam Britten for their photos.

To the authors who's words of encouragement meant so much: PD James, Santa Montefiore, Anne Dunhill, Jenny Patrick and Felicity Price.

To the Italian people of Castel Vittorio and Pigna especially Claudio, Silvio and Gloria Lanteri and Marisa De Montis.

I am deeply indebted to Sylvie Reiss for giving me her story.

None of this would have been possible for me without the inspiration of my exceptional daughter Emily and my tolerant husband Tim. I am ever grateful for their constant love and their belief in me.

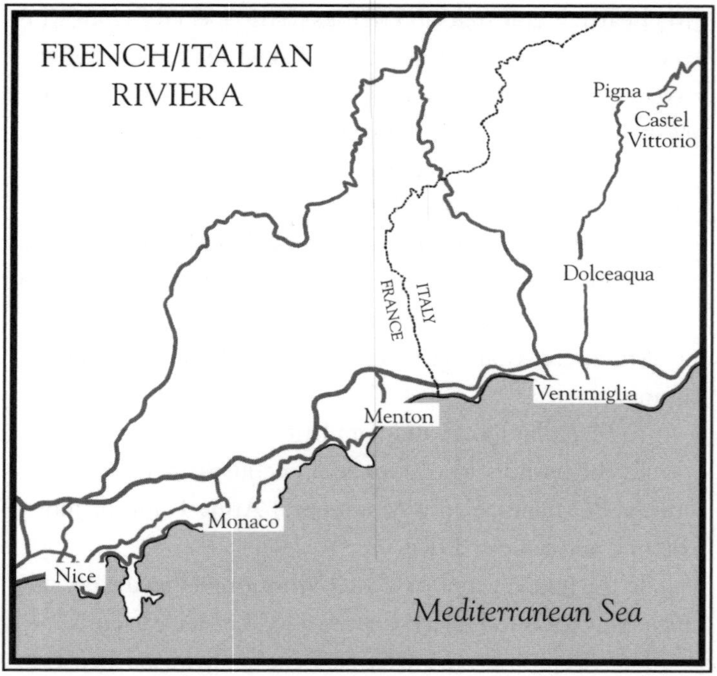
FRENCH/ITALIAN
RIVIERA
Pigna
Castel
Vittorio
Dolceaqua
FRANCE
ITALY
Ventimiglia
Menton
Monaco
Nice
Mediterranean Sea

Prologue

"I don't believe it! Mum you were adopted! How could you have kept this from us?" Sarah sat rigid, focussing on the familiarity of the elegant silver candelabra as she grappled to respond to her daughter. Dam Hugh! Opening his big mouth – it was typical of her overbearing brother.

"I'm, I'm sorry." she stammered.

"It's okay Mum, don't cry, just, tell us about it?"

Sarah's son, Nicholas had leant over and laid his arm protectively around his mother's trembling shoulders. Hugh and his wife sat riveted to their seats as the drama Hugh had provoked, unfolded. Then Sarah finally found her voice.

"Okay, I'm going to tell you, but Flo be quiet, just this once and listen! First, your Uncle Hugh had no right to announce this, as it's none of his business. Secondly adoption is a complex matter and it was MY adoption not my children's, nor my brother's. So how I've dealt with it is my business".

"But Mum..."

"No Florence but nothing. It may take me a minute to compose myself but please shut up and let me get on with it."

Sarah turned to face both her children who sat to one side of her at the table. "From as young as I can remember, I always knew I was adopted. Mum and Dad regularly referred to me as their 'special adopted daughter'. In retrospect I can see my parents handled it all very well. But in reality, I didn't fully comprehend what the word 'adopted' meant 'till I was about ten years old. We had a new girl join our class half way through term, and the class busybody informed us all the next day that this girl was 'adopted'. She spat the words out as if it was a contagious disease and I felt so humiliated. When I arrived home that day I demanded that Mum tell me what it meant. She gently explained I was really hers and Dads but that another lady had given birth to me. The tainted words of the stupid girl at school were all consuming; I demanded Mum and Dad never mention the word 'adopted' again and I guess from that point on I wrongly embraced the shame."

Sarah paused, anxiously rubbed her hands together, and then nervously pressed them up to her mouth.

"Did Dad know?" Florence gingerly queried.

"Yes, and he encouraged me to tell you both, but I wouldn't ever consider it. However, once he knew his cancer was terminal he pushed the matter."

"Rightfully so," Hugh arrogantly interjected, assuming he'd gained the sympathy of the room. They all ignored him.

"Dad's been dead for eighteen months! What's held you back, Mother?"

"There no need for sarcasm Flo, if you must know I agreed to Uncle Hugh's invitation tonight, as after dinner I intended to discuss it with you; just the three of us that is." She shot a look at her brother. Nicholas took the floor. He was the opposite to his fiery artistic sister. Like his late father, he tended to be methodical, pragmatic and quietly spoken.

"Mum, I think once we all calm down, I'm sure we can live with this, even if it is a little late in the piece. Uncle Hugh is correct. I've been diagnosed with diabetes, and have been asked if it's hereditary, so it's a very good reason for me to have known that you were adopted."

He spoke without malice. "I'm truly sorry Nick." Sarah cleared her throat, raised her voice a notch and straightened in her seat.

"But may I finish please? The grief counsellor I've been seeing has suggested I make a few life changes and the reason I've been with Uncle Hugh today was to go through our parent's old documents, as I've decided to try and find out who my birth parents were."

"Go on Mum, don't stop now! Did you find anything?" Flo was captivated.

"Hugh, do you mind bringing the file in please?" Sarah's tone had softened as she spoke to her brother. As Sarah handed her son the file, he warmly recognised his grandfather's neat hand writing. On the cover, it read 'Sarah's Adoption'.

"Turn to the last page." Sarah's voice had tempered. Flo stood behind Nick, both children fervently reading through the old document. The last page was obviously a copied birth certificate.

Sarah Maria Orengo
Date of Birth: 31/05/1955
Place of birth: (blacked out)
Birth registered: Golders Green, North London
Mother: (blacked out and DECEASED hand written in capitals)
Father: Mario Orengo.

PART ONE
ALLESSIA

Menton, French Riviera, 1944-1945

One

"What were those girls up to now?" Their giggles sounded as noisy as a flock of seagulls. Hopscotch was meant to tire them, not stretch their vocal cords. Allessia rested back on the park bench. She closed her eyes to avoid squinting into the low Mediterranean sun and seized the moment to indulge selfishly in her own thoughts.

Old Jean Claude was perched on the adjoining bench watching the pétanque game that his friends were playing close to the young girls hop scotch. He'd mumbled something.

"What are you saying Jean Claude? I can't quite hear you!"

Edging across so he was directly next to Allessia, he pushed his white garlic-scented, moustache close to her ear.

"If I were you I'd be very wary of that Marseilles farmer who's taken over the property in front of yours. They say he bribed officials to get it at that price, so he'll be looking at yours next."

"Thanks Jean Claude, don't worry, my Joseph has been keeping an eye on him."

Attempting to mask her anxiety, she gave the old man a goodbye peck on his ruddy, wrinkled cheek then quickly moved over to wind up the hopscotch game.

"Mama, Mama please can I have a gelato? Please, please."

Allessia's daughter Sylvie jumped up and down like an excited kitten as they left the pétanque terrain. Sylvie was eight years old, an only child with dark curly hair and large brown eyes; happiness and curiosity radiated from her perfectly oval face. She clutched her mother's hand tightly, but quickly dropped it once they were in sight of Giovanni's Gelato Parlour.

Giovanni's had been selling ice cream in Menton since Allessia first used to visit, nearly twenty years previously. Like Giovanni, Allessia was born and brought up in Italy, just across the border from Menton. She met her French husband Joseph Reiss at the border market when she was just 15 years old and for her it was love at first sight. Joseph and his family were Jewish and it had taken two years of family arguments before both sets of parents had eventually conceded to the couples mixed religious marriage.

It used to be so simple. The border was just a formality. While the French believed their wine was the best, there was no doubt that the Italians always made the best gelato. Why should it all have to be different because those fascists in Berlin and Rome said so?

"Bongiorno Giovanni. The usual for my little one, please."

"Ah! Allessia you look as beautiful as always."

"And Giovanni you're as charming as always, and, before you ask, just one scoop!" As Allessia followed Sylvie out of the parlour Giovanni lifted the counter lid, and sidled up beside her, his kind, wrinkled eyes full of concern.

"My dearest friend, things are not looking good, many of our Jewish friends have left town, you should all be on your way."

Allessia prickled defensively. "My Joseph has the view that most of what they are saying is just hearsay or rumour."

"I pray to the Blessed Virgin that is true." Allessia gave a forced smile at Giovanni's parting comment and then took her daughter's free hand as they walked briskly up the street.

Allessia's looks were those of a typical northern Italian woman. She stood a mere five feet two inches tall, her long black hair was loosely braided and her deep brown eyes complemented her sun-tinted glossy olive complexion. She'd spent the first seventeen years of her life cocooned with her close knit family in the Italian hill top medieval village of Castel Vittorio. Since then Joseph had influenced every part of her life. To please him, the only make-up she wore was Rubinstein red lipstick which accentuated her full, sensual lips. The last nine years under his influence had added the extra polished veneer of French chic to her naturally striking appearance.

The family villa was only a ten-minute walk from Giovanni's. It nestled in the midst of a large garden, up a gentle slope, with colourful views across Menton to the sea. Sylvie had finished her ice cream and skipped ahead arriving first at the ornate wrought-iron gate. It creaked loudly, as with the full force of her small frame she struggled to push it open.

The fragrant path that led from the gate to the family villa and their small hotel was Allessia's pride. Her contribution to her husband's family home and business had been lovingly to design and plant a welcoming perfumed approach. The small eight-room hotel shared the pathway and sat just behind their villa. The grounds had been neat and tidy when she first arrived, but the gardens had lacked structure. Placing tubs of lavender and citronella, interspersed with exotic flowering succulents bordering the path, Allessia had managed to create a grand impression – more than the property actually delivered. Climbing jasmine clung to the fence beside the path, emitting its delicious fragrance, whilst neatly clipped boxed hedging gave a feeling of structure to the borders of the property.

"Happy Birthday Allessia" her mother-in-law, Ruth, greeted her with a big hug.

"Thank you. I didn't expect anyone to remember considering what we're all going through."

"On that subject, where's the Little One?"

"In the back garden, in her secret hiding place, with her baby." They both smiled.

"I think it best to wait 'till after dinner to give her the bad news. Let her enjoy the cake first."

"Oh Ruth, you shouldn't have gone to any trouble, but, as you have, did you use the last of the sacred chocolate?" Ruth was reassured to see a brief return of her daughter-in-law's dry sense of humour. Allessia adored Ruth, who was a woman who inspired confidence. She always stood tall and, although matronly she was self-assured. Her pure white hair never publicly left the constraints of the severe bun, tied at the nape of her neck. In contrast her faded eyes still radiated happiness from behind her wire-rimmed spectacles, and her soft mouth was rarely without the warmth of her generous smile.

The door flew open and Sylvie held up her bedraggled looking doll.

"I kept the secret Grandmama! I never told Mama and look, my baby is all dressed for the birthday party. I can't wait for the cake; please say it's chocolate. Are Gramps and Gran Orengo going to bring Mario with them? I can't wait to play with him again." Her words spilled over themselves.

"I'm sorry Little One; Mario won't be coming this time. Gramps is coming alone and will be leaving early in the morning. Please go up, have your bath then you can put your special party dress on."

"It's not fair!" She stamped her small foot and stormed off.

The Reiss villa wasn't as grand as some of its neighbours, but the rooms were large enough, stylishly decorated, predominantly in the favoured colours of neighbouring Provence, pastel blue and soft shades of lemon. Downstairs was a salon, a large kitchen and a washing room. Upstairs there was a bathroom and four large bedrooms, three of which enjoyed sea views.

The villa had always basked in loving family warmth, but the divided opinions had soured the once, comfortably, bountiful atmosphere and Allessia's dread of the following day dampened the joy she normally would have felt on her birthday.

"Happy Birthday beautiful girl." Allessia's father-in-law Daniel joined them. He handed her a bunch of tiny white and lemon daisies tied with some old string.

His six foot two inches towered over Allessia in giant fashion. He was extremely tall for a French man, and totally bald with a perfectly shaped, bronzed head that shone above a deeply furrowed brow. His eyebrows were grey and bushy like two fat furry caterpillars; the butt of many family jokes.

"Oh Daniel thank you, I'm going to miss you both so much."

He took the posy from her hands, laid it on the table and pulled her to him in a tight hug. The three of them sat together as Ruth poured out hot chicory essence which was what passed for coffee. As he unconsciously stroked his eyebrows Daniel asked Allessia about her day and how she thought Sylvie would react to the news.

"Come on Daniel, what else are you really trying to ask me? I know you well enough to recognise the signs of your daughter-in-law diplomacy. Ask what you like."

"Well my dear, I don't want to ask you anything, rather say something. There may not be another chance after tonight.

When Joseph first wanted to marry you it wasn't that we didn't like you, or that we're particularly religious, but our hesitation was that mixed marriages can be so difficult, not so much you being Italian, more us being Jewish. We both want you to know you are the best addition to this family that we could have ever wished for. Whatever happens, please know how much we love you."

Allessia, humbled by his words took both her in-laws' hands, giving them an affectionate squeeze. "You didn't need to say that. I know you love me, but thank you – it means a lot to hear it. Let's just get through our last night together as happily as we can."

Allessia had excused herself to tidy up before dinner. She sat in front of the dressing table brushing her hair, attempting some enthusiasm into dressing up a little. As she scrutinised her face in the mirror she felt a sense of loss for her youth. She could see that more laughter lines had made an appearance around her eyes and the dimples on either side of her smile had deepened, well on their way to becoming wrinkles and regularly she found herself plucking out the odd grey hair. At least she hadn't put on any weight. Once she'd applied her signature red lipstick she felt a little more confident. She offered herself a brief smile in the mirror before heading back downstairs.

"Sylvie, you may get the special cutlery set out tonight and give each piece a shine before you place them." Allessia had tried to keep things as normal as possible. They'd all gathered in the kitchen, the true heart of their home, the mouth-watering smell of fresh baking pervaded the room.

"Yes Mama, but what icing is Gran going to put on

the cake?" Sylvie was washed and dressed in a pretty pink pinafore dress only worn on special occasions.

"The birthday cake only comes out when all the main meal is eaten. You'll see the icing then. So you had better be hungry tonight."

"Where's the birthday girl?" Joseph called out as he walked in with a huge bunch of lilies. "Happy birthday my Darling" he laid the flowers on the sideboard then kissed his wife passionately.

"That's yukky Papa. You're being so sloppy" Sylvie shouted as she squeezed between her parents' embrace.

"Okay a big kiss for you too my angel in pink." Joseph swung her up and gently planted a kiss on her nose. Allessia's husband was tall, handsome and rugged. His rapidly receding hairline resembled his father. But the similarity ended there – unlike his father, Joseph's was a little like an ostrich. He didn't want to believe the German propaganda and was reluctant to leave his family home and business.

At around six p. m. the old Orengo truck pulled up outside. Allessia quickly slipped out of the kitchen so she could have a few words in private with her father.

"Papa, is everything organised for the morning?" Her father lovingly embraced her with both arms and whispered his reply to her in Italian.

"You don't have to do everything your husband says, you and the little one can come tomorrow as well. Your Mama and I only want to know you're safe."

As Allessia inhaled the familiar tobacco fragrance that clung to her father's clothes and heard the soothing lilt of her native tongue, she experienced a brief reprieve.

"Papa I've been over it all a hundred times in my mind

and I've decided we must stay together; I think Joseph will be safer if he's with a Catholic wife."

Her father Luigi Orengo was only forty-eight years old, but hours spent working outdoors coupled with the stress of the war had emphasised his bad posture and aged him prematurely. He stood only two inches taller than Allessia but despite everything he still had a full head of rich brown hair. The rest of the extended Reiss family greeted Luigi at the door. He wearily took a seat at the table, then took a large envelope out of his tatty satchel and kissed his granddaughter as he handed it to her.

"Look Mama look! Mario has drawn me a picture, and written me my very own letter." Sylvie's smile was infectious enough to lift the sombre mood, at least momentarily.

"Don't you read it Mama, I can do it by myself, I know my Italian very well."

She proudly read out the few simple words from her ten-year-old cousin and then basked in the applause that followed the demonstration of her linguistic skills. When the first course was finished Daniel stood up and tapped his glass to gain everyone's attention.

"Oh no Grandpapa, not one of your too long speeches, we need to eat up so we can have the birthday cake!"

"Sylvie I want you to sit quietly and listen very carefully."

At the sound of Grandpapa's serious voice Sylvie was wide eyed and sat perfectly still.

"Terrible things are happening to Jewish people because of this war. We don't know if everything we hear is true but I believe we must protect ourselves so Grandmama and I will be leaving Menton in the morning and we must all keep it a secret, especially you Sylvie, as we don't want to get anyone else into trouble for helping us. You mustn't even tell your very best friends. Okay?"

Allessia pulled her chair up closer to her daughter, for she could feel the child's fear as the adult's sombre mood enveloped the room.

"Where are you going? How long will you be away?" Sylvie's baffled questions sounded small and fragile.

"Gramps Orengo will take us with him early in the morning. We'll stay up in Castel Vittorio with him and Gran." Daniel maintained his authoritative stance.

"But Grandpapa, that's all the way to Italy." Sylvie was on the verge of tears.

"Nonsense, it's just across the border. You can come and visit us dear child when we all agree it's safe." He shot a questioning glance at his son.

The two women retreated out to the cooking area.

"Allessia, please reconsider; please keep the pressure on Joseph to see sense." The tears glistened in Ruth eyes as she whispered to her daughter in law.

"I've tried, but he just won't believe the Germans will oust the Italians and occupy this part of France. You know how passionate he is about this hotel, what more can I do?"

They'd wrestled to contain their emotions as they finished icing the birthday cake. It created a distraction and it put a smile back on Sylvie's little face. The family sung a subdued Happy Birthday before mother and daughter blew out the candles.

"Grand papa, I have an idea. As I am not allowed to go to proper school now, why don't I come with you and Grandmama – just for a holiday?" Sylvie added to the conversation as she started on her second piece of chocolate cake.

Allessia immediately interjected. "Sylvie, you're only half Jewish on your father's side. I'm Roman Catholic which is what you are as well, so you'll be safe here with us and besides you're our little girl and we want you with us."

Joseph anxiously continued, "Sylvie, it is very important you say you are a Catholic to anyone who may ask you questions. You remember taking your First Holy Communion with the other children? Well, that makes you Catholic."

The five grownups hadn't touched their cake. Each sat quietly, their strained faces betraying their inner turmoil. Once Allessia had finally tucked her daughter into bed, the adults huddled closer around the table and spoke in hushed voices.

"Joseph, please reconsider coming with us tomorrow. Allessia and Sylvie may be Catholics but with a name like Reiss you're so obviously Jewish." Daniel was desperate.

"Papa I just don't believe it will be as bad here in Menton as perhaps in other parts of the country. I'm sure a lot of it is exaggerated. Besides you built this business up and I'm damn sure I'm not leaving it for the Germans or any of the Mussolini henchmen to take. The minute we show weakness, we'll lose it all."

Allessia had listened to this same conversation in many different forms over the past few weeks. The question was continually gnawing away at her like a nagging pain: were her in-laws right? She now believed her husband was allowing his wishful thinking and pride to cloud his judgement. Despite the tension and the strong differences of opinion, they all shared a tender kiss as they finally said goodnight.

Ruth placed her arm around her husband as they sat together on the large bed they'd shared for over thirty years;

their careworn faces softened by the glow of the single burning candle.

"Daniel we just have to accept this situation. We don't want to part with bad feeling tomorrow. Joseph hasn't experienced the same anti-Semitic sentiments that you did before you moved here. I guess it's because we've been more or less accepted by the extended family and community He just can't believe the worst of them. She rested her head despairingly on his shoulder.

"This may be our last night in this bed, in this house. Oh Ruth! I'm so frightened for our son, but he's his own man and you're right. Tomorrow our goodbyes must all be without judgement, regret or blame."

Two

Allessia had been up since before dawn. She had made some hot tea with mint from the garden, packed a lunch for the three of them and had just taken the croissants out of the oven when Daniel and Ruth arrived downstairs with their two small suitcases. Every possible precaution had been planned and discussed so as not to draw any attention as they left the house to make their getaway across the border.

"Good bye just for now." Sylvie still wore her pyjamas as she held her Grandpapa tight.

"Now, my little Angel. We're all saying our goodbyes indoors, no shouting or waving once we go out to the truck. We don't want the neighbours to notice anything." Daniel gently kissed her, then Allessia. He no longer contained his emotions as he hugged his son.

"We must go now. The border guard I bribed finishes his shift at 8am and we must be through the tunnel by then." Luigi Orengo interrupted the poignant little scene.

He went out first with the bags – one covered by his coat. Then the other two quickly joined him in the cab of the truck. Daniel, Allessia and Sylvie watched from the window fraught with misery. In a bid to stay as silent as possible, Luigi let the old truck just roll down the hill, only starting the noisy old engine when they'd reached the bottom.

"Madamee Gueone will be here at ten with a new set of school lessons for the week Sylvie, so hurry up and get dressed please." Allessia attempted to stick to normal routine as far as possible.

"Mama I still don't understand if I'm Catholic, why I had to be excluded from school. I don't even know what excluded really means! I was the only one it happened to, I'm sure Madamee Gueone hates me. It's not fair!" She jammed her hands onto her hips.

"Sylvie! Don't speak to me that way. Madamee Gueone does not hate you or why would she put herself at risk to bring your lessons here each week. I've told you it was the new Italian government that has taken over Menton. It made the rule about half-Jewish children. It won't be forever little one." Allessia's voice softened as she reminded herself that it was essential to keep things as calm as possible. "Just get through one day at a time" was the last thing Ruth had said to her that morning.

"All the guests have finished breakfast. There are just the two checking out. I'll be in the garden so let me know once Madamee Gueone has gone. Then I'll watch over Sylvie doing her lesson, if you are okay to do the rooms?" Joseph too, was determined to keep busy.

"It won't take me long, thank goodness as those Italian soldiers are so fastidious in their rooms, it makes the job easy." Allessia poured them both a strong tea from the old pot.

"Don't be over familiar with those soldiers Allessia. We can't trust them. They are occupying our countries as an act of war."

As Joseph walked out to the garden Allessia watched him through the window, while two of the soldiers passed him on the path. They deliberately ignored him. A few months before he would have reacted to such ignorance and bad manners, but now he said nothing.

The soldiers passed the house in silence as Madame

Gueone arrived at the door. Allessia acknowledged them with a lukewarm smile.

"Bonjour, Madame Gueone. Please come in and join me for some tea. There's still plenty in the pot." Allessia found it heartening to spend time with Sylvie's intuitive teacher.

"Madame Reiss, I can't express just how continually embarrassed we are at the school at the Council's reluctance to take any kind of stand with these occupiers, especially over a little girl attending school."

As Madame Gueone spoke, her plump chin wobbled in a jolly way. The children called her 'Madame wobbly' behind her back. However she was a precise, strong woman and fiercely protective of the children she taught.

"We really appreciate your support, but it's important we don't draw any attention to ourselves under the circumstances, especially with our family name being so obviously Jewish." They cut the conversation short as Sylvie appeared at the door.

"Madamee Gueone, how are my friends? I miss them. It's lonely here and now I haven't got Grandpapa to take me to play at the pétanque terrain."

Allessia quickly interjected. "Sylvie, Madame's not here to discuss your friends and your play time. She's here to look at your exercises from last week. So quickly now, fetch your book from the salon." As she refreshed Madame's tea she prayed the teacher wouldn't enquire about her in-laws. For half an hour Sylvie diligently listened and responded to her teacher. Allessia breathed a sigh of relief once she'd left, then called out to Joseph "Your turn Professor Reiss, my turn as the maid."

A week had passed since Daniel and Ruth had left.

Allessia took time out to accompany Sylvie for some playtime with her two special friends near their usual spot at the end of the pétanque court. Sylvie's usual happy-go-lucky personality had taken a battering but Allessia tried her best to maintain the status quo.

"Bonjour Allessia. Jean Claude tells me your father-in-law has rushed off to visit his sick brother is Lyon. Is he on the mend?" One of Daniel's friends called out to her.

"Well we haven't heard. I think it's quite serious so he'll most likely be away a while." Allessia blushed as she replied with her lie. Their conversation was interrupted by an increasingly loud roar, coupled with vibrations that caused tremors through the loose pebbles under their feet.

As they looked along the promenade a fleet of large heavy trucks was in clear view. They were being driven towards town. Each truck was open-backed, menacingly filled with soldiers sitting jammed stiffly side by side, their upright guns with attached bayonets.

"Mama, Mama! Who are they? There are hundreds of them. We counted ten trucks already!" Sylvie and her friends had rushed to Allessia's side.

"Now girls, it's time to finish playing. These are new soldiers from the German army. You must go directly home, now!" Fearfully, Allessia grabbed her daughter's hand and moved swiftly.

"Mama, you're hurting me. Let go." Allessia suddenly realised she had her daughter's small hand in a desperate, steely grip.

"So sorry Little One. Mama got a fright that's all. We must hurry home."

The noise generated by so many large motor vehicles reverberated across Menton. Joseph had run down from the hotel to the villa just as his wife and daughter arrived home.

"Don't panic Allessia. We must keep calm for all our sakes." His father's words rang in his ears.

Having eaten most of the evening meal in silence, they were disturbed by a loud knock at the door. It was an Italian soldier.

"Signore, we must inform you that our entire unit will be leaving tomorrow, except for two of us, so we no longer require your accommodation. The German army are replacing us as occupiers."

He turned to leave and although Joseph didn't really want to rock the boat he couldn't help himself. "Excuse me but can you give us any more information about the German intention for Menton? We have all felt the Italian Army has done a balanced job in difficult circumstances."

The officer yielded to this patriotic flattery "Well Signor Reiss, that's not what Hitler thinks. He believes our leader Mussolini has let the Italian and French partisans get away with too much and that we've not achieved the desired results with our occupation of this part of the French Riviera. So, apparently they are now dealing with it, and all but the liaison officers must be gone in twenty-four hours." He turned and hurriedly stomped off.

Allessia couldn't speak. Real fear had arrived and clung like a mould in her mouth. Once she had settled Sylvie and ensured she was asleep, she led Joseph into the salon and closed the door.

"Joseph we can't stay now. What are we going to do, I'm extremely frightened?" Her voice faltered, and she struggled to suppress the taint of blame.

"I agree, I have been desperate for a peaceful solution but now I think we should leave as well. We must try and keep as much of all of this as we can from Sylvie and we must protect her. I'll sort things out in the hotel and ask Donata and René if they'll watch over the property until we come back, so we can be gone by the end of the week." Joseph's tall body stooped in defeat as his eyes filled with tears of impotent humiliation.

Sylvie had sensed the danger and she stayed close to her mother. Four days had passed since the Italian soldiers departed. The only place Allessia could be totally open with Joseph was in their bed whispering, out of earshot of their daughter. Their bedroom was pitch black except for the light of the half-moon glistening palely onto the bed through the half closed shutters. Allessia's supressed anger had made it difficult for her to respond to Joseph's advances, but she listened attentively as he spoke about the Germans.

"I guess it's not possible to understand Hitler unless you can understand his hatred of everything we hold sacred."

Subtly, she attempted to create a verbal barrier to avoid lovemaking, but as Joseph continued to talk he began to stroke his wife's long dark hair. "My Darling you've given me such happiness. I'm sorry if I've made the wrong decisions, but what I believe is just and moral is clearly not what will keep us safe. I've lost control of even our personal circumstances. We'll be all sorted to leave the day after tomorrow. Let's try and keep the packing to just three suitcases so we can carry them ourselves if needed. If in the meantime if anything should happen to me, be strong. Be very stoic for Sylvie's sake."

Allessia's reserve had all but gone, and her heart was breaking. Too many words had already squandered precious time. Joseph kissed her gently at first, but as his kisses become more passionate she disguised her reluctance, slipped off her nightdress and feigned her response. Sex was the only comfort she had to give.

Three

It was a characteristic autumn Menton morning, fresh outdoors with the garden fragrance now replaced by the subtle aroma of wood-burning fires. Even without heat, the sun had illuminated the day. At breakfast Allessia and Joseph had tactfully informed Sylvie they were going on a holiday to Italy and once Allessia had packed her small manageable case, the little girl ran happily to her secret hiding place with her doll.

"Sylvie seems more her old self today, the bait of playing with Cousin Mario helps." Allessia and Joseph sat having one last coffee before they departed.

"Yes, she seemed in a rush. A busy bee with her doll, oops should I say baby." They both smiled in mutual acknowledgement of their daughter's play speak.

Suddenly there was a loud, abrupt bang at the door; which was simultaneously pushed open by a tall officer wearing the German uniform.

"Are you Joseph Reiss, a Jew?" He barked in French with a heavy German accent.

Joseph jumped to his feet and; in a bid to control his trembling he clutched his hands in front of him.

"I am Joseph Reiss. I am a Jew but my wife's not. She's a Catholic. " He blurted out.

"Well! You'll have to prove that to me."

Joseph immediately opened the drawer and showed the officer the birth and baptismal certificates for his wife and daughter.

"Why would any girl want to marry a piece of shit like you, Jew?" He shoved Joseph in his chest.

Allessia gasped. Joseph quickly recovered and stood upright.

"You, Jew, are coming with us."

He grabbed Joseph's arm. Joseph pushed him back.

"Where are you taking me?"

Hearing the raised voices, six soldiers, all armed, went running into the house.

"Get the Jewish pig. Put him in the truck."

The officer had punched Joseph's face and when Allessia ran to help she was roughly shoved across the room, and then smacked in the mouth.

"Get off him. What's he done? He's lived in France all his life. He's a French man." She shouted desperately, as the blood spurted from her split lip.

"He may be a French man but he's a Jew. We don't want any dirty Jew pigs where we're living." His captor brutally shoved him through the door.

"Papa, Papa! What's wrong? Leave my Papa alone."

At the sound of her daughter's voice Allessia had pushed past the soldier and rushed out.

"Sylvie, run back to your special place. Quickly now! These are bad men. Go now and hide."

Thankfully the soldiers made no move towards Sylvie and after a few seconds of horror she bolted back to her hiding place. Joseph stood in the back of the truck, his hands bound and flanked by four soldiers.

"I want to look closer at your certificates Madame Reiss."

They moved back into the kitchen. Allessia shivered as she handed him the papers.

"I will need you to supply me with your mother's and your grandmother's birth certificates within two weeks at the town hall. You must ensure you give them to me personally. I am Commandant Hesse."

He then marched out the door. Allessia followed in desperation.

"Where are you taking my husband? Where's he going?" She was frantic, shaking, with anger.

"Nowhere you will ever see him! Shut up and make sure you deliver what I've asked."

As the truck drove off Allessia's eyes were fixed on her husband, his head-wound bleed profusely, and his familiar rugged face drenched in helplessness and despair. Only when the truck was completely out of sight did she surrender to her terror. Consumed by dread and grief, she collapsed to her knees, her heart torn with uncertainty and loss.

Allessia, unable to control her shock, had frantically stumbled up to the rear garden, when she heard the lone whimper of her only child. Sylvie was curled up in a ball and encased in her tiny hiding place clutching her doll. "Baby, it will be all right. Mama will save Papa from the bad soldiers. She will call us soon and the doctor will make Papa better."

"Come on Little One. Come inside with Mama." Allessia gently pulled her from the small space, picked her up and barely managed to carry her and the doll into the house. They huddled together on the sofa seemingly unaware of their surroundings. Allessia had no words of comfort for her daughter. It was all she could do to manage to hold her physically close. The outside door had been left slightly ajar. She heard a soft knock; stiffened and stood up. Sylvie cried out.

"Hush child, it's not the Germans." Allessia moved to respond just as a soldier pushed open the door.

"Mama, it is a soldier! Please don't let him take you!" Sylvie was hysterical; her voice reaching a high-pitched scream.

"I'm not here to hurt you". The Italian soldier spoke firmly in Italian.

Allessia held Sylvie securely.

"Sylvie, quieten, this is not a bad soldier. You know Sergeant Balio who has been staying at the hotel. He's a friend."

The sergeant held his cap in his hands.

"We're so sorry for what's happened Madame Reiss. Apparently a neighbour of yours reported that your husband is Jewish.

Allessia's hand clung at her forehead. "Who?"

"We don't know." The sergeant cut in. "Someone nearby."

"What will happen to him?"

The sergeant shifted uncomfortably on his feet. "The German soldiers are instructed to incarcerate all Jews into work camps that have been set up in Germany. I don't personally hold with their politics." His face was honest. "But there's nothing I can do to help."

He moved towards the stove.

"The Italian army will be almost gone from Menton by tomorrow and you may have to accommodate German soldiers. Some of them are reasonable. I believe you have seen the worst today; now let me make you some tea."

Allessia stayed silent. He filled the battered kettle. He managed to find the tea box and encouraged both of them to sip the hot liquid.

"My Mama always said tea helped deal with shock. Perhaps you can give me the address of a friend, who I can contact to tell what's gone on here, and who can give you some support?"

Allessia finally managed to respond in her first language. "Thank you Sergeant Balio. You're most kind, but we've a telephone, so I'll call my friend. Those Nazis have demanded I present them with my Mama's and Grandmama's birth certificates. I don't know how I can achieve this as my family home is in the village of Castel Vittorio at the top of the Nervia Valley across the border." Her voice was barely audible.

"I've a soldier friend who's stationed in Pigna, just below your family's village. Let me see what I can organise for you. It's the least I can try to do. Write down your family's details." His face was full of empathy as he reluctantly left with Allessia's scrap of paper. Sylvie had returned to the sofa, and, now curled into the foetal position, her eyes in a fixed stare. Allessia's hand shook as she picked up the phone.

"Hello Donata, this is Allessia. Please can you come to our villa straight away? Something terrible has happened."

Donata, was Allessia's best friend, Italian-born and also married to a French man. Within a half an hour Donata had arrived. To keep out of earshot of Sylvie, they spoke out in the garden. Donata listened, shaken, as Allessia recalled her horrific ordeal.

"You know the Cohen family well; the German soldiers took them all yesterday from their home. Except their youngest daughter – we don't know where she is."

Allessia mentally counted about twenty Jewish friends and acquaintances in Menton. "Well I suppose they'll all be together which will make it a bit easier."

Once back inside Donata insisted that Allessia ate some of the fresh bread she'd brought, even if only to encourage Sylvie to leave the sofa and do the same.

"Come Sylvie, eat some bread and cheese then I'll walk you to the gelato parlour and buy you the biggest chocolate gelato you can eat." Sylvie registered no acknowledgement. Timidly, she left the sofa and lent up against Allessia as she toyed with a piece of bread.

Donata wasn't beautiful; plain was the word Joseph used to describe her. She was a little overweight, her hair a bit too fine, with a habit of squinting because she refused to wear her glasses. However her eyes were kind and she was always practical and organised in a crisis.

"I can't tell you everything will be all right". You'll have to pull yourself together enough to look after your daughter and keep the hotel going. You won't be able to leave now. They'll be watching you. Joseph would have full faith in your ability to adapt, Allessia. Do it for him and for Sylvie's future."

She handed Allessia a cup of sweet tea.

"Thank you for coming so quickly, you really are my best friend; things will never be the same until my Joseph returns to me but I'll make sure we are both here waiting when he does."

A few days passed and Allessia was encouraged to see her daughter was slowly recovering. Allessia created a layer of protection between Sylvie and the outside world. Sylvie was more demanding than usual, but Allessia welcomed the distraction, as, apart from the household chores, Sylvie was all she had to get her through the day.

Allessia had been reading Sylvie one of her favourite stories when there was a knock at the door. Cautiously Allessia called out.

"Who is it?"

A familiar voice responded, "It is just me, Sergeant Balio."

She immediately ushered him in.

"I have your Mama's and your Grandmama's birth and confirmation certificates; the local policeman helped us, and coincidently he turned out to be your cousin." He smiled as he handed over the large brown envelope.

"Oh this is wonderful. I can't thank you enough. How was my family?" She beckoned him to sit.

"I'm sorry. I can't stay. I'm here on the pretence of the 'hand over' to my German counterpart, but he's already suspicious. Very little was said to your family and its best you don't ask me any questions so that no-one is compromised or put at risk. I won't see you again. I'm sorry there's nothing more I can do to help."

He gave her hand a gentle squeeze as he left. The sense of loss swamped her. Allessia quickly retreated to the toilet to avoid Sylvie. Once she'd composed herself she returned to the envelope, and looked through the certificates. Disappointedly there was no note from her Mama. First thing the next morning Allessia dropped Sylvie at Donata's villa, and then walked hesitantly to the town hall. When she stated to the German soldier, in charge at the reception area, of Commandant Hesse's request, she was rudely told to wait at the end of a queue.

With her hand perpetually moving to her brow, Allessia nervously paced for over a protracted hour before being ushered in to face the repulsive, odious excuse of a man. He sat bolt upright, behind a large oak desk, his body stiff, his face fixed with a sneer across his lips. The German flag was mounted in an over–bearing, arrogant fashion, on the wall behind him. His hair was disgusting; shorn sharply on all three sides, the crown looking as if it had been dipped in black ink, and then smothered in greasy jelly. The pupils of his eyes were beady pin-points, as if pierced with pure evil.

"So, all your certificates seem genuine Madame Reiss."

To her relief he handed them back to her.

"Now, there's another matter of which I need to inform you. We will be commandeering your hotel for the housing of our soldiers – mind you, only non-commissioned soldiers and file privates. We wouldn't allow any of our officers to stay in a former Jew hotel! Their bare costs will be covered and you will be expected to serve them breakfast each day. My Sergeant will come and discuss further terms with you. Now you are dismissed."

Allessia was too stunned to reply. She nodded, clutched on to her certificates and swiftly exited the office without pausing until she was well clear of the town hall. Her chest pounded and she struggled for air; each step was a challenge. She finally reached a park bench where she sat until she felt composed enough to collect Sylvie.

Allessia recognised the knock of fear; it was hard, inevitable and consisted of at least three loud bangs that shook her kitchen door. The uniforms of the two German soldiers lacked the decoration of her previous visitors. The taller one opened the conversation.

"Madame Reiss, I'm Sergeant Schmidt. I've been instructed to inform you that I and five of my soldiers will be staying here from now on." His tone was polite and his French passable.

"Very well Sergeant Schmidt. I'll take you up to the hotel and show you the rooms immediately if that's suitable?"

"You've a very beautiful garden." The Sergeant attempted small talk after she'd shown them the rooms and handed over the keys. The fee he offered for the rooms would barely cover her costs. The five other soldiers moved off while the Sergeant lingered, his attitude lightened.

"Madame I understand how difficult this is for you, but please accept this assurance from me. While I'm here, providing you meet all our requirements, no harm will come to you or your daughter." He didn't wait for a reply.

Allessia's time was taken up keeping the wood range fired for the constant washing, and sourcing affordable food suitable for German-style breakfasts.

No pastries and coffee for German soldiers; they would eat practically a full breakfast with sausages, eggs and toast. It was clear to see why: their rations served in the army mess during the day were very meagre and the little money they received didn't go far for an evening meal in the local brasseries.

She had to call on favours from friends and trawl the market stalls to procure the needed supplies. At least all this activity provided some distraction from her constant fear.

Two weeks after the last of the Italian liaison soldiers had left, there was an almighty explosive bang, so loud and ferocious it echoed over the entire town. Sylvie rushed into the kitchen.

"Mama, Mama! They must be bombing us." She clung to Allessia's legs.

"It's okay Little One. Let's not over-react. We're both unharmed. I'll phone Donata and see if she knows what's happened."

"Hello Allessia. Yes I do know, I just heard, and I'm so infuriated. The Italian partisans have blown up the road at the entrance to the border as they want to make it difficult for the Germans to get their food supplies through from Ventimiglia. They haven't considered the French and us Italians on this side. How the hell will we get our food supplies now its winter?"

"Oh my God Donata, what will happen to Sylvie and me if I can't provide for those damned soldiers?"

Allessia's feared what she could do. Four of the market stallholders she shopped with received all their vegetables, eggs and sausages from Ventimiglia. It was the first town across the border and supplied most of Menton's fruit and vegetables. She would have to stretch what little food she had even further.

After a few days searching, Allessia had only managed to procure a dozen eggs, but because rabbits were quite bountiful in the hills surrounding Menton she had learnt to make rabbit sausage. She had disguised it with lashings of herbs and seasoning to imitate the Italian pork ones the Germans usually ate. As they'd eaten them without complaint she felt a surge of confidence with this small success.

Allessia was having a coffee break when the phone rang.

"More bad news I'm afraid. The curfew this time." It was Donata.

"What! The curfew – no one pays that any heed." Allessia remarked.

"I agree, none of us paid it any real heed with the Italians soldiers' occupation. In fact I never heard of anyone being arrested for breaking it the entire time they were here. But last night that all changed. Seven people were shot."

Allessia gasped "Who?"

Donata continued. "There were five in the same family,

you probably know them, the Bourbellion's. They live just up at the beginning of the Borrigo valley. They were celebrating a birthday and had two friends visiting. All the lights were on in their apartment and the curtains open and also the front door open, as a couple were outside chatting and smoking. The German contingent in charge of enforcing the curfew turned up shouting in German. Apparently they didn't fully understand what the soldiers were saying. From what I've heard there was a bit of a skirmish. The soldiers left, returning about fifteen minutes later with a squad of ten armed men. They dragged all seven occupants of the apartment outside, lined them up under the street lights and shot them. This morning on my way to the market I was passing the town hall when that Commandant Hesse announced with a megaphone that any resistance or retaliation to his soldiers would be severely dealt with. They're barbaric."

Four

Madame Gueone's teaching visits had ceased. Both she and Allessia had agreed it was best not to draw any unnecessary attention to Sylvie. The nuns who ran the Menton orphanage had offered to take Sylvie. Allessia had discovered that amongst the genuine orphans they had an additional fifty Jewish children hidden, all with new non-Jewish names. This was where the youngest Cohen girl was placed.

To date the Germans had shown no interest in the rather run-down children's home. Allessia couldn't even consider this alternative, as the time she spent with her daughter was sacred and her only motivation. Her own existence was devoted to securing Sylvie's future. The atmosphere in the town was tense. Fewer and fewer locals gathered at the usual places to chat and discuss the daily goings on. Food was scarce and although the tunnel to Italy was open again, there were so few workers in the Italian market gardens that there was very little produce. Allessia was on polite terms with Sergeant Schmidt who was billeted with her and she noticed he had Sunday afternoons off and usually sat in the garden by the hotel reading and smoking smelly French cigarettes. Allessia had observed meals were one of the few enjoyments the men had.

"Hello Sergeant. I was wondering if I could have a word with you about food."

"Yes Madame Reiss. Speak freely."

Allessia respectfully sat on the bench beside him.

"I've a lot of free space and fertile land here in the garden and I feel confident, with help, I can construct a simple hen house. Then, if I could travel to my family across the border in Italy and bring back some hens and a rooster and perhaps a goat then I'd be able to provide you all with much better breakfasts."

He shot her a quizzical look.

"So how would you build the hen house?"

Allessia was prepared. "I already have some wood and trellising in the shed and I'll ask my friend Donata's husband to help me put it all together. The hens can roam in the garden but it is best they lay their eggs in the same place each day."

He was impressed. "So how will you get to your family's village?"

She was making progress. "The same friend has a small truck. If you would be able to use your influence to provide the truck with a pass, say for two days. I'll give you my word I'll return with the hens, goat and fresh vegetables at no extra cost to you."

He paused thoughtfully for a moment and then pronounced he'd let her know during the following week. After some difficulty with the Menton switchboard Allessia was finally connected with a friendly Italian operator whom she knew slightly. She assisted her with a phone call to the police station in Pigna, where her cousin Bartolo was the local police officer. The police station housed the only phone in the area and Pigna was located directly below her family village of Castel Vittorio.

"Allessia, so good to hear your voice. No, I can't really speak but I can listen to you." She outlined her plan.

"Don't you worry. The hens, the goat and much more will be waiting if and when you arrive. Even, if I have to steal them myself."

Once she'd replaced the receiver, she felt empowered by a new sense of defiant excitement. Donata and René, her husband, were happy to help. René agreed to visit the next day to build the hen house. He also had his own agenda for going through to Italy. Donata had agreed to cover for Allessia at the hotel for two days. The crucial part to Allessia's plan would be the border pass from Sergeant Schmidt. By Thursday a rough looking hen house was constructed next to the fence in the garden. Good timing because the Sergeant arrived at Allessia's door around eight o'clock that evening with the pass.

"I have arranged to be on border duty myself on Sunday morning to ensure it all goes smoothly. But its best that you're not friendly with me and please do not use my name."

Allessia chose not to tell Sylvie until Saturday evening that they'd be travelling the next day. She'd planned to make no mention they would be visiting the family until they were well across the border. René and Donata arrived at seven p. m. in the morning. Allessia's anxiety level rose, as she hadn't heard the gate creak. What if Sergeant Schmidt wasn't on duty?

"Mama, where will we get the hens from? Can the goat be my own pet?" Sylvie had very rarely travelled by motor vehicle.

"Yes the goat can be your pet if you can catch her. Now you must keep as quiet as you can while we pass through the border and don't say anything to Sergeant Schmidt. Do you understand?"

Even at the early hour the border was busy, with two lanes that vehicles could pass through with a soldier directing each vehicle alternatively to the next available booth.

Panic set in as Allessia couldn't view the faces of the soldiers in either booth. How would she know which one Sergeant Schmitt was in; what if they were directed to the wrong one? René shared the same thoughts.

Then, as it was their turn to be directed to a booth, the right hand booth door opened, out stomped Sergeant Schmitt, and after a word in the directing soldier's ear they were smoothly pointed through his channel. He said nothing and just looked at their pass and waved them through.

"Phew Allessia, that was close. The Sergeant was as good as his word. I can't wait to see Donata's family and finally have fresh potatoes and wine. Your parents will be over the moon to see you and their grandchild."

Sylvie couldn't supress herself.

"Mama Mama! Are we going to see Grandpapa?"

Allessia swiftly responded. "Yes Gramps and Gran Orengo. But it's another secret Sylvie that you must keep."

She shot her an overstated frown.

"Oh yes Mama. Just like our other secret. I understand."

Allessia studied René as he attentively steered the truck along the tricky road. René was as plain as his wife; in fact they were like bookends. He had fine mousy hair, and his lower lip drooped a little as he spoke with a slight lisp. Allessia had to strain sometimes to catch everything he said. If René picked up on any indication about the senior Reiss's being hidden in Castel Vittorio he chose not to comment.

Donata's family had a small vineyard near Dolceaqua. So once he'd dropped Allessia and Sylvie at Castel Vittorio, about ten miles further up the valley, he would return there to spend his time with his in-laws. The Italian border town of Ventimiglia looked tired and in need of repair as they passed through. Allessia hadn't visited her childhood home since before the war and Sylvie had never travelled this far since she was a baby. Once through Ventimiglia and before the turn-off to the Nervia Valley René pointed out the ancient Roman ruins to Sylvie.

"Many hundreds of years ago that was an outdoor theatre where the Romans held plays. The Italians are very proud to have preserved this important monument – let's hope after all this time it doesn't get bombed." Allessia, feeling so much more relaxed, then chipped in. "And just there opposite is the hospital where you were born." Sylvie grinned.

The first village after Ventimiglia was Dolceaqua where Donata's parent's vineyard produced red, fruity wine that was sought after throughout the area.

"See that bridge Sylvie, that's where my wedding photo was taken." Allessia pointed out the romantic, stone-arched bridge that led across the river to a Castel ruin. At the next tiny village of Isabalona, there was a delay. An old man was struggling with his reluctant horse and cart, which had blocked the road. This gave Allessia a chance to point out to Sylvie the big, wooden water-wheel that slowly turned on the other side of the river – one of her favourite childhood memories.

Pigna, the last village before their destination, bustled, but not with locals. Any happiness had been short lived once Allessia spotted the distinct German helmets that seemed to be dotted everywhere. Sylvie buried her face into Allessia's lap.

"The Germans are so angry with the trouble the partisans are causing up here that they're determined to force them under control. I've heard they've taken over the Gabani Villa as a head quarters." René's voice was tinged with fear. Dread enveloped the cab of the truck and they decided against any stop at the police station to visit Bartolo. René clung to the steering wheel and Allessia cocooned Sylvie in her coat on her lap and stroked her reassuringly. Once they were clear of Pigna Sylvie sensed her mother's body relax.

"Mama I have to pee, please stop!" She sat upright.

Allessia glanced at René.

"What do you think?"

"I think we'll be okay, just make it quick."

Allessia squatted Sylvie beside the truck with the door obscuring her from the road.

"Mama, René! It's a magical castle just like in my book. Look! Look!" Sylvie pointed up above them to Castel Vittorio; her excitement was infectious. A fleeting smile brushed across Allessia's face. "Well, not exactly a castle. The tower you can see is the bell tower next to the Church. But it can be magical. I thought so when I was your age." She fell silent as she gazed up towards the rooftops and the pinnacle of her childhood home. "We all had so much fun growing up here."

The ancient, remote village perched proudly with its rough terracotta roofs terraced into the skyline. Enhanced by the low-hung mist, the height of the clock tower was exaggerated and it appeared to almost touch the clouds. Allessia thought fondly of her child-hood wrapped in the warmth and safety of Castel Vittorio, playing for hours with the other children in the narrow, cobbled streets. She'd never felt the sense of isolation outsiders had commented on. For her the village represented the security, predictability and belonging that came with a close community.

The truck groaned as it wound its way up the steepest side of the hill. They had to park at the base of the village as there was no way a motor vehicle could travel through the narrow fourteenth-century streets, built when donkeys and mules were the only mode of transport.

"I won't come up with you if you don't mind. I'm keen to get back down to Dolce Aqua. I'll be here Tuesday morning at eight a. m. to collect you and the menagerie" René assured. Allessia was relieved; she had no wish to expose René to the fact that Joseph's parents were hiding there.

Sylvie held tight to her Mama's hand as they embarked on the enchanting short walk up to her family home. The houses were built entirely of stone; mostly three or four stories high, with door mantles constructed of heavy, wooden beams that sat very low. Most of the villagers were naturally short and taller visitors had to duck down to enter. The entrance doors were extremely thick – made of dense native, knotted wood. The architecture hadn't altered in three centuries. Many of the buildings had more recently been divided up into family apartments with one floor providing for one generation of the family, while wealthier villagers had an entire building as their family home. A pretty square, with a few market shops and the natural spring-water well was the main meeting place of the village.

Allessia and Sylvie stopped briefly in the square to chat to Allessia's old aunt, who gave them a big toothless smile. Aunty was traditionally dressed in black – a distinguishing sign of her mourning for her late husband. Her black headscarf held back her thick, wiry, grey hair and her stocky, bandy legs were clad in knee-high woollen stockings.

"Mama I thought it was only men that could grow moustaches!" Sylvie declared as they walked away.

Allessia cut the conversation short, as she was anxious to move on. The steep stairs took them even higher towards the Church and the bell tower. Tomatoes were laid out in the sun on flat, cleaned pieces of stone beside the steps – a local way of preserving the vegetable for winter. Once dried out they were stored in jars with olive oil. Sylvie reached out to take one.

"Don't touch Sylvie! They're not yours. We will be at Gran and Gramps soon. There'll be plenty to eat."

As they passed the Church, Sister Margarita walked by and greeted them as old friends.

"I heard you were expected. How wonderful for your parents. I can see you are rushing. I won't keep you. God Bless!"

Allessia responded with a thankful smile.

As they turned the corner behind the bell tower, Allesia's childhood home stood in full view. She was heartened at its façade of colourful window boxes and intricate lace curtains appeared as familiar and welcoming as always.

Five

Allessia and Sylvie were seen through the curtains before they reached the door. Within seconds the Orengo's had their daughter and grandchild enveloped in their arms and everybody seemed to talk at the same time with tears of joy. Once inside, Allessia's parents gave their own welcome. Feeling the strong arms of her Papa and father-in-law around her, Allessia experienced some moments of respite from her constant fear. However Sylvie was quite overcome with the intensity of the new emotion and crumpled like a little wisp onto the large, sunken armchair.

The reunion was complete when Allessia's brother Massimo walked in, accompanied by his wife Carla and son Mario. Sylvie appeared to find her tongue as Mario squashed on the big chair beside her.

"Hello cousin, I always wanted to see what your house was like 'cause you've been to mine two times before." she whispered shyly in French.

"What's she saying Papa. I can't speak her language." Mario replied frustrated, in Italian. Sylvie frowned in concentration, then after a minor struggle responded in understandable Italian.

"Don't worry, I can speak to you. I am half-Italian you know!" The adults abruptly stopped talking their attention turned to the children as they effectively bridged any language or cultural divides between them.

"Why don't you two have a quick snack of bread and tomatoes? I'm sure Sylvie must be hungry after her journey?

Then, Mario, you could show her around the village. But be back within an hour for lunch." Gran Orengo clapped her hands to hurry the children along.

Mario was ten years old two years older than Sylvie. His thick, black, straight hair was cut very close to his head. Only slightly taller than Sylvie, he appeared more grown-up and walked with his head held high and carried an aura of purpose. Allessia escorted the children to the door then listened for a moment as the cousins sorted out their pecking order.

"I will show you most of my favourite hiding places but you mustn't tell Mama or Papa as they're secret. The other boys mostly know about them, but no girls. Because you're my cousin I guess it's different and will be okay." It was clear who would be in charge.

Back inside without the children, Allessia's initial intoxication of family love abated. She knew she would have to retell the unthinkable tragic details of Joseph's brutal abduction. Rekindling the memory was too painful; before she could finish, she'd lost all control and wept, gasping for air. Her father held her, while the others sat crestfallen close by.

Daniel's face had turned a dull shade of grey as he heard how his only son had been degraded and brutally abused. The tears were followed by a prolonged silence. It was Massimo who moved things on. Allessia's brother, although typically short like most from the area, had broad shoulders and exceptionally muscular arms. A deep scar etched in his chin, gave him a slightly sinister look. But he only needed to flash a brief smile to expose his warm and caring nature.

"There's nothing we can do just now except pray to both

our Catholic God and your Jewish God. The children will be back soon. I'm sure you all agree we should protect them, especially Sylvie, from any more grief. We've only two days together. Let's try to make them as happy as possible."

They all nodded in agreement. The two Grandmamas went into the kitchen to prepare the lunch, while Gramps headed down to the basement to choose some wine. Allessia sat close to Daniel.

"You did all you could to make him leave. He truly believed the best of everyone and I am living with hope in my heart he will return to us. You too must have hope." She tenderly embraced her father-in-law's arm.

They were interrupted as Sylvie and Mario burst into the room.

"Grandpapa! Grandpapa! I'm having such a good time. I love it here. Maybe I could stay here forever – 'till Papa comes home?"

Daniel scooped his granddaughter up in his large arms and kissed her cheeks as he attempted to disguise his sorrow.

"Little Angel! You have two whole days to play with your big cousin, and then you must go back with Mama, as she needs your help in Menton. Mario will show you where you will sleep tonight and where the washbasin is. So both of you, get those dirty hands washed, then lunch will be on the table."

Lunch was a veritable Italian feast. Mozzarella and sun dried tomato with a little fried red onion, with a full array of antipasto starters, followed by porcini pasta, then a crumbed veal cutlet. Ever since they'd received news of their daughter's imminent arrival, much thought has gone into preparing her favourite dishes.

"Gosh Gran! You have so much food here at your house. We never have this much food in ours, the soldiers in our hotel get the best sausages for their important breakfasts and Mama only sometimes gives us meat."

Sylvie's innocent comments raised concern in the family, but Mario was oblivious.

"It must be exciting having the soldiers living at your house. I bet they have big guns."

So far Mario had never had to leave the safety of the valley. Since the Germans had arrived in Pigna he'd never been allowed further than Gordale, the gardening allotment down the hill.

"Well!" Sylvie replied "They're really bad men. The ones that hit Papa and took him away – they were very bad. Mama says we must just be polite to the ones living in our hotel so they won't hurt us."

Dewy-eyed Ruth steered the conversation in a different direction by asking Sylvie about her lessons. Then Allessia lightened things by embellishing the tale of how René and she built what looked like a poor excuse for a hen house. The family had agreed they would spend the next day together, with a picnic lunch, working on their allotment at Gordale.

Because of the stony ground, many of the villagers had their own plot of gardening land in Gordale, which was located just down the hill within the Castel Vittorio County. Their plots were alongside those of professional growers who lived in the few houses that had been built there.

"Is it safe for you to be seen that far from the house Daniel?" Allessia was hesitant.

Her father replied. "We feel confident that no one left up here now would have any reason to 'finger' us to the Germans. Your cousin down at the police station keeps his ear to the ground and there is no suspicion that we have any Jews hidden in the valley."

Carla and Massimo met them at the base of the village with their antiquated truck. The large picnic baskets full of freshly baked bread, cheeses, prosciutto, wine and cakes were placed securely on the back. Mario hauled Sylvie up onto the back of the truck; the two Grandmamas and Massimo joined them in the cab. The others followed on foot.

The morning was crisp and refreshing. Allessia enjoyed the small talk with Carla, her sister-in-law. They had been friends from birth, having lived close to each other through their childhoods. She listened to the light-hearted gossip about who had married whom and it shifted her invariable, fearful thoughts to lighter plains. Carla had been the only girl in her family and she tended to be a little self-absorbed, but Allessia understood her. Her thick rich brown hair framed a pair of large brown eyes that complemented her rubenesque body. Her womanly appearance at an early age had seduced Massimo. From the time when they were all teenagers, he preferred a woman who was a little on the plump side. He'd never even considered dating or chasing any other girl, Carla had been everything he desired.

"Sylvie, hurry up! I want you to see my tree hut. Don't stay near to Papa and especially Gramps for too long. They'll try and get you to help them; it's so boring, all that digging and weeding." Mario took her hand as he led her further up the hill, away from where the family were setting up for the day. At the allotment Allessia's mother showed her the fresh plantings with the latest addition being the runner-bean tepee.

"Mario has already nearly knocked it down. He wants to use it literally as a tepee imagining he's a Red Indian."

All three men got stuck in with the shovels, turning the soil, ready to plant a new lot of seed-potatoes. Ruth and Gran especially enjoyed each other's company, checking the pumpkins and covering the general weeding. Communication didn't seem to be a problem, despite the language barrier.

Before they left, one of the residents of Gordale arrived at Massimo's truck with three cages of hens, plus a rooster in his own cage. All the way back to the village, Sylvie's contagious giggles at the bird's antics was shared with the extended family.

Everybody rose at dawn. It was a much colder day. Massimo and his family joined them for breakfast. Gramps had gone off to fetch the goat. Daniel and Ruth took Sylvie to one side to tell her how proud they were that she was helping Mama at the hotel. Allessia, whilst appearing to tidy things at the bench, discreetly listened-in to her daughter and father-in–law's animated conversation.

"Grandpapa! Why are you wearing that funny hat?"

"Grandmama knitted it for me. She only had bright red wool; she says she can see where I'm hiding a mile away. I feel the cold on these autumn mornings," he said as he touched his bright new headgear. Allessia smiled across at her mother-in-law who acknowledged the humour with a purposeful wink.

There was a crowd waiting as René pulled up in the parking place. Massimo helped him pack the four cages of hens, a live goat plus two large sacks of potatoes and other vegetables alongside his already substantial load on the truck. Allessia had prepared herself for riding home as part of the menagerie. Rugged up in several layers, plus a coat, hat and gloves, she joined the animals on the back of the truck to keep the goat controlled.

The Orengo's and Reiss's were pleased they'd said their personal goodbyes at the house, as a crowd of neighbours had gathered to wish Allessia well. Allessia chuckled to herself, as she imagined the comments they'd all would have made about her on the back of the old truck as it meandered down the valley? Chicken feathers flew, the goat bleated like a starved baby, and there she sat amongst it all. Despite the cold and her fear, she'd felt a brief sense of happiness.

As they passed through Pigna, Allessia caught a glimpse of her cousin in his police uniform. He waved out with a forced smile as the truck chugged past.

"René", said Sylvie, "I am going to give all my hens names you know. They'll be my pets. Mama says it is my job to collect the eggs." It was evident what a change of air had achieved for the small girl. Allessia was nearly blue with cold by the time they'd arrived at Ventimiglia so René pulled up by a café to revive her with some hot chicory.

"Thanks! I feel a lot warmer. Now my concern is whether Sergeant Schmidt will be on duty." Her newfound bravado had suddenly deserted her.

"The important thing is, Allessia, to maintain your confidence, I really can't afford to be questioned too closely as my personal papers aren't actually in order." Sylvie listened intently.

"Mama, the soldiers won't hurt us will they?"

"No, Little One but you must sit very still and no matter what is said, even if we tell a lie, you must say nothing. Do you understand?"

Sylvie's eyes had lost their sparkle as she slipped her thumb into her mouth. It was ten a.m in the morning by the time they reached the border. It crawled with soldiers and a long queue of vehicles waited on the French side, where it appeared most of their attention was directed. When the old truck came into view with its own circus on board, there was no way they would slip through unnoticed. Allessia's obvious feminine presence provoked two young soldiers to promptly approach the truck. They went straight to the driver's door.

"So, what are you doing with all these supplies? Get out of the truck immediately and show me your papers," The first soldier snarled.

Allessia didn't hesitate; before René answered she had jumped off the truck.

"Please, officer, I don't mean to be rude but this man is just driving me. I am assisting some of your superiors." Allessia stood her ground and forced a smile through her shivering lips. She'd secured their attention.

"So, what have you here, young woman? Are you opening a new restaurant?" He'd looked across to his colleague for acknowledgement of his clever humour.

"No, Officer. Sergeant Schmidt requested I source provisions for my hotel where he and his team are staying. I'm not sure exactly when, but soon, he must prepare to entertain some officers from Paris."

As Allessia had anticipated the soldier had been of no higher rank than Sergeant, and to avoid any consequential discipline he efficiently waved them through. She was relieved to have her feet firmly on home ground. René moved the hens and rooster up to their new home and in a bid to rejuvenate her enthusiasm, allowed Sylvie to lead the goat.

No sooner had René and Donata left than Sergeant Schmidt knocked at the door.

"I'm pleased to see you completed your mission, Madame Reiss. As a reward for my assistance in this exercise I would request you cook a special evening meal for my men and me. In addition, please provide the wine. We will expect to eat tomorrow evening at eight p. m. in the hotel dining room." He turned and walked out.

Six

Allessia aggressively sorted through the vegetables. Her anger stuck in her throat. Why should her family's food feed her enemies? Her thoughts wandered to Joseph, what would they be feeding him? She so wanted to believe he was alive. Then she pushed this thought to the back of her mind as she planned the meal. She must restrain her anger.

Papa had given her four roasting-fowls so she decided to use two of them to make coq-au-vin as it would stretch the meat further, especially tasty with fresh vegetables and dauphin potatoes, which would now be possible with the cheese and fresh cream. She prepared it all in advance then left it to slow cook whilst she returned to the villa.

Sylvie had an early supper and Allessia had read her a bedtime story.

"Now, Little One you must stay in bed, I'll just be up at the hotel cooking the soldier's dinner. Don't answer the door to anyone. If you hear a knock, ignore it. If it's anyone we know they'll see the lights on in the hotel and will come up. Are you clear on this?"

"Mama, I won't let anyone come in. I'm a big girl now; tell me what time you'll be home so I can look at my clock if I wake up?"

Allessia responded with a grateful hug. "Well I'm sure I will be back by half past ten as I'll leave the dishes until the morning. But you should be well asleep by then."

At eight o'clock sharp the six soldiers sauntered into what was usually just a breakfast room. Allessia had set the table with all the best napkins and silver. She wished to please Sergeant Schmidt in case she needed to ask more of him another day. At the same time she had to clearly define her formal role as the hotelkeeper.

The soldiers had leaned near to her each time she brought out the meals. As they drank more, the more advantage they took. While she cleared away the plates, they were burping competitively and they all laughed as one large man stood and farted. He then attempted to fondle her bottom, but she swiftly sidestepped him. She strained to stay silent.

"The chicken is excellent Madame Reiss, but we need some more wine."

"I'll just put the dessert in the oven, Sergeant, and then bring you the last bottle I have."

Relieved at the sergeant's subtle intervention, she scurried off to the kitchen, stalling for time. She had just placed the apple pie in the oven when she was startled; the Sergeant was directly behind her.

"Madame, what do you mean your last bottle of wine? You Italians always have wine. Don't lie to me after all I've done for you."

Frightened, she opened the cupboard to show him there was only one other bottle left. He then proceeded to open all the kitchen cupboards and only came across a bottle of cooking wine and some Limoncello.

"Well maybe you are telling the truth. I'll take all this out to the table anyway; my men won't know the difference. They just want to drink tonight and forget the war."

By the time she'd cooked and served the apple pie, three of the soldiers were totally drunk. Although they were speaking German a few French words were thrown in.

Allessia clearly caught the heavy sexual innuendo and knew she needed to move fast.

It all happened so suddenly. Allessia had just finished clearing the dessert plates and was thinking it would soon all be over and the soldiers would be off to their rooms to sleep it off. The soldier grabbed her so fast she had no chance of escape; he had her arms painfully locked behind her back. His breathing was fast and frantic; the strong stench of red wine and garlic momentarily invaded her senses. Brutally he dragged her along the hall, then forced her into the small reading room. Using his free hand he pulled his trousers down. His penis was fully erect and he was undoubtedly roused by Allessia's raw fear.

As he removed his hand from her mouth to grab her breasts she screamed at the top of her voice. Sergeant Schmitt rushed in. The big soldier bore down on Allessia, whose her dress was ripped and her breast exposed. The soldier had torn her panties off and was attempting to penetrate her.

As the sergeant pulled the large drunken soldier off Allessia they all heard Sylvie's scream. "Mama, Mama where are you?"

He dragged the astonished soldier out by his arm berating him violently in German. The drunken soldier could barely grip his unbuttoned trousers, in a bid to cover his exposed nether region. Allessia staggered out of the room. Her blouse was torn, with all the buttons missing. She swiftly covered her chest to conceal her bra, then, with the other arm, held Sylvie tightly.

"I'm not going anywhere Sylvie, I promise you. I'm alright. It was an accident."

Her words came out in unmanageable gasps.

Then the Sergeant interrupted.

"I apologise for my soldier's behaviour. He can't handle his drink, no harm done. You may return to your Villa. We will say no more of the matter."

Allessia glared, repulsed at the German. The vision of the soldier's hideous erect penis with its distended blue veins was still fresh in her head. She could barely compose herself. She scooped Sylvie up in her bruised arms, desperate to reassure her. Once they were inside the safety of their villa she attempted to placate her fractured daughter with a lie.

"The naughty soldier became a little drunk on the Limoncello. We were playing a game and I accidentally ripped my blouse."

"Mama, when I saw my clock said 11.30 and you weren't in your bed I came to look for you. That soldier's a bad man. I hate him, I hate them all. I want them to go. I want to go back to Castel Vittorio. There are no Germans there. Please, Mama?"

Allessia offered no response. She had cleaned herself up and then made them both a hot drink. Sylvie had finally fallen asleep in her arms in the early hours of the morning.

The next morning Allessia's only choice was to leave Sylvie sleeping while she returned to the hotel to prepare the soldiers' breakfast. Her pride gave her strength. Not one soldier could look her in the eye. She felt some reprieve that the beast that'd attacked her had not shown up at the table. Once she had served the coffee Allessia rushed back to the villa, desperate to arrive before Sylvie woke up.

First, she'd made a quick phone call to Donata.

"Good morning Little One. I have a treat for you today."

Sylvie took a minute to respond. "Am I going back up to

be with Grandpapa?"

"No, that's not possible just now. But Donata is taking you to play with her nieces today. You know them – Francis and Fifi."

As she'd cleaned up at the hotel delayed shock had set in. Allessia shivered as she reflected how close it had come to yet another disaster. Thank God Sylvie had screamed when she did.

Seven

When there was any lull in Allessia's busy day the nagging pain of deep sadness for her absent husband and uncontrollable angst haunted her thoughts.

She rarely ventured into town and was careful not to attract any attention to herself, but was so desperate to know anything of Joseph that she decided to brave the visit to the Red Cross centre to see if they could give her any information about the Jewish camps. As she walked towards the square she observed how Menton had lost its spark. The local's walked with their eyes cast downward and there were no men playing pétanque. Winter had subdued the summer blooms and there was a sorry absence of the regular old gossiping women around the square. Sadly the colourful carousel horses were faded and alone; without music or children, silent and abandoned.

"Allessia, is that you?" Madame Gueone greeted her; the teacher seemed a lot thinner than last time they met.

"Bonjour, Madame Gueone. Yes it's me. I just wear a head scarf, you know, to try and look as invisible as possible." Allessia's hair was tucked under a dark brown scarf that Ruth had left behind.

"How's Sylvie?" Madame Gueone inquired in her soothing, caring voice.

"Well, all things considered she's fine. I'm here trying to find out any news of where Joseph may be being held, but the Red Cross centre seems to have closed."

Madame Gueone replied with a sigh. "Ah yes. Any organisation or Church that supports the Jews, or what the

Germans call "undesirables", has been banned I'm afraid."

Allessia then lowered her voice. "I would have thought he would have somehow written me a letter at least to tell me where he is." Her eyes began to water.

"Don't think harshly of him. He may have written to you. Very little post is getting through. My brother-in-law's a postman at the main Menton post office and told us the Germans have two soldiers daily checking most of the incoming post and if anything is suspicious or connected to relatives of the camps, they destroy them. They're evil men, Allessia." Madame dispensed with her usual formal farewell and gave Allessia a hug.

As the weeks passed, Sylvie adjusted to the changes. She visited the hens daily and seemed to chat a lot to the goat. Allessia managed to teach herself and Sylvie how to milk the goat but many buckets were kicked over before they mastered the skill. Five days after Allessia's visit into town, Madame Gueone appeared at the door.

"Please come in, Madame. Let me call Sylvie. She'll be so pleased to see you."

But Madame pressed her hand.

"No, Allessia, best not. I shouldn't be seen here. I mustn't stay.

I mentioned to my brother-in-law about you, and coincidentally one of the soldiers at the post office was away last week. The one left inspecting the post couldn't keep up and kept having cigarette-breaks. My brother-in-law grabbed as many letters as he could and shoved them in the checked bin each time the soldier left the room. And guess what he found? He was too scared to deliver it to you himself, with the soldiers being in residence, but I've brought it. Please tell no one. We can't afford to compromise ourselves in any way."

She took the letter from her handbag, kissed Allessia's cheeks and then quickly left.

Eight

Allessia didn't recognise the handwriting on the envelope. The postmark was French from somewhere called Drancy and there was no return address on the envelope. It contained a piece of scrappy paper. As she opened the neat folds she instantly recognised the faded writing. Her heart soared with exhilaration. She clutched the letter as if it contained her very last breath and sunk back onto the chair near the window. It had been written in very light pencil and at first glance was a little difficult to read.

My Dearest Allessia,
I pray with all my heart this letter reaches you. One of the guards has an Italian wife from our area, who, so far, has been a little sympathetic towards me. It's my hope that he'll be true to his word and post this. I also had to give him a bribe; thankfully my fellow prisoner, who has lost all his family, was able to help me with this. I've so many things to say to you it's difficult to know how to begin.

Most of all I miss your warmth and touch. This outweighs the physical pain and hunger I'm suffering. I can hold on to life knowing you and our angel Sylvie are alive and well and that one day I'll hold you in my arms again.

These Nazis are brutal inhuman beings. The cruelty and murder that they inflict on us is beyond belief. They force me to do tasks of physical work twelve hours a day. As long as I can continue to perform I get to stay alive. I try not to feel sorry for myself, as there is always someone worse off. The chap in the cot beside me witnessed the murder of his parents, his wife and child by the SS. He cries out in his sleep most nights. None of us can offer any solace. I thank God I know my parents and you two are safe and well.

The camp, is called Drancy, located one hour out of Paris. But how long I'll be here, I'm not sure. A lot of the men who arrived with me have been sent on to camps in Poland. The main one is called Auschwitz, so I assume it is only a matter of time until I'm sent on there.

Most nights I experience vivid dreams. I dream of your beautiful face with its dimples and your wonderful body. I remember how round and warm you were when you carried our angel Sylvie in your belly. I hunger to make love to you with my soul and for you to understand I'll never be complete without you beside me. Whatever happens to us always remember how deeply I love you and our precious daughter. Please carry me in your heart every day. Knowing that will keep me fighting for life. I will try and write again soon. Kiss Sylvie from me and tell her how much I love her.

Your husband forever,

Joseph

Allessia wept tears of love mingled with regrets as she re-read the letter. She longed for her husband and her buried passion.

"Mama, has the bad soldier hurt you?" Sylvie stood at the door watching her mother. "You are making such big crying noises you're frightening me. Shall we get Aunty Donata?"

Allessia smiled through the tears.

"No, Little One. They are tears of happiness really."

Sylvie accepted the explanation, and joined her on the sofa.

"This is another secret you must keep. I have just received a letter from Papa."

Sylvie's big brown eyes opened as wide as saucers.

"Mama, when is he coming home?"

Allessia cautiously considered her answer.

"Not 'till the end of the war. He told me to give you a kiss from him and tell you how much he loves you." She embraced her daughter with closed eyes as she struggled to remember her husband's touch.

Nine

Donata and René had a secret wireless. The Germans had banned radios, but René risked listening to the BBC Radio broadcasts across France and Italy, which were often the only way they could hear news from across the border. Dolce Aqua and Pigna were both mentioned. It was speculated that there might have been hundreds of Italian casualties. Allessia rose from her sock-darning to answer the phone. She was tempted just to let it ring, as she only ever seemed to receive bad news.

"Oh my God! Are your parents okay?" Allessia could not quite take in what her friend was telling her.

"We don't know any more than that. It all happened yesterday. René says the chap in the tabac told him that the Germans are posting lists of the dead in the town hall in the morning. Will you come with us?"

Allessia couldn't sleep. She dwelt on all the unthinkable possibilities of who may have been killed, including Massimo. At least the broadcast didn't mention Castel Vittorio.

At breakfast the next morning Sergeant Schmidt appeared much more agitated and difficult than usual. Each week the soldiers had looked more worn and downtrodden. The amount they'd been paying for their lodgings, already meagre, had decreased. It barely covered their daily breakfasts. As soon as the soldiers had left for the day, Allessia and Sylvie anxiously headed off for the town hall. The whole town seemed to be there. She spotted Donata and René across the hall and as she finally managed to push in beside them, the Commandant stood up on a podium to speak.

"The German army lost many brave soldiers in this skirmish. We will not tolerate being undermined by either the French or Italian resistance. They're all criminals and anyone protecting them or assisting them in any way will be shot. Out of respect, I am posting the lists of the dead we have been given by the local police from Ventimiglia."

Everybody pushed forward to read the list of about 200 names. The soldiers moved them back, forcing them to queue in an orderly fashion. Many people screamed and cried out as they reached the lists. Others rushed to comfort them. René and Donata were directly in front of Allessia and Sylvie. The lists were in order of village and as Allessia looked over René's shoulder she could clearly see Castel Vittorio listed. Donata screamed as René read out her brother's name. When Allessia finally approached the notice-board the name Orengo jumped out at her in at least ten places. She trembled. Her whole body had spun out of control and, as she held on to Sylvie's shoulder to steady herself, she was oblivious to the little girl's confused expression and was compelled to look closer. Her brother, her parents, her cousins, Daniel and Ruth Reiss's names were all listed. The shock was beyond endurance and she collapsed on the floor still holding on to Sylvie.

"Mama ,Mama please stop crying, open your eyes, please get up."

Eventually a kindly neighbour gently encouraged her to her feet and guided the bereft mother and child back to the hotel.

Allessia had no memory of leaving the town hall that day. Having found herself at the Villa both she and Sylvie had fallen onto the sofa. The little girl murmured softly to her doll.

When Allessia finally noticed the moon had risen she managed to feed her daughter some soup, then they both fell into disorientated sleep in Allessia's bed. She was roused at seven a.m. the next morning with Sergeant Schmidt yelling for her from downstairs because there was no fire or hot coffee waiting for him.

Still in her clothes from the previous day she rushed to the hotel. She used the gas burner and quickly toasted yesterday's bread and fried the eggs and sausages. It took every ounce of control for her not to tip the hot coffee pot in the sergeant's lap. Very disgruntled, the soldiers hastily ate the breakfast

"Are you sick, woman?" he barked at her.

"No. I'm trying to cope with the deaths of my family. Your bloody army murdered them all two days ago." The venom in her voice immediately silenced him.

As the soldiers left the hotel the Sergeant stayed back.

"I'm sorry for your loss, Madame. We've all lost family and comrades in the past weeks; please do not concern yourself with us tomorrow. We'll make arrangements for our breakfast at the patisserie." His tone sounded genuinely apologetic. Allessia blanked him. She was past fearing the Germans; there was almost no loved-one left for them to destroy.

Five days had passed since the news of the massacre. Allessia preferred the numbness of shock to the reality of the trauma, but for Sylvie's sake she had to go through the motions of the daily tasks. No one could offer comfort. Donata and René were in the same state of grief. Most

Menton families had been affected by the conflict across the border. Allessia was so fragile she had begun to doubt her own sanity.

Allessia and Sylvie were revising Sylvie's lesson for the day when there was a barely audible knock at the door. "Who is it? "Allessia called cautiously. The response was the soft mumbles of a female voice.

Warily she opened the door.

There stood a hardly recognisable Carla and Mario. The sisters-in-law fell into each other's arms. Mario stood a shadow of his former happy self, and he was mute. He showed no recognition of Allessia or Sylvie. He just stared into space.

Once they had composed themselves and Allessia had managed to make a pot of tea, she suggested Sylvie take Mario up to her room or outside to show him the animals in the garden. The two women clung to each other. United in their grief Allessia could feel Carla's bones where her weight had dropped away. She was spent with grief and bitterness had engulfed her like a potent smell.

Once they'd finally unclasped each other, they sat down at the kitchen table. Carla was desperate to share her story, which poured out. "Massimo was home on one of his rare visits. He was hell-bent on fighting for his rights and had become a fully entrenched partisan fighter, with his Papa's blessing. He had told his Papa and Daniel it was getting risky for them to venture anywhere near Pigna as the Germans were everywhere and angry. But you know what they're like: this will be our last time until after the war. They all so loved the gardening.

"So the rest of us decided we'd go as well. There were

about thirty of us including the full time gardeners that live in those old dwellings at Gordale. As we walked down the hill that girl Anna skipped past, all done up in her Sunday best, high heels and all. Mario informed me she was off to meet her boyfriend Angelo.

"Massimo had said Angelo was in his unit but he wasn't bright enough for the strategic stuff and a bit too handy with a gun. When we arrived Massimo teased Ruth about her bean-tepee and the size of her beans.

"Luigi had everybody pull together to heap up the leaves and old branches and we lit the fire for the burn off .Mario had run off following Anna. He had a full view of the road from Pigna and of Anna and Angelo kissing when he first saw the soldiers."

Carla was overcome and covered her face with her hands.

"Please go on Carla, I can see it's difficult but I have to know everything that happened, just take your time," Allessia pleaded.

"Well, it's funny what sticks in your mind. I remember Luigi joking with Mario that he wouldn't be seen dead in a bright red hat like Daniel's, and that it must be true love for him to wear it." She paused again, letting out a protracted sigh before she continued.

"The fire had been burning about thirty minutes when Mario came screaming 'The German soldiers are coming Papa, a whole heap of them'. At the same time we all heard a huge bang. Massimo yelled for everyone to move fast and hide, but they didn't really take it in and milled around. He shouted at me directly to take Mario and hide as we were in immediate danger. Mario grabbed my hand and pulled me to Ruth's bean tepee. I wrapped myself around him, he curled into a ball, and the overgrown foliage on the sticks concealed us. I had my hand over his mouth and told him 'whatever you hear, do not speak or move' and for once thank God he did as he was told.

"We heard loud stomping as the soldiers crunched their feet, running to the allotment. I could hear Massimo arguing with the one in charge. Then I heard Luigi pleading. But the Germans were just angry; they had no reasoning. We heard popping sounds. They shot them all, then when some didn't die in the first burst of bullets they shot again 'till their massacre was complete. Mario and I were drenched wet. It was only later, because of the smell, it dawned on me we had both peed ourselves."

She took another break letting out a loud sob before continuing. Allessia sat transfixed and speechless. Then Carla managed to go on.

"It seemed like hours we didn't move, then we could hear a woman's voice and I vaguely recognised it as Sister Margarita. I extracted myself from the hiding place and told Mario to wait. I could see Massimo lying face up on the cold ground. I tried to warm him, but he was gone. Then I heard a scream like a wounded animal. It was Mario: he had emerged from the tepee and stood transfixed. All four grandparents appeared to be lying on the ground asleep. Luigi's eyes were just staring, wide open. Ruth was so still and her face had almost gone. There was just flesh, like raw meat, where her face had been.

"Daniel's bright red wool hat seemed to have dripped red all down the side of his face. We could hardly differentiate where the hat finished and the blood started. It was a mass of red. I felt someone's arms holding me. It was Sister

Margarita. She was speaking but she didn't make sense. I could see Bartolo holding Mario in his arms, but it was all in a haze. Then I passed out."

Carla wept in Allessia's arms. Allessia still had so many questions to ask but understood it would all take time. She made them some sweet, strong tea, and then gently prodded her sister-in-law to carry on.

"It only took minutes for those bastards to march up our hill and murder thirty of our family and our people. And, if that wasn't bad enough, after burning most of the Gordale houses to the ground they stomped up to the village and lit several fires in the houses on the lower level. Our apartment was badly burnt.

"Bartolo arrived first at the village. Seeing the smoke, he assumed that was where the soldiers had directed their attack. He was pretty sure that Angelo had hurled a grenade at the troops as one of them had a superficial wound. That was what had provoked a whole massacre, the bloody stupid fool. Bartolo, Sister Margarita and the few old people left up there managed to put the fires out. Then they came and found us."

"What about their burials?" Allessia asked tentatively.

Carla paused, taking a little more time to compose herself.

"The Priest from Pigna said we must bury everyone as soon as possible so we had a mass funeral yesterday. They're all together in the hillside cemetery. He told us death was a change, not an ending. For me it's ended. Once they were buried I knew I couldn't stay in the village with Mario; he's been mute since it happened. All our possessions were destroyed in the fire. We were staying in your family house, which was all intact. I thought if we had a change of environment he may recover in some way. Bartolo managed to bring us as far as the border and we walked from there."

Carla's tears had dried. She vacantly stared across at her sister-in-law with dead eyes. Sylvie had taken Mario up to see the goat and the hens.

"Have you lost your voice, Mario? Once, when I had a sore throat that happened to me."

Confused by his demeanour, Sylvie instinctively carried on chatting. She showed him the hen-house and pointed out the direction of her secret hiding place. He followed her back to the house but with no verbal response.

"Mama, Mario can't talk, he must have a sore throat."

Allessia took her daughter's and Mario's hands in each of hers and knelt down in front of them.

"We've all had a bad fright. It's very sad because we've lost all our grandparents and Mario has lost his Papa. It will take us all time before we feel better. Mario and his Mama will stay here and if Mario doesn't want to talk then you will just have to talk for him."

Carla took over Daniel and Ruth's room and the two Mamas made the small spare room into a suitable space for a boy. They shared all the hotel duties, the gardening and the cooking and managed to stretch the limited food supply.

It was a month before Mario found his voice. Sylvie had ignored the fact that Mario never answered her questions, and often didn't seem to notice her presence. She seemed naturally to know just how to rally him, because he followed her, even if it was at a distance. He would eventually turn up wherever she had decided to play. She gently coerced him in a simple child-like manner. The children collected the eggs and milked the goat but Sylvie had not yet shown Mario her secret hiding place. She'd decided she would, but only when his voice returned, as anyone who visited her special place must promise never to tell.

Despite him not speaking, Sylvie loved having her big handsome cousin join her on her daily jaunts. He'd been busy playing with the goat, so she slipped off to her special place. It was surrounded by plants and shrubs with an entrance so tiny that only a child could squeeze through. Being completely dry, Sylvie kept a couple of dolls and a tea-set Grandmama had given her, inside.

"So this is the secret hiding place. It's not very secret!" Mario said as he squashed in behind her.

"You can only come in here if you are invited! You must promise never to tell!" Sylvie turned round.

"You talked Mario! You talked!"

Mario was inspecting the doll. "Yes I think I will be speaking from now on. This doll has no panties on."

Sylvie grabbed it off him. "Don't be rude. Don't touch my dolls."

Ten

From then on, lavished with Sylvie's love and affection, Mario went from strength to strength. He talked at breakfast, lunch and dinner and soon took over as the leader with his younger cousin. With René's help, they built a tree hut, which superseded the secret hiding place. Nearly every afternoon they invented a new game that involved Mario always emerging as the hero.

"Children seem far more resilient and quicker to heal then adults" Allessia commented to Carla, as they watched the tree hut activities from a distance.

"I don't think I'll ever heal, how can I? The person I used to be doesn't exist anymore. It's all down to Sylvie; when he's with her, he blooms. She's like a little mother, a best friend and cousin all rolled into one. I wish he was like that with me." Carla spoke with a dollop of bitterness in her tone. Allessia had observed how Carla unnaturally clung to her son; her need greater than his.

It had been four months since the massacre at Gordale. Rumours were circulating daily that the Germans would soon retreat from France. The air raids over the Riviera by English and Canadian planes became more frequent. Although frightening, most of Allessia's friends agreed the combined strength of the two foreign nations was their only hope of liberation.

Sergeant Schmidt and his men had snuck out in the dead of night leaving unpaid rent. It had made life easier for the women. Now all the food they grew would be their own, with vegetables and eggs left over to sell in the market. On April 24th 1945 Allessia, Carla and the two children took their produce to the main Menton market. Sylvie and Mario relished these excursions as they enabled them the opportunity to play with other children. Each day Sylvie had taught Mario some new French words and he had mastered the language well. They had just set up their small stall when they heard the loud rumble of trucks.

"Mama, Mama! The Germans are leaving, Mario was shouting, along with many of the other children.

Allessia and Carla rushed out towards the main road in front of the market. The noise was deafening as at least fifty heavy army trucks rolled out of town towards Nice. The dust they roughed up engulfed Menton like a storm cloud.

"Are you thinking what I'm thinking, Carla?" Allessia shouted in Carla's ear to be heard above the din.

"I wouldn't get your hopes up just yet; you know how things are, never what they seem." Carla cynically responded.

"We won't celebrate just yet. Let's wait 'till it's official." Allessia declared in a bid to quell the over-excited children.

They were eating lunch the following day, when they heard the first shouts. Allessia rose to open the window and could see a man waving a bottle of wine and shouting. "The war is over! The war is over! Germany has surrendered!"

Not fully believing what she'd heard she scuttled out the door with Carla and the children in tow. Several people on the street hugged in joyous relief, then joined the man with the wine bottle. She directed her question at a neighbour she recognised. Is this true? Have the Germans surrendered?"

A huge smile crossed the neighbour's face as she responded. "Yes. We're free. The British and Canadians have defeated the Germans. We're rid of them. Vive la France!"

Mario and Sylvie were caught up in the joy, dancing about and parroting "Viva la France! The war is over!" Then Sylvie quietened for a moment.

"Mama, now it's finished, when will Papa be home?"

Allessia didn't answer her daughter. The question was left hanging in the air.

The whole of Menton celebrated. The market had been festooned with blue, red and white balloons in addition to copious amounts of tatty bunting that had been stored away since a pre-war Bastille Day. Stalls had been moved back and a large central area cleared as a party venue. Everyone had brought plates of home-made food and wine. Some of the old men had put together a small band, with violins, mandolins and a badly tuned trumpet. They attempted to play dance music. From the very old to the very young they clapped, danced and enjoyed bursts of release after years of tension and fear.

A month had passed since the war officially ended. Many of the locals who fled were returning to their homes. Many displaced, confused people were arriving on the Riviera, as it was easier to survive homeless in a warm climate. Carla had been quiet for a few days so as they were having their ritual morning tea, Allessia decided to talk with her.

"Carla, is everything alright? You seem to be distracted of late. Is it something you can share?" Although close, they respected each other's boundaries.

"I'm sorry. It's just that I've been struggling with a decision and I didn't want to discuss it until I had it all clear in my head. I feel secure, being here with you and Sylvie but I keep thinking about what Massimo would want me to do.

I know he and his Papa would want us to be in the family home and for the Orengo's to be a part of Castel Vittorio for generations to come. Both our families have lived there since the fifteenth century. The Germans really will have won the war against us if I desert everything that our family has spent lifetimes building."

A few moments of silence passed before Allessia replied.

"I agree with you, however I can hardly bear to think of life here now without you. You two have been beacons of light in our darkness. But I agree Massimo and Papa would want that. We have a duty to the future of the Orengo family".

"You don't mention Joseph much, but I'm sure he's always on your mind. My main concern is you hold it all in and if I am not here you don't have anyone close,"

Carla cautiously added.

"I don't talk about it because the ache for him is like a sharp, never-ending pain in my heart. When I visit the Red Cross room and I don't see his name on a camp death list I still have hope, but day-by-day it's fading. A part of me thinks I should come home to Italy with you, but I have my duty to the Reiss family to keep this home and business going for when Joseph does return."

They shared their awakened sorrow by sitting close, lost in mutual thoughts of the family they would never see again. Sylvie cried in dismay, almost hysterical when Allessia informed her Mario would be leaving. "He can speak French well now, Mama, and he has lots of friends at our school. Please, please don't send him away."

Mario stormed off to the tree hut.

"Perhaps you should go and talk to him?" Allessia suggested to Carla.

"No, I know my own son. He needs to think through what I have said. I'm sure he'll come back inside soon. He knows I'm always right."

As the women prepared the supper Sylvie, who'd finally calmed down slipped out to find her cousin. The children didn't appear back until well past the usual suppertime.

"Sylvie and I have had a talk, and we won't upset you any more about us returning to the village. But please promise that Aunt Allessia and Sylvie will visit us a lot." Mario spoke demonstrating a maturity beyond his years.

"Darling, they will come as often as they can, and you can come back here any time."

Bartolo arrived a few days later to drive the Orengo's back to their Italian home.

Eleven

Allessia had five paying guests at the hotel. The tariff was nowhere near the amounts that the hotel commanded before the war, but she'd weighed up the costs and it was her only option of income. Every day displaced men and woman turned up at her door asking for rooms, offering to pay once they'd found paid work. She felt guilty as she turned away these bedraggled strangers. Her new-found stealth for survival and the safety of her only child outweighed any charitable intentions she once may have harboured.

Many of the men who came to the hotel suffered post-war trauma. Allessia's close shave with the drunken German soldier had left her suspicious and wary of everyone. She believed now she was free to choose who she accepted as guests, her preference being for married couples and any government officials who required long-term lodging.

Allessia could see how much Sylvie missed Mario, but as the days passed back at school, she blossomed and took up with her old friends. Allessia allowed her to join them down at the pétanque area. Jean-Claude had been watching as the girls unsuccessfully attempted to scratch hopscotch squares on the cracked concrete with Sylvie's pencil.

"Young Sylvie Reiss, just what are you up to? Pencils are few and far between just now. I am sure you need that for your school work." Sylvie looked up at her Grandpapa's old friend, and understood the humour in his voice.

"Well, Monsieur Jean-Claude, we're not allowed any chalk from school and Mama can't buy any. Everything is rationed." She politely replied.

"Well if you meet me here tomorrow at the same time I think I may be able to solve your problem."

Allessia was beginning to panic. Sylvie was over an hour late. She'd regretted allowing her any freedom even though she was with Jenny. Still, they were only nine years old. Then Sylvie burst through the door

"Mama I'm so hungry! We saw Monsieur Jean-Claude, Grandpapa's friend. You know with the smelly moustache. He said he'd have a surprise for us tomorrow." Sylvie seemed almost back to her old self.

"Slow down Sylvie! And first of all tell me why you're an hour late."

"But, Mama, I was only playing with the girls, just like we always used to. I'm okay, I'm nine now. Their Mamas let them stay out longer!" She began to sulk.

"Well, I will talk to their Mamas and we will have to make some rules."

Allessia had no wish to share her fears about the tramps and vagabonds. Her greatest happiness was Sylvie's laughter. The next day when the three girls arrived at the pétanque area, Jean-Claude was waiting to greet them.

"Monsieur Jean Claude, where's our surprise?" They spoke in unison.

"Here are three new pencils for your school-work." They didn't manage to conceal their looks of disappointment.

"However if you come this way I've something to show you." He moved down to the hopscotch area.

"Oh, Jean-Claude! It's just what we wanted. Thank you! Thank you!" They all gave him a hug before he re-joined the other men.

"Amazing how you can please a woman with a can of white paint!"

Allessia continually wrote to all the government and Jewish organisations that the Red Cross had recommended to her, but she received no replies. So far, none of the Jews who left Menton had returned. The fifty Jewish children up in the Menton orphanage all had parents when they arrived there, but it seemed they were destined to be true orphans. Each week that passed more information came out about the German concentration camps and the deaths of hundreds of thousands of Jews.

In a bid to cheer Allessia up, René offered to babysit Sylvie and keep an eye on the hotel while Donata took Allessia to the reopened cinema. Before the main film, a Pathé newsreel was shown and Allessia couldn't take her eyes off the screen. The camera had recorded walking skeletons, barely recognisable as human beings, waving as the allies liberated them from a German camp. It was followed by footage of rows and rows of dried, withered bodies, encased in filth, hollow shells of men left to rot like discarded vegetables in a mud-sodden field. The commentary went on to tell how they suspected millions of Jews, and others deemed undesirable by the Nazis, had been gassed and killed.

"Do you want to leave?" Donata clasped her friend as she saw her sway at the same time as a coating of sticky perspiration emerged on her brow.

"I must get out now. I think I'm going to be sick." They only just reached the outside pavement before Allessia vomited.

"I'm so sorry Donata to spoil everything. It's just too horrific knowing one of those men could be Joseph." Her mouth felt dry and bitter.

"Let's get you some water!" Donata guided her across to a seat near to the water fountain. Allessia took a few sips.

"Shall we just sit a bit? It'll be best if Sylvie is asleep when you get home." The women sat motionless on a park bench.

"If there's a bloody God, where is he? Christian, or Jewish, how could he let this happen?" Allessia was incensed.

"Because there's evil and Hitler was the devil himself. Try not to lose your faith Allessia. You have Sylvie and she's a part of Joseph."

For nights afterwards the visions of the rows of skeletal men haunted Allessia's dreams and her eyes carried black rings from so little sleep. She lost weight as the thought of eating food made her physically sick

Allessia changed. Only a tiny speck of hope for Joseph lingered in a far off corner of her consciousness. She had decided it was time to talk to Sylvie.

"Little One, I need to tell you grow-up things about this terrible war. Many Jews have been killed in the Camps that Hitler forced them into. Nobody knows just how many have died. It's been six months now since the war ended and as none of the Jews from Menton have returned, I'm afraid we may have to assume that Papa may not come back." She paused, and allowed the information to sink in.

"Mama, don't talk like that, lots of Jews may have died, old ones like Grandpapa and Grandmama but not Papa, not my Papa; he's a big strong man and he'll come home, I know he will. Why would he be killed? He's a good man and he's my Papa. I'm not going to talk about it. I am going to play in the tree hut." Then dismissively, with no sign of tears she ran off. A few days later, Allessia had just finished the peaches she had been preserving when she heard Sylvie shout.

"Mama, Mama! Naomi's Papa has come home. He has no teeth, but he has come home." She flung open the door. "He was in one of Hitler's camps and he's come home. It took him forever 'cause he had to walk most of the way."

Allessia quickly wiped her hands, hardly believing what she'd heard. Anxious excitement bristled through her body as she steadied Sylvie by firmly holding her shoulders.

"Now, Little One, quietly, tell me all you know."

Sylvie dropped her school bag and sat on the kitchen chair.

"Well, you know Naomi who lives with the Nuns; she's in the class above me. She told us at playtime that last night a man turned up at the orphanage, just before it was dark. Mother Superior wasn't going to let him in because he had no teeth and he was all dirty. Anyway, he said he was Naomi's Papa and finally they let him in and Naomi said at first she didn't remember him but when he talked to her she knew it was him. Mama, if he is alive maybe Papa is too?"

Allessia's heart lifted. She hugged her daughter.

"I'll go and visit him tomorrow and see what he can tell us. Now, have some bread and jam."

Once Allessia had finished the breakfasts for the hotel guests and said good-bye to Sylvie at the school gate, she walked around the port towards the border. The orphanage was nestled up above the port. It had been a long time since she walked beside the sea. On the beach front she could see several men bathing in their underpants. They had obviously been sleeping rough and this was their daily wash. Their dirty clothes and meagre possessions were left in scrappy piles on the rocks. Allessia fantasised that Joseph was somewhere bathing in the sea or a river doing the same as he made his way home.

She took the short-cut up to the orphanage through the ancient olive grove. The olives were no longer picked and it had been converted into a public garden. It evoked further memories of Joseph and how, during their courting days, they would sit up there holding hands and talking about their future.

"Madame Reiss! Come in." Allessia struggled to remember the name of the nun who greeted her.

"I would very much like to talk with Nathaniel Cohen please. I am assuming he's still here?"

The Sister avoided answering the question. "Just wait here please and I will bring Mother Superior." She scuttled off up the marble-floored corridor.

"Madame Reiss, I'm sorry to keep you waiting. Sister Mary is very nervous about visitors here, as we were so strict about discretion during the war, especially with all the children we had disguised." The Mother Superior gave out an aura of serenity coupled with self-confidence.

"I would like to talk with Monsieur Cohen. My daughter told me he'd returned."

"Of course, I fully understand your situation. But first I must tell you he's in a very bad way. Not only is he physically ill, but I suspect mentally very fragile, so we'll keep him here and care for him as long as is needed. By all means chat with him but please, make this visit as brief as you can."

Allessia followed Mother Superior down the austere corridor to a sunny courtyard. She tapped lightly on a set of adjoining glass doors. "Nathaniel! Are you awake?" She called softly.

"Yes, Mother. Please come in."

Allessia followed directly behind her. She barely believed

the man sitting before her was Nathaniel. He appeared to have halved his previous body weight, most of his hair had fallen out and there were red scabs covering his sunken cheeks and the backs of his hands. All of his teeth were missing. She managed to smile.

"Hello, Nathaniel. It's me, Allessia Reiss."

His response was slow. "Yes I know you Allessia. I haven't quite lost my mind yet. Not entirely anyway." He gave her a gummy grin.

"I will leave you two for a while. But please, Nathaniel, you mustn't tire yourself."

Allessia pulled up a chair next to the bed.

"As soon as I was able I was going to visit you, but all of my strength finally gave out when I arrived here and could see Naomi was safe." He paused to catch his breath.

"We had all given up hope that any of you would return. It's been over six months since the war ended." She didn't want to push him.

"Allessia, I know what you want to hear. I can't tell you anything about where Joseph may or may not be now. As you know we were taken on the same day and both ended up in Drancy. As Joseph and I were healthy and strong, they kept us there and worked us to near death. Joseph was amongst a big group they'd just herded onto a train heading for Auschwitz Camp in Poland. But the Allies were well on their offensive by then, targeting any German transport. And the train carrying all the prisoners was a casualty of an attack. From what I heard, not everyone was killed. Many fled. And that's all I know." He began to cough.

Allessia waited 'till the cough had subsided.

"So, Joseph may be out there somewhere, hurt?"

She looked into Nathaniel's eyes, pleading for more.

"I wouldn't hold out much hope. I was one of about fifty still alive when the allies liberated us. It was just sheer bloody mindedness and desperation to see Naomi again that got me back here. There are thousands of displaced men and it is impossible to get on trains without tickets. None of us have any money and many people found the sight of us so offensive they just didn't know how to react."

Allessia sighed as she placed her face in her hands. Nathaniel reached his bony hand out to touch her.

"The thing I can tell you, as a fact, is how much Joseph thought about you and Sylvie when we were in that terrible place. The only thing that gave him strength was that you were waiting for him. I knew my Nelly and my boys were dead, they had long been taken to Auschwitz. My only hope was that the Sisters had succeeded in keeping my girl hidden up here."

Mother arrived at the door. "I think Nathaniel needs to rest now. You may come back as often as you wish Allessia. But best for short periods to begin with."

Allessia bent over and kissed her husband's dear friend goodbye.

Twelve

It was December and the trees had lost their leaves and the blooms had deserted the garden. All around Allessia and Sylvie people prepared for Christmas. The town lights had been resurrected and the shop windows were bursting with Nativity scenes, angels and Father Christmas. With little enthusiasm Allessia had done her traditional Christmas baking, with Sylvie helping stir the chocolate mixture for the log cake.

"We will have to make gingerbread men cookies – boys for Mario and angel ones for me, Mama. And I want chocolate ones as well please!"

Carla and Mario were expected on 20th December and Sylvie had counted the days 'till her wonderful cousin arrived. The tree-hut had been adorned with old Christmas decorations that looked sadder by the day as they faded with the rain. Allessia attempted to join in the spirit of the festivities but the empty place inside her heart couldn't be filled. At least twice a week she made the trip up to the orphanage.

"So now you're well on the mend, when will you and Naomi return to your house?" The two friends sat beside the fire in the small salon Nathaniel and his daughter used as their own.

"Mother Superior thinks I should wait until it's a bit warmer in March, as my chest still rattles a little. She's been so kind. What do you think of my new teeth?" He flashed a big smile showing his shiny, white Bakelite teeth the latest invention from England.

"You look back to your old self. The food must be good here as you've certainly gained weight." She poked his tummy and returned the smile.

"Would you and Naomi like to join Carla, Mario, Sylvie and me on Christmas day? I know it's not a Jewish celebration but we would love to have you."

"Thank you, Allessia, but there's been so much preparation here. The Nuns go all out at Christmas for the children, and Naomi is really looking forward to it. She feels the other children are her family now."

During these visits they rarely mentioned Joseph. But in a strange way she felt close to her husband by being with his friend. Sylvie's state of excitement was driving Allessia crazy; every second word seemed to be Mario and the talk today was all about the Christmas tree.

"Mama, I know we have a sort of a Christmas tree at the back of the garden. But the man in the market is selling proper ones. You know, they are pointy at the top."

Allessia counted to five before she responded.

"Little One, we don't have money to be buying a tree when we have our own growing in the garden. Once we decorate it I am sure it will look just wonderful and I have bought you three different colours of crepe paper to make decorations."

This distracted Sylvie who then set herself up with glue and scissors.

She had been back and forth to the gate since eight a. m. watching down the road. It was about eleven a. m. when Bartolo's truck finally pulled up outside the villa.

"Mama, mama! They're here!"

The Villa appeared to take on new life with the return of the Orengo's. The children's chatter and giggles echoed through the house. Allessia felt a sense of inner warmth, comfortably relaxed by the fire with Carla, sharing their children's antics.

All the permanent hotel guests had gone off to family for the Christmas period so Allessia felt very indulgent, only having the four of them to concern herself with. Carla's once plump face looked pinched and withdrawn. Allessia observed that under the surface the bitterness within Carla had firmly taken root.

"Can I say or do anything to help you Carla?" Allessia feebly attempted to offer some respite.

"No Allessia nothing helps. I'm aware we maybe the lucky ones to have our children alive, but you and I both know we are just masquerading. Who else would care about our pain? I will hold on to and protect my Mario for as long as I have breath, but for myself, when death comes I'll welcome it like a lover."

Allessia was dumbstruck. A stony silence had engulfed the room.

It was interrupted by Sylvie's shouts.

"Mama, Aunty Carla! Please come now. Mario has found Papa's axe and we need your help to chop down the Christmas tree."

The women grabbed their coats. With the vision of Mario and an axe they broke into a run across the hard cold earth.

"I've waited 'till you got here but I think I am strong enough to chop it!" Mario was poised with the heavy cleaver.

"Okay, but just chop it half way through. Then we will push so it falls towards the fence," Allessia instructed her nephew. Mario then demonstrated his brute strength. One chop, one big push and the tree went down.

"Bravo, Mario!" Allessia sung out.

Mario, ignoring his Mama's stare, beamed with pride, at his Aunty and cousins applaud. As they dragged the tree back down to the villa Allessia was unable to suppress her emotion. It had always been Joseph's job. Despite being Jewish he loved to involve himself with the delight of this happy tradition. Allessia checked herself as she realised her thoughts were in the past tense.

The entire population of Menton appeared to be squashed into the Basilica, in the old town for midnight Mass. The gilt frescos glistened in the glow of the hundreds of candles that framed the statues of various Saints around the Church.

The burning incense, being both a French and Italian tradition, created a smoky haze, which mingled with a pleasant pungent fragrance and enhanced the atmosphere of this dramatic holy place.

There was standing room only for latecomers. Allessia, Carla and the children had seats by the choir, which, assisted by the acoustics of the vaulted ceiling sounded gloriously melodic. Sylvie was singing along at the top of her voice to her favourite carols while a slightly embarrassed Mario barely opened his mouth.

The next morning Allessia awoke to an excited Sylvie standing at the end of her bed, "Mama, Mama, please can we open the presents?"

As she followed her eager daughter downstairs her own sadness and loss threatened to overwhelm her.

Carla had joined her, and sensing she needed to make an effort reassuringly patted Allessia's back as they affectionately watched the two over-excited children race to open the gifts under the tree.

Around two p. m. they sat down to the gourmet Christmas feast.

"Look Mama I've found a charm." Sylvie held up the small silver heart Allessia had concealed in the Christmas pudding.

"Yippee! I can make a wish!" She closed her eyes.

"I wish if Papa doesn't get here in time for Christmas day that he will make it for New Year's Eve." She spoke out loudly and then added an Amen as if she'd said a prayer.

"The wish won't come true if you say it out loud," Mario interjected.

"Yes it will 'cause I said Amen," she snapped back at him, full of self-belief.

Neither woman said a word.

Thirteen

Boxing Day passed and the two families fell back into their comfortable rhythms together, making the most of the ten days they had before Carla and Mario would leave and the hotel guests return. Allessia and Carla had packed up several small parcels of leftover food and along with the children they visited the railway station where many displaced men and some women had been sleeping rough. Most of the men had been given warm clothes and food and had gathered around a roaring fire which burned in a large, used petrol drum. They flirted and joked as the two attractive women handed out the food parcels. But the children held back, keeping their eyes on their Mamas from a safe distance. "I'll stay over here with Sylvie," said Mario. "You know how scared she gets."

"I just hope somewhere out there someone did something kind for my Joseph," Allessia confided to Carla as they walked back to the Villa. It was the end of 1945 and of twelve months of horror. Allessia reflected that nothing could ever be worse than this year. They had planned to stay in for New Year's Eve, to celebrate as a family. The children had gone down the street to visit friends and Allessia was lost in her thoughts, when Carla interrupted by handing her a coffee. They were disturbed, as they heard Mario's desperate shouts. "Mama, Aunty Allessia! Quick! Come now! It's Sylvie. "

Both women rushed outside.

"What is it Mario? What's happened?" Allessia filled with dread.

The boy turned and pointed.

"Look, its Sylvie. She's holding that dirty tramp's hand and bringing him up here."

Sylvie was in easy view a few metres down the road. She held the hand of a grubby man in filthy ragged clothes; his pants appeared too short, he was void of socks and had some old rope tied around his middle in an attempt to keep his faded worn coat fastened. His head was shaved and his pale face covered in dirty rough stubble. Man and girl walked slowly up towards them. Allessia's panic subsided once it was apparent her daughter was unharmed.

"Maybe he's one of the chaps from the railway station. She probably just wants to give him some food. "Allessia relaxed as she walked down the hill towards them.

"He must have a hurt leg or something. He's struggling a bit with that limp," Carla added.

"She was gone for ages before I found her. And she was holding that tramp's hand." Mario's voice betrayed him, he was scared. Carla firmly took his hand. They moved nearer. Allessia couldn't quite make out exactly what Sylvie was saying to the bedraggled man, but she caught her soothing tone. As they stepped closer she saw he wasn't one of the tramps she recognised from the railway station.

"Sylvie, tell us who your new friend is." Allessia was almost face to face with the sad, dirty excuse for a human being. At the same instant her daughter spoke, Allessia recognised something familiar about his eyes.

"Mama, he's not my friend! He's my Papa. I told you all he would be home today!"

PART TWO
REBECCA

London, 1954

Fourteen

Rebecca waited apprehensively on the platform at Paddington station, still not entirely convinced she had made the right decision to leave London. But she was desperate to get away from home. To take the option of a working holiday on the French Riviera had sounded like a great way to evade her mother, but Rebecca harboured some suspicions about her host, her second cousin Aaron.

Her pushy mother had grasped onto Cousin Aaron's suggestion with both hands. She'd viewed it as an advantageous way to save face. It would be perceived as a 'finishing' year for Rebecca, without actually paying to attend a finishing school. The Samuels weren't in the same financial league as many of their peers. Her mother was bitterly disappointed she lacked the privilege of class, so she constantly unearthed ways to maintain the façade.

Rebecca's silent qualms were interrupted by the noisy arrival on the platform of her grandparents and Aunt and Uncle.

"My girl, my girl you are so young to be going so far." Her grandfather's wiry white beard scratched her cheek as he hugged her.

"Don't fuss Dad; she's on her way now, we've already had this conversation." Rebecca's mother butted in.

"Don't forget to write in your smart new dairy; it's very special, I bought it from Harrods." Her Aunty Hannah had cheerily chipped in.

Once all the family had expressed their emotional Jewish farewells and then moved on to discuss the merits of the

French Riviera, her father had discreetly led Rebecca out of earshot and pressed some pound notes into her hand.

"You'll be okay my girl, I'm sure you may even meet a suitable husband in France, don't take to heart all your mother's match-making, just be your own person."

His eyes welled up; he embraced Rebecca one last time, and then guided her back to the group. Aunty Hannah had her back to them as they approached, but Rebecca heard the conversation clearly.

"She's so young and naïve, are you sure she'll be safe on foreign soil?"

"Well, what else can I do with her? She's not like the other two, she's almost an embarrassment."

Rebecca bit her top lip over her crooked teeth, as she felt the hurtful sting of her mother's tactless reply. Her father had attempted to rescue the situation as he'd loudly called his wife's name, but the damage was done. Rebecca hurriedly stepped into the carriage as a shot of steam bellowed out and the guard blew a loud blast on his highly polished silver whistle.

Although she'd quickly lost sight of them all as the steam engulfed the platform, her families noisy distinct goodbyes could be heard until the train finally chugged out of the station. Rebecca found her seat located in a private compartment which she would share with two other passengers' .The first to arrive was a thin, balding man who wore an ill-fitting suit, thick, dirty spectacles and smelt of whisky. They were joined by a bulky middle-aged woman carrying a basket, who bustled about, reminding Rebecca of her mother. The woman 'tut tutted' to no one in particular, then nestled her large bottom onto the seat.

"You're very young to be travelling on your own," the fat woman commented once she realised that Rebecca wasn't connected to the alcohol-fragrant gentleman.

"I'm seventeen and going to help in my cousin's hotel, and improve my French for a year in Nice," Rebecca had responded politely in an attempt to sound grown up. Then in a bid to stem the conversation she excused herself to use the toilet.

As she critically studied her reflection in the murky, toilet mirror her mother's words rang in her ears "That hair Rebecca, it needs to be kept under control; you can't have it flowing all over the place. Try those new hair curlers I bought you; anything to get you looking better." Rebecca scrutinised her eyes, which she viewed as her best feature. Large, brown and round, they seemed to compensate for her slightly crooked top teeth which insecurely hindered her smile.

Her slim figure still lacked the breasts she would prefer, and her crop of thick, unruly, dark wavy hair, had been the bain of her mother's life. Her mother criticised most things. She'd desired her daughter to marry a nice Jewish boy who might have hopefully been a little higher up the north London social scale than the Samuels. But, according to the professional 'match-maker' her mother had engaged, Rebecca's problem was her attitude.

She'd sighed out loud as she sat on the closed loo seat and thought of the obnoxious match-maker and some of those ugly men with whom she had to have tea. Never in a million years would she even have considered kissing one, let alone marrying. She'd enjoyed her school French lessons, art and writing, all of which she'd hoped would improve, so it seemed a reasonable alternative to take Cousin Aaron's offer.

For the remainder of the journey, to avoid conversation with her fat companion, she pretended to be engrossed in writing in her new leather-bound diary. Once the train had pulled in near the ferry terminal at Southampton, Rebecca felt deflated. The ship didn't look at all exciting and romantic as she'd imagined; it seemed oversized, industrial and detached. She found a seat near an open door to the deck. Once at sea she felt brave enough to wander about. On a seat further along she noticed another girl about her age who looked slightly hesitant. Rebecca gave her a half smile, to which the girl responded.

"Hello, are you travelling alone as well?"

"Yes, I'm Rebecca Samuels from London, 'how do you do'." She extended her hand.

The girl replied, "Pleased to meet you, I'm Sandy, where are you off to?" She played with her fringe as she spoke, and her eyes widened in a slight stare as she shook Rebecca's hand. Rebecca imparted to her new friend the abridged version of her adventure to Nice.

"How wonderful, I'm going to Nice as well, to live with my father; he's French and divorced from my English mother. He feels sure with my grasp of the language I should be able to get a job there and live with him."

Sandy's blonde hair was tied up in the latest ponytail, with a thick fringe that just stopped short of her eyebrows. She wore a sloppy blue sweater and narrow black cropped slacks. She appeared to have perfected the modern look. Their conversation was relaxed and frank and Sandy disclosed to Rebecca how her mother had decided to marry again and wanted her daughter out of the way. Sandy saw her father twice a year, but could never remember living with him as her parents had parted when she was tiny.

"I'm a bit apprehensive about it but even though we're a bit awkward together I know he really cares for me."

Rebecca was fascinated how each time Sandy completed a sentence she widened her eyes.

"I've never been away from home before, but my Mum was driving me mad with the obsession of getting me married off and, well frankly, I want to have a good time first. We're Jewish and in my family's social circle if you don't have the brains for extended education and a profession then you need to marry well." Rebecca halted, not wishing to sound disloyal.

"Well at least your Mum was interested enough to try; I just feel my Mum wanted to get rid of me. What's your cousin in Nice like?"

"I only met him the once at my brother's bar mitzvah; he's more like an Uncle as he's about my Dad's age. He's owned a hotel in Nice since the end of the war; I liked him initially but then after he had a few drinks I found him a bit sleazy – however his wife will be there too, so I think I should be okay."

Sandy was to spend two nights in Calais with a family friend, whilst Rebecca had been booked in at a bed-and-breakfast place for one night before she caught the train to Nice. After they'd exchanged addresses they'd agreed to meet at Sandy's father's house in a week's time. The French countryside captivated Rebecca's imagination. From the train window she gained momentary glimpses of her new country. There were few animals as the train rumbled along, mainly crops and fields of unidentifiable greenery.

The smoke from the steam engine created a pleasant haze in front of her window which added a dreamlike appearance to the constantly changing scenes. Then it all began to feel very foreign. After the first four hours she was less distracted, and a sense of unease set in as she realised just how far she was from home.

When the train finally arrived at Gare de Nice, Rebecca's anxiety abated a little. Like Paddington, the station was busy and noisy, full of people who all seemed to push and shout. It took Rebecca a few minutes to gain her bearings as she had to walk down the stairs on the platform to get across to the main station on the other side of the tracks.

Fifteen

"Rebecca! Rebecca! over here!" Cousin Aaron's words in English boomed out above the foreign rabble. Aaron looked a bit of a sight. At five feet eight inches tall, he was only slightly taller than Rebecca. He had a little pot tummy which he attempted to hide under his smartly-tailored jacket, but the two buttons done up appeared strained. In contrast, his trousers which were just a bit too baggy, with the hems falling a little far forward on his shoes. Despite this 'crumply' look he stood very straight, with a full head of black hair and he had a confident manner as he took Rebecca's suitcase.

"Hello Cousin I'm very pleased to see you." He responded by kissing her on both cheeks.

"Nice station is always like this. It's the main hub for trains departing to all over France. Here's the car, let's get you to your new home. Best you call us Aunt and Uncle as we are nearer your parent's age, if you are okay with that?"

His words and his kisses had felt uncomfortable, and seemed to linger with stickiness on her cheeks. In contrast, his Citroen car was sleek and comfy and smelt of new leather.

"Over on the left is the Negresco Hotel. Hotel Samuels is a baby in comparison, but we benefit by being located in the same area." His commentary smacked of self-importance.

As they drove along the famous Promenade Des Anglais, Rebecca was mesmerised. The sea appeared just how she'd read about it in travel books. Pure azure blue and tipped with a white froth framed by what appeared to be a neat line of golden sand and tiny stones. People were very well dressed; men sported the latest double-breasted suits, some in lighter shades such as caramel and cream. They seemed to saunter rather than walk along the promenade and many wore straw panama hats. Without exception, the women all emulated movie stars, their eyes shaded and framed with fashionable sunglasses, their heads crowned with either a large sun hat or a colourful silk scarf.

Rebecca's senses went into overdrive; she imagined that she was alive in a page from the glamorous 'People' magazine. The exterior of Samuels Hotel was typical of most of the surrounding buildings. Four stories high, painted off-white, the full-length windows flanked with duck egg blue shutters and a grand, central, front door entrance. In the reception area there were polished wood floors surrounded by extravagant plasterwork and cornicing; but it had a modern and spacious feel to it all. There were fifty-five guest bedrooms all together.

"Welcome Rebecca to Hotel Samuels. So I finally get to meet you! I'm your Aunty Liz." A short, slim, blonde woman offered her handshake to Rebecca.

She responded politely, but detected a hint of hypocrisy in her greeting.

"I'm very pleased to meet you, thank you for inviting me."

Uncle interrupted as he arrived with the case.

"Let's get you up to your room, and then tonight we can all eat together."

Rebecca's room was on the top floor in what was called the servants' quarters, but despite the somewhat lowly reference, the room had a wonderful view. It was large and airy and the bed was covered with the latest soft gold candlewick bedspread and matching cushions. The furniture was classic French. The best feature was that she had sole use of the adjoining bathroom.

Dinner gave Rebecca a chance to see how the restaurant worked and the opportunity to study her Aunty at close quarters. She was immaculately groomed, only spoke when necessary but seemed to be frosty towards Rebecca.

"We thought it best to first go over what we expect of you. And then you can ask any questions." Uncle started. Then Aunty interjected.

"You will be expected to assist with setting the dining room for both breakfast and dinner. This will mean a six-thirty morning start, as breakfast is served at eight a.m. Dinner is at seven-thirty. Our standards here at the hotel are high, so every aspect of the set table must be immaculate. You will initially work with Ronnie, who will show you what we expect."

Her words had a certain tone. Uncle appeared to ignore her and then took over. "We have many widows and single, older women here, mostly from England, and it will be your responsibility to run any errands for them, accompany them when required, and generally ensure their stay is pleasant, so that they return each season and spread the word to their friends. You may have the weekends off."

Rebecca had just plucked up the courage to ask about the stipend, when Aaron beat her to it. "You will receive one hundred Francs a week and have time off, by prior arrangement, when you find a suitable French class to attend. Saturdays and Sundays will be your days off. We must insist on you telling us where you are going and with whom. And you must be in by ten p.m."

Rebecca thanked them and inwardly reflected there not much change on the rules front from home in London. The meal of coq-au-vin was delicious, but the atmosphere between her Aunt and Uncle was conspicuously awkward.

"It's been a big day for me. Many thanks for dinner. I'll be in the dining room sharp at six-thirty to meet Ronnie in the morning."

As they exchanged their goodnights, Rebecca looked directly into her Aunt's eyes. They weren't actually frosty at all, they were sad, as if something or someone had extinguished their light. Rebecca kissed them both, and then left for her room. Rebecca's next few days were filled with new tasks and the frustration of not being able to make herself fully understood. Ronnie was a great help, as he was English and spoke fluent French and Italian. There was, however, something a little odd about him. He was immaculately groomed with his hair greased down in the modern style but so much so it almost over shone. He wore his uniform with pride but walked in an affected way; what Rebecca's Mum would call a 'mince'. He reminded Rebecca of an actor in one of the pantomimes her family attended at Christmas time. She half-expected him to shout out accordingly, but he didn't shout, he spoke very softly and kindly and showed her all that was expected of her.

"Thanks so much Ronnie, I know I've been quite useless; I seem to be getting the hang of it all now, I do however find my Aunt a bit scary. I'm glad it isn't her showing me the ropes."

Ronnie beamed. "I'm enjoying the company; you're a shy wee thing, but you'll be an old hand soon. Don't mind your Aunt, she's okay really; things aren't quite what they seem." Rebecca paused, as she waited for him to enlighten her, but he just finished his coffee and moved on to his work.

Sixteen

On Sunday morning Rebecca, armed with a map, ambled off to find Sandy's house, which was situated in the old town. Nearly all villages on the Riviera had an old quarter as well as a more recently built area. Nice old town dated back to the 13th Century and lacked many of the modern services such as a good sewage system. Initially it all fascinated Rebecca, but many of the street names were unreadable and could hardly be called streets, just narrow, dim, alleys; badly lit, with a persistent odour. After an hour of getting lost and slightly panicked, Rebecca finally made out the street name she'd been looking for. She gave a cautious knock, and was mightily relieved when it was a smiling Sandy who opened the door.

"Bienvenue! Welcome to our home!" She greeted Rebecca like a long lost friend. "You're in time to eat; Father always cooks a proper meal for Sunday lunch."

The aroma coming from the kitchen immediately made Rebecca feel hungry and homesick at the same time.

"My family in London always had Sunday lunch as well. Father insisted that one day a week we all put the effort into eating together." As she entered the small, cosy kitchen, Rebecca could see Sandy's father bent over the bench as he whisked something loudly in a bowl. When he turned she couldn't help but notice his slightly blood-shot eyes and stained, brown teeth that were superseded by a huge warm smile. He had a slightly faded look about him. His clothes, although they had once been of the latest style, were now dated and had seen better days.

"I am so 'appy you can join us for lunch. Sandy, please pour us all some wine."

His English had a strong French accent and he dropped all his 'H's.' But to Rebecca's ear it sounded attractive and funny at the same time. After the delicious lunch, Sandy's father, having drunk far too much red wine, quickly fell asleep in his chair.

"Father's main problem is the wine. Mother always said that, but he's always kind and still manages to go to work each day." Sandy's voice had been full of reservation, as she pulled at her fringe and they lingered on their coffee.

"When are we going to go out on the town?" Rebecca chipped in, steering the conversation onto a brighter note.

"Well I've given it some thought; I've had a good look around Nice and I think we should aim high if we want to meet some exciting types. What do you think?" Sandy's eyes widened.

"Me? I'm open to anything. What's the plan?"

"Well on Saturday let's meet just along from the Negresco Hotel at about seven p.m. You'll need to be dressed up as smart as you can, with some spending money. I should have the details sorted out by then; I feel confident we can pull it off, so I will tell you the rest when we meet."

Seventeen

There were several hotel guests that needed assistance and they all fussed a lot, but Rebecca coped. She took the view that they were similar to many of her parents' Jewish friends, as they all liked to use an excess of unnecessary words and energy to achieve very little result. Almost on a daily basis she was required to visit the old town, which was where the seamstress lived, the dry-cleaners and, most importantly, the doctor, who had a business almost exclusively administering to the Samuels Hotel guests.

"They're all a bunch of hypochondriacs! I'm sure they are just seeking attention!" Rebecca told Ronnie, after her third accompanying visit to the doctor in as many days.

"Well they don't have husbands anymore; some of them never had husbands, so they crave any male attention; and let's face it Becca, that doctor is so handsome."

Ronnie had a way with words that made Rebecca giggle, and she loved her new nickname. Saturday came round and Rebecca tapped on Ronnie's door.

"Is that you, Ma Cherie?" He responded

"No I am not Cherie. I am Becca!" They both laughed at their silly joke as he opened his door.

"Now, where shall I go to buy the best dress in Nice?"

Ronnie was thoughtful. "Well I guess it depends on your budget. But if it was me, I'd head straight for Galleries Lafayette. Second floor. Ladies fashions."

Armed with his instructions, most of her savings and all of her first week's wages Rebecca set off to Galleries Lafayette. It was the first time she'd ever shopped for clothes without being accompanied by her mother. As she walked to the newly built department store, she keenly observed the style of the weekend lady shoppers. Nice was far removed from the style in North London. French women invented the word 'chic' and that was how Rebecca intended to look tonight.

On entering Galleries Lafayette a whole new world had opened to her. Her first encounter, just inside the door, was an entire department devoted to cosmetics and perfume. There was an overwhelming fragrance of Paris de Nuit. The interior décor was avant-garde. She observed the well groomed, immaculately made up assistants in lilac uniforms offer squirts of perfume to equally well groomed, attractive customers. Rebecca began to feel inadequate, as if she was a less than beautiful interloper.

Once she'd stepped out of the lift on the second floor she was confronted by two of the most beautiful frocks she'd ever seen. They were dressed on store mannequins, one black and the other red. The red one, waisted with a full skirt, was hypnotic. She decided first to view a few more dresses on the rails before enquiring to try the red one. But everything else had paled into insignificance compared to her first choice. It was "V" necked, sleeveless with a large, black, patent leather belt; the hemline sat just below the knee and had a stiff layer of netting underneath to create the full-skirt look that was so fashionable. The shop assistant approached her.

"Bonjour Mademoiselle. Je peux vous aider?"

Rebecca had been daydreaming, so automatically replied in English. "I'm just looking. But do you have my size?"

"You are English, no? I will speak English for you."

She'd sounded condescending and superior, but

Rebecca only cared about trying on the divine confection of red crisp cotton.

"I have it in several sizes on my stock–rail, I think you are a size ten." She beckoned Rebecca to follow her to the fitting room area.

"Here Mademoiselle! The price is on the swing label!" She handed her the frock.

It had the feel of new cotton and was lined in the softest satin. Rebecca loved the way it glided down her torso as she slipped it over her head. She studied the full effect in the large gilt mirror, then decided as she'd almost gnawed away her top lip, no matter what the cost, she must own the frock.

"This is the most beautiful I have ever felt in my life. It's like magic!" she murmured.

"Does Mademoiselle need assistance?" The assistant had been close to the door.

"No thank you. I'll take the frock."

There was a swift change of tone.

"Merci beaucoup, Mademoiselle. Perhaps I will serve you on your next visit?"

The rest of the afternoon Rebecca had spent deciding which way to wear her hair; after flicking through a smart fashion magazine a guest has discarded, she'd decided on a high ponytail.

"Uncle, I'm meeting my friend Sandy and we are going to her favourite brasserie," Rebecca reported to her Uncle as was required, but had added the part about the brasserie so it all sounded safe.

"Well, you look very beautiful, my Dear!" He'd stood a bit too close for comfort, and, as he spoke, she smelt his stale breath which reeked of wine.

"Remember your curfew of ten p.m." he called as she moved quickly out the door. Sandy was waiting at their agreed spot.

"Sandy! You look wonderful! We match!" Sandy wore a black, taffeta, waisted frock, a similar style to Rebecca's, but with a scoop neck and small cap sleeves.

"Now, this is my plan. I think we should aim high, go where all the fashionable people go. For that reason I've chosen the Negresco Hotel. We'll walk into the bar; as we are unescorted we'll have to fake it. I'll do all the talking, just follow my lead. The main thing is to appear as if you've visited hotels this grand all your life."

Rebecca didn't get a word in, but she was enthralled by Sandy's sense of humour and adventure and elated to follow in her wide eyed wake. The hotel foyer was magnificent. Opulent was not even near to describing it. There were polished, cream, marble tiles, thick, red, velvet drapes, caught back with gold tassels, elaborate, sunken sofas, all crowned overhead by giant, shimmering, crystal chandeliers.

"Heads up Rebecca." Sandy whispered as they walked across the foyer to the bar.

"Bon soir Mademoiselles. Je peux vous aider?" Even the maître d' was resplendent in his green frock-coat with large gold buttons.

"We're meeting our uncle here; he may be a little late, so please, could you show us to a table?" Sandy announced rather than informed in near perfect French.

"Certainly Mademoiselle. Follow me please." He led them across the crowded room. Most eyes in the room turned to watch as the stunning, youthful duo were shown to a comfortable table in the corner.

"We will both have a Martini please," Sandy spoke confidently to the maître d'.

"What's in a Martini Sandy? I've never had one," Rebecca whispered once he was out of earshot.

"Neither have I. I just saw Ava Gardner order one in that film 'The Killers'." They both burst into a fit of giggles.

"I really have to pee. Can you see where the lav's are?" Sandy pointed to the other corner of the room.

"Oh! I have to walk across the room again; I don't think I can do that!"

"Don't show your shyness, just keep your head up, try not to bite your lip and look straight ahead with confidence!" Sandy said. Rebecca timidly left her seat. It felt like a long trek across to the other side of the bar.

She'd only looked straight ahead. It was the poshest lavatory she'd ever seen. All gilt-edged, heavy-framed mirrors, deep, marble sinks with gold Swan taps. A fat, black maid with shiny, red lips and an over-teased, high hair-do was positioned next to a polished, marble table on which stood an array of perfumes. She handed visitors a towel immediately after they had washed their hands and offered them a spray of perfume.

Rebecca was very impressed. Just as she'd thanked her for the towel she spotted the small silver saucer containing various coins and realised she was expected to tip. "I'm sorry! I left my handbag at the table." This was met with a subtle, cynical smile before the maid ignored her and greeted the next visitor to her domain. As she walked back to her seat Rebecca was more relaxed and felt confident enough to have a keen look around the room. The ambience smelt of luxury; the thickness of the wallpaper was tinged with gilt that set a sumptuous background for the heavy-framed, historic paintings that adorned the walls; the glass doors to the terrace were edged with heavy brocade and featured elaborate, gold door handles.

The seated, chatting guests reminded Rebecca of a scene from a movie that had been lavishly coloured. She took her time to walk back; she gazed around the room taking in the glamorous guests' clothes, jewellery and hairstyles. Then suddenly she'd become aware of her own presence within this scene. Her eyes had randomly locked on a man sitting close by, who stared back at her intently with a disturbing smirk, so she'd quickly averted her gaze. But then she'd recognised the same dubious smirk on several of the other male guests. It was as if they'd suspected she didn't really belong. She quickened her pace, eager to get back to the reassuring, secure company of her confidant friend.

As she rushed to sit down the waiter arrived to place the Martinis on the table. He bent down directly next to her as she straightened up in her chair and looked intently into her eyes; his eyes were amazing, deep brown and twinkled with excitement.

"Bellisimo!" was all he'd said, and then he beamed at her, as he revealed a smile full of clear white teeth.

"Goodness me Rebecca! Look at your face; it's gone beetroot, you're blushing!" Sandy burst into giggles.

"What does 'Bellisimo' mean? He's so handsome!"

Rebecca had attempted to compose herself by taking a sip of the Martini, which was slightly difficult given the olive balancing on a toothpick in the glass.

"It means 'beautiful' in Italian, silly. I was watching him, watching you. He could have brought the drinks over a little sooner but he waited and followed you over. You really look striking in that dress Rebecca!"

The effect of the alcohol had lowered their reserve, and the volume of the giggles increased. "We'd better slow down with our drinks. I'm not sure we will be able to afford a second one." Sandy attempted to be practical.

Rebecca was a little concerned, as she hadn't a lot left after spending so much on her frock. "Look! Mr Brown Eyes is still looking over in our direction, I wonder if he'll talk to us."

Rebecca had appraised him as he worked around the room; he seem to glide effortlessly, as he held his silver tray, stopping to collect an empty glass or give a customer a smile as he took the drink orders. He wasn't particularly tall, about five feet seven inches but he'd walked with a swagger of purpose. His hair was cut short, close to his head at the sides, with quite a thick, long 'mop' on the top of his head parted at the side and lightly greased with the latest Brylcream.

Sandy wittily commentated as they discreetly observed the guests dotted around the bar. About three-quarters of an hour had passed and they knew they must leave. Sandy beckoned the maître d'.

"It seems our uncle has been delayed; please bring our bill as we think it best to go and look for him." He returned promptly with the bill on a silver tray and left it on the table.

"My God! How much money have you got Rebecca? This is triple what I thought it would be!" The girls were in a blind panic as between them they didn't have enough cash to cover the two cocktails. Suddenly Mr Brown Eyes the waiter had appeared beside them.

"Just put what cash you have on the tray. Then get up

and leave as confidently as you walked in. Then meet me at Café Fontaine on Rue de la Tour at nine p.m."

He'd said all this in French which Sandy quickly translated. As instructed they put the money down, rose and walked across the bar. Once out on the Promenade they fell into fits of laughter.

"That was so exciting! Wasn't he brilliant?" Rebecca cooed as they flopped down on a pavement seat.

"Well, we have the red dress to thank, I am sure!" Sandy quipped. "Let's go and see if we can find this Café Fontaine." Arm-in-arm they moved off in the direction where many of the cafés and brasseries were located. They easily found the small establishment with its red and white awning and the tables had matching red gingham tablecloths, the blackboard menu offered very affordable prices. It was eight forty-five. The girls decided to take a seat and order a coffee.

"I've found two francs in the bottom of my bag. So at least we can pay for the coffee if he doesn't turn up," Sandy commented as she fossicked in her bag. At five minutes past nine a Vespa motor scooter roared up and parked on the pavement right next to the café. Mr Brown Eyes had an equally handsome companion-riding pillion.

"Bon soir. I'm Mario, and this is Claudio my best friend. We are Italian, but we speak French very well." They sat themselves down. Both boys were similar in height and hairstyles, very typically Italian but Claudio appeared the more confident as he lit up a cigarette and placed his other hand cockily on his hip.

"I'm Sandy and I can speak French, but not well. This is Rebecca and she speaks only a little French; we're both English."

Mario had taken the seat next to Rebecca and he gazed at her intently while she nervously bit her lip and sipped her coffee. The boys ordered crème caramels all round. Sandy continued the conversation as Rebecca appeared to be mute.

"Where are you from in Italy?"

"We are from villages across the border called Castel Vittorio and Pigna. They are very near each other, up above Ventimiglia. The French management at the Negresco love Italian waiters as we are so charming, and we are able to live in the staff quarters. We have one hour off now for our break."

Claudio was full of pride and humour. He smoked continuously and his words lacked subtlety, but he'd spoken quite understandable French, and Sandy assuredly translated everything for Rebecca. She struggled to find her tongue but eventually managed to offer a few stilted French words. The two couples exchanged polite information about each other over the next forty minutes.

Mario carried a purposeful expression on his face. His voice had a sincere quality, which had reassured Rebecca. After the boys had paid the bill Mario took Rebecca's hands in his.

"Please, will you meet us here next week? We will arrange a longer break. We will be here at eight thirty." He spoke in a new yielding voice, quite different from his demeanour with the hotel customers. Sandy enthusiastically interpreted.

Rebecca coloured, as she replied. "Oui Mario. I would love to."

Claudio had posed the same request to Sandy. As they'd all stood up to say their goodbyes Mario gently pushed Rebecca's lip from its 'bite' position with his forefinger then softly brushed her cheek with a delicate kiss. "Bella, Bella!" he whispered, before they roared off.

"He may be a little short, but he's so handsome and he has a wonderful smell!" Rebecca leant against Sandy, both girls gazed into the darkness.

"Claudio too." Sandy dreamily replied.

"I've never had a boyfriend; I've never even been out with one without a chaperone before," Rebecca confessed. Sandy smiled. "Well there has to be a first time for everything!" Then Rebecca glanced at her watch.

"Oh I have to go! I'll be late otherwise. Thanks so much Sandy. See you tomorrow." The girls had arranged to meet for Sunday lunch, but due to lack of funds, Rebecca had invited Sandy to the Hotel to join her at the staff lunch. Uncle Aaron intercepted them as they walked into the staff dining room.

"Well! Who have we here Rebecca, a beautiful French friend?" He'd moved disturbingly close to the girls.

"No Uncle. This is Sandy; she's half French, half English. Her father lives here; we met on the train," Rebecca responded politely as she attempted to keep moving.

"Slow down girl. There's no rush. We aren't very full in the restaurant today so why don't I treat you both to a smart lunch. After all you are my family before you're staff." There was no way out.

"Thank you uncle," she reluctantly responded. He ushered them to a table for four and informed them he'd join them once most of the guests had been seated.

"I'm sorry Sandy, I didn't want him around; let's quickly talk about our Italians before he joins us." They stifled their giggles. "Our Italians – I like the sound of that!" Sandy lowered her voice as she looked around to ensure Uncle was out of earshot.

"I have another plan." She paused. "Hurry up! Don't mess about. Tell me!" Rebecca prodded her.

"Well, Our Italians get Sundays off, so, I thought, when we meet them on Saturday evening, we could tell them we are visiting Hanbury Gardens on Sunday and maybe they would like to meet us there."

"What and where is Hanbury Gardens?" Rebecca was intrigued.

"They are famous botanical gardens just across the border in Italy. We could catch the fast train to Menton which takes about forty minutes from Nice, and then a bus across the border and up the hill to the gardens." They were interrupted as Uncle Aaron offered them the alternative of chicken or roast beef. True to his word he joined them for the main course.

"Where's Aunty Liz today?" Rebecca quizzed. "She has a headache so is up in her room resting," he replied bluntly, as he offered both girls a glass of wine.

"No thanks Mr Samuels, I don't drink wine." Sandy covered her glass with her hand. Rebecca took her lead and followed suit.

"You're welcome here any time Sandy." His slimy eyes flicked up and down her body as he spoke. When lunch was finished, so was the entire bottle of wine. Uncle's words were slurred and he insisted he'd walk Sandy to the door. As Rebecca said goodbye, he walked between them and attempted to kiss Sandy on her lips.

"Thank you for lunch Mr Samuels and see you next week Rebecca." She spoke assertively, her eyes wide and flushed with indignation; she'd firmly pushed him away indicating she preferred a handshake rather than the inebriated kiss.

Once Sandy had left, Aaron referred his inappropriate attention towards Rebecca. She'd felt disgusted and panicky as he draped his arm around her shoulder. Then the cavalry arrived in the form of Ronnie.

"Mr Samuels, I need you to give me some advice please on the wines for the menu this week. Could you come to the cellar and cast your eye over them? You are so much better with wine choices than me." He winked at Rebecca, and had inclined his head to indicate she should make her move, as he'd steered his inebriated boss away. About an hour later there had been a tap on Rebecca's door.

"Who is it?" she cautiously answered.

"Just me Becca," Ronnie called as she opened the door. "I won't stay long but I just wanted to check you're okay. Our boss really does seem to have a problem with the drink, and the girls, if you know what I mean. It's caused big problems with Mrs Samuel's who actually isn't as bad as she seems; he treats her very badly."

Rebecca absorbed these comments before she responded.

"Why didn't you tell me all this before? I thought we were friends!" She was hurt.

"We are friends! It's just that I didn't want to plonk it all on you early in the piece. He's your uncle, or cousin, or whatever and I don't enjoy putting him down; it's just that I think you should keep your distance from him when he's drinking." He gave her a hug and she warmed to him again.

"Sorry Ronnie! I just got a bit of a fright; I've never encountered behaviour like that before. My parents don't drink much .My mother say's I'm naïve." They sat side by side on the bed.

"I had my problems when I first came here and Liz and

Aaron were very kind to me when I couldn't get a job anywhere else, but I've watched him deteriorate over the past few years, all to do with the booze. Enough of all that! Let's change the subject. Tell me, how did your big night out in the red dress go?" Ronnie's face was full of expectation.

"Well, I met the most handsome man, he's called Mario and he has the most beautiful brown eyes." She pretended to swoon.

"Lucky girl! Wish I could wear a red dress and meet an Italian. Best keep him under wraps, especially if he's Italian as well as a gentile." Ronnie gave her another hug and minced off.

"He's a strange one sometimes." Rebecca pondered. The week dragged by for Rebecca. It felt like an hour didn't pass without her thoughts wandering to Mario. When he'd kissed her cheek her whole body had seemed to tingle; when he'd looked so intensely into her eyes it had made her feel she was the most special person in the world. On Saturday, she'd tried on all combinations from her wardrobe, unable to decide what would really impress.

"Ronnie, are you in?" She tapped on his door.

"Yes 'Becca. Enter!" He sat on his bed, draped in a floral pink Kimono. Rebecca managed to suppress her surprise.

"I think I need your help. I can't decide what to wear tonight and tomorrow, and it's so important I get it right. If you were taking me out, how would you want me to look?" He stood up with hands on his hips and walked in a circle around her.

"You want me to be honest with you Becca?"

"Of-course! We're friends!" He sat back down on the bed, patting for her to join him. "Well actually, I can only look at you from a woman's view really, as I feel like a woman on the inside."

Rebecca was a little taken aback, and gave an involuntary gulp before she spoke. "I'm not quite sure what you mean but go on."

"You've probably heard of people like me. They call us homosexuals or 'poofs' in English slang".

Rebecca paused, chosing her words carefully.

"I've never met a poof before but how will it stop us being friends? It doesn't bother me! We Jews get called some pretty awful things too; besides you can be more like my girlfriend then!" He immediately embraced her.

"Thank you for saying that, I don't think you're naïve, you're just honest. I struggle with the way I am, and as much as I've tried I can't change, so I've learned to accept myself." His wrist seemed to droop. "Back to your original question, let's be objective now, first, you must wear your hair down. Curl it a little for bounce. Wear a skirt tonight and those modern pedal-pusher slacks tomorrow."

Rebecca returned to her bedroom to wash and set her unruly hair in rollers. "Maybe Mother was right." She said out loud and smiled to herself. By seven-thirty she was finally ready. She had chosen a black, cotton skirt with a stiff net-petticoat underneath. She had tucked a crisp white fitted shirt in at the waist, using the wide, patent leather belt from her new dress.

As she couldn't locate her Uncle, she sought out her Aunty in the kitchen and reported to her that she'd be joining Sandy for a meal and would be home at ten.

"Okay. Have a nice time won't you! Enjoy being young!" Auntie's warm comment surprised Rebecca. Maybe Ronnie was right. He hovered near the front door to catch her on her way out.

"Becca, your hair is perfect! Shiny and with a bounce, oh! You do look beautiful! Take care! Italian men are full of charm but usually with no responsibility." He pecked her cheek as she walked out. The girls met at the line of seats on the Promenade des Anglais nearest to the Negresco which was only a short walk to the Café. It was a perfect summer evening, still daylight but softened with a dusky haze.

"I love your hair down like that. It looks great!" Sandy shared Rebecca's excitement.

"I love your sweater. So modern!" Sandy wore a black sweater in stretch type fabric, which she'd pulled down to expose one shoulder.

"It cost me the earth. It's from Paris, but Father helped me out. I just love it." Like Rebecca she also wore a full, black, stiff-cotton skirt. It was bordered at the hemline with a white pattern. The two girls linked arms as they walked towards the café, and relished the obvious glances their presence provoked from men along the way. Just after eight-thirty the Italians arrived and suggested they order the salad nicoise, the local delicacy, and rosé wine.

"I practise my English very good!" Mario declared, as he took Rebecca's hand.

"I practise my French too!" Rebecca hesitantly replied. They mostly talked as a foursome as Sandy translated and the Italians attempted to introduce English words.

"We're going to Hanbury Gardens tomorrow and were wondering if you'd like to meet us there? We could bring a picnic lunch." Sandy winked at Rebecca.

"Yes!" Both boys responded at once. "Great! The train

leaves at ten-fifteen. Shall we meet you at the station?"

Mario answered "No, we'll meet you at Menton station at eleven, if that's okay?" The hour and a half passed too quickly; Mario had held Rebecca's hand, rubbed his leg against hers and brushed his lips on her cheek several times. As they stood by the scooter to say goodbye, he kissed her on the lips.

"That was the most wonderful sensation I have ever felt," she murmured to Sandy after the boys have left. "My lips are actually trembling!"

"So that was your first proper kiss!" Sandy exclaimed.

"Yes, and I loved it."

Eighteen

Sandy had packed the picnic basket and Rebecca had contributed the lemonade that Ronnie acquired from the hotel kitchen. They'd just made the train in time.

"Let's get a seat on the seaside!" Rebecca was still on a high from the previous evening. Neither girl had taken the trip along the coast before. The train passed through all the chic Riviera towns: Villefranche, Beaulieu-sur-Mer, Eze-sur-Mer. It stopped at the principality of Monaco, where several smartly dressed couples boarded, also armed with picnic baskets. Rebecca had found a brochure in the hotel foyer about the gardens and shared the information with Sandy during the journey.

"Apparently Lord Hanbury fell in love with the Riviera when he first visited about forty years ago. He purchased the land on the Italian side of the border, as it was much cheaper than on the French side. After building his Villa he started importing interesting and exotic plants from all round the world. He owned a shipping company in the Far East, so I guess that helped. His son now opens the gardens to the public."

"Thanks Becca, you sound like some sort of travel commentator for the BBC."

Rebecca grinned. "Even my Uncle recommends a visit as a day trip to the hotel guests so he was okay about me visiting; but I omitted to tell him who else was coming!" The Italians had waited on the platform in Menton to meet the train. They looked so different out of their uniforms.

They wore wide-legged flannels with turn-ups, white shirts and navy blazers; both had slim neckerchiefs tied at their necks. Mario's was navy with white spots.

"Bonjour mes amis! Come this way." Mario greeted Rebecca with a kiss to her hand, as Claudio said something Rebecca didn't quite catch to Sandy.

"He's saying they have a surprise for us." Parked close to the station were the boys' motor scooters. "We are to ride pillion with them up to the gardens," Sandy informed Rebecca. The bikes had been cleaned and polished and had neatly-rolled, plaid picnic blankets clipped on the rear carriers.

"I don't know about this! I've never been on a motor scooter before. Perhaps I'll catch the bus and meet you all up there." Rebecca faltered. Sandy translated, but it had been immediately obvious to the boys that there was a problem with Rebecca.

Mario placed both his arms dramatically around her and spoke perceptively into her eyes.

"You are the most precious person I have ever met. Do you think I would put you at any risk?" He then tenderly kissed her, as Sandy translated. The drama of his words, compounded with the kiss had achieved their purpose. Without further resistance, Rebecca submitted. Once Mario had secured the bike clips around his rolled trouser legs she mounted the bike and, as instructed, held tight around Mario's waist.

No one could have described to Rebecca how exhilarated she would feel. Once her initial fear had subsided, it was replaced by pure enjoyment as they speed up the hill towards the border. Her ponytail bellowing out behind, she indulged in the stimulation of her body as it pressed so close to Mario, and the sensation between her thighs as she straddled the leather seat. It was a quick 'hello' at the border to the border guards – both boys being regulars – and just a quick glance at the girls' passports, then the scooters sped higher up towards the gardens.

The landscape on the Italian side revealed quite a difference. The houses appeared more ornate, many with borders of decoratively embellished, plaster trims under the roof eves, larger terraces with prominent, potted palms, but not quite as neat as the French side. Rebecca felt she has entered a whole new world. The boys paid the small entrance fee in return for a map of the seventy acres of gardens; after some debate between Mario and Claudio, they all agreed to visit the Hanbury Villa first.

Equipped with the rolled picnic rugs and the squashed picnic basket, they navigated the hundreds of steps to the bottom of a small valley.

"What an enchanting house! It's so different to the architecture in France," Rebecca commented. "Well of course! We Italians are known for our style, this is typical of a grand Italian Villa. And one thankfully that the Germans didn't destroy during the war."

Claudio's chest puffed out as he took Rebecca's comment as a personal compliment. "Actually it took an Englishman to create this garden and home, not an Italian!" Rebecca joked at Claudio's arrogance. "I won't translate that bit Rebecca. It's just their way," Sandy added, under her breath.

They moved on to a spot designed for outdoor eating, it had a small wrought-iron and tiled table, with a bench either side. Sandy set out the sandwiches, which were baguettes cut in half with ham, cheese and tomato fillings.

The food looked sad, a little squashed and unappetising. The boys removed their blazers, and then cynically viewed the baguettes; nevertheless they were eaten.

"Try this!" Mario took out the bottle he'd rolled inside the picnic rug. "It's wonderful wine from the village near ours called Dolce Aqua." They all took turns to swig the red wine from the bottle. Rebecca was reluctant at first, but once the other three had a sip she joined in.

Mario sat close to her and gently kissed her neck and stroked her hand. Meanwhile Claudio had stubbed out his cigarette, and laid his rug out, he and Sandy were engaged in a passionate embrace.

"Come with me!" Mario took Rebecca's hand; they walked until they'd found a small, private area. It was surrounded by bushes and covered in soft dry green moss. Rebecca felt giddy and light-headed; the wine had had the desired effect. Mario laid out his rug and pulled Rebecca down to join him.

"Mario you are the first man I have kissed!" She blurted out; she just hoped that he'd get the right meaning.

"Bella, Bella! Take off your shoes," he responded. They'd both kicked off their shoes and lay side by side; they gazed upwards, contemplating the trees and the clouds. Then very slowly Mario had begun to kiss her neck, and then he moved to her lips; all the time he gently rubbed her back with his hand. Next he'd moved to her thigh and she wished the amazing sensation would last forever; her desire grew with his as he carefully unbuttoned her blouse.

"It is okay Tesoro. You are so beautiful. I just want to see all of you."

He removed his own shirt, and kept kissing her, his tongue

explored her mouth; he unzipped her trousers, pausing to look at her lying on the rug with only her white brassiere and matching lacy panties on. "I want you so much Tesoro."

Rebecca felt such wonderful sensations as Mario stroked her body; somewhere in the back of her mind there was hesitation. But these doubts soon expired. As he rubbed her breast, her nipple become rock hard under her bra and her pleasure heightened to the next level. She had passed thinking through any consequence, her arousal now matched his. He managed to unhook her bra, and then gradually transferred his kisses to her breasts. She gave herself over to him.

He slid her panties off and touched the secret-most part of her body; she closed her eyes as he lay on top of her. The extended pleasure out-weighed her initial pain and then the explosion that happened seemed to be both in between her legs and inside her head; it gave her, all at once, a feeling of satisfaction, relief and love like she had never before even imagined. When it was over, they'd laid in each other's arms, touching and caressing until the sun had moved away and they were chilled.

Before they started back to join the others Mario took both her hands.

"Rebecca! You are my woman now, I love you." He had tears in his eyes. "I see many sad things in my life, now I want to have happiness with you; you're so different to Italian girls. I'm sorry for my English, but it is important to me that you know you make me happy." He'd paused. He looked serious without his smile.

She squeezed his hands. "I understand your English; I promise I'll try and make you happy and I love you too."

As they returned to join the others Rebecca's guilt set in. It eased as Mario chatted to her softly in Italian, and offered her his charismatic smile. The girls needed to be back in Menton to catch the four p.m. train. At the station Mario asked Sandy to translate.

"I can't wait until next weekend to see you. Please, can we meet maybe on Wednesday when I finish early at ten?" Rebecca nodded and asked to make it near Samuels Hotel, then added,

"I will have to sneak out but I'm sure Ronnie will help me." Once on the train the girls were keen to discuss their new boyfriends. Sandy opened the conversation.

"Claudio wanted to go all the way, but I was too scared about getting pregnant. Next time he said he would have one of those 'rubbers'; but Father would kill me if he knew." Rebecca, although reluctant to expose her inexperience, had to ask. "What's a rubber?"

Sandy laughed. "I forget you are only seventeen. I didn't know much about sex when I was your age; you seem to have grown up so much since we first met. A rubber is a thing the man puts over his 'you-know-what', so when you do it, you don't get pregnant."

Rebecca nodded, and then she cautiously responded with limited details of her afternoon activities. Guilt and shame had replaced the lust she'd only a short time before, willingly indulged in.

"Sandy, do you know what 'Tesoro' means?" "Yes, that's easy. It means 'my darling'."

Nineteen

It was Monday morning. Aunty had gone off on a shopping trip and to meet a friend for lunch. As there were only a few guests in residence Uncle had invited her to join him for lunch. "We're very impressed with your work so far Rebecca. You're doing well." Uncle initiated the conversation mainly about work so Rebecca relaxed; however as he finished the first bottle of wine things started to deteriorate.

"You're a very beautiful girl Rebecca. I'm not your Uncle really you know, I'm only a cousin. Your Aunty Liz is a bitch; I should never have married a gentile, and I should have listened to my family."

They'd finished the main course and Rebecca didn't want to hear any more. He'd leaned too close. "Thank you for the lunch Uncle, but I must finish my letter to Father. So please excuse me, I'm so full I can't manage dessert today." She stood up to leave and struggled to appear calm so as not to aggravate him.

Rebecca was relieved once she had reached the sanctuary of her own room. She had just finished the letter to her parents, when her Uncle burst in. "Rebecca, Rebecca! Just give me a little cuddle. Come on now! I've been good to you." He lunged over towards her, grabbed her arm with one hand and roughly touched her breast with the other.

"Get off me! Let me go!" she screamed. "Come on now. It won't hurt to let me kiss you!" His breath reeked of red wine and stale cigarettes.

"Leave me alone." With all the strength she had, she

pushed him back, but he had a vice-like grip on her arm. Suddenly Rebecca became aware there was someone else in the room. "Come now, Mr Samuels. I don't think you're very well." Ronnie placed his hands firmly on Uncle's waist and pulled him away from Rebecca. Something seemed to jolt in Uncle's blurry brain.

"Piss off you poof. I'll visit my cousin if I want to." He'd let go of Rebecca and he stumbled out of the room. "That was close Becca; I think you should consider going home to your parents. You are vulnerable and young. He really is out of control."

Ronnie closed the door and turned the lock. "Also from now on keep your door locked!" Rebecca was tearful, but more with anger than any pain.

"It's just such a shock!" She said as she allowed Ronnie to give her a comforting hug. "He's an alcoholic and a man who isn't happy with his lot; and from what I'm observing, he's getting worse." They sat side-by-side on the bed.

"Oh Ronnie! I can't go home. I'm so in love with Mario; we had such a wonderful time yesterday!" Her face radiated youthful love. "I can tell by that desire in your eyes what this Italian means to you. But be careful! These Italian boys mainly live for the moment; they nearly always end up marrying Italian virgins!"

Rebecca prickled. "No! Rebecca, you didn't sleep with him did you?" She paused for a minute; the colour rose in her face.

"Well we didn't sleep at all. But I think we went all the way; no one ever told me about all the details. Anyway, you can't get pregnant if you only do it once?"

Ronnie was circumspect about his answer, as her statement convinced him just how innocent she really was.

"First, let me say I don't doubt you love each other. I for one am a hopeless romantic and I'm in no position to make judgements on behaviour and matters of the heart. But secondly, you can get pregnant by just doing it once; so from now on take precautions. Do you know what I mean by that?" Rebecca nodded.

"Yes. Sandy told me about some 'rubber' things." Ronnie let out a little sigh. "Well at least one of you has had some sex education!"

On Wednesday Ronnie had said he would leave the kitchen window unlatched, as it was low enough and wide enough for Rebecca to climb through after her rendezvous with Mario. She could slip out the kitchen door before ten, but would need to be back by eleven, as after that, it would most likely be locked. Mario waited a few yards up the street. He carried a brown paper bag.

"Good evening Tesoro. I've been so excited to see you. I am sorry for my English." He spoke a mixture of English and French words.

"I am sorry for my French and Italian. I missed you so much Mario." He took her hand. "We go to the park!" It was a warm night, with very few people around. They sat on a park bench, which caught the light from a street lamp.

"Here, have a grape, they are from my valley in Italy!" He popped a grape into her mouth. "Let me give you one!" Rebecca repeated the process, but Mario softly held her fingers in his mouth with his teeth and rubbed his tongue over them.She blushed as the sensation tingled all over her body.

"Mario, we must be careful!" He released her fingers. "Yes Tesoro! I'm sorry I rushed you; please don't think me bad. We must be careful when we make love again. I will be prepared! You are so special."

His unguarded words helped alleviate Rebecca's shame. For an hour they chatted in their funny mix of languages and held hands and kissed. Rebecca contemplated telling Mario about her Uncle, but didn't want to spoil the evening. It was eleven-thirty, by the time Rebecca approached the kitchen window, and it was all in darkness. True to his word Ronnie had left the latch unlocked. She hoisted herself up onto the window, steadied herself with one arm and pushed open the window with the other and squeezed through, landing on the zinc bench. She'd locked the window and, just as she stood up, the light was flicked on. Uncle stood there and she smelt the booze before she saw him.

"So where have you been my lovely. Sneaking out with some man, no doubt?" As he moved towards her, Aunty walked in. "Ah here you are! Aaron you've had enough tonight. Come on. Off to bed! Hello Rebecca, time you were probably in bed as well. We have six new guests arriving on the early train." She skilfully led her drunken husband out of the kitchen.

Twenty

The following Sunday morning the foursome met on the promenade with bathers and towels. The girls confidently rode pillion and they zoomed off to the beach. Villefranche was a popular village about five miles from Nice. The waterfront was dotted with tourist hotels and restaurants favoured by English visitors. The boys knew of a less populated spot with some evergreen, over-hanging trees for shade.

They had procured the picnic lunch from the hotel kitchen. It was a wonderful selection of cold salad leftovers, all carefully packed in small containers. They lay the containers out on a towel.

"We're eating food fit for a princess because that's who ate some of this last evening at dinner!" Claudio announced proudly. "You are our Princesses!" Mario added, as he kissed Rebecca's hand.

"It's all so delicious. Much better, than my English squashed sandwiches," Sandy said. "I think we can safely say the Italians are better at food than the English." The boys beamed at Rebecca's comment. Most of the day was spent swimming as the boys continually competed for attention and tested who could swim the fastest. Claudio had brought a pack of cards and as he cockily dealt the hand; he looked very comical with his cigarette stuck to his lower lip jutting up and down as he made wise cracks. He always impressed Sandy, who adored him. She pulled at her fringe and gazed at him with her special wide eyed look. She laughed and encouraged his every move, which provoked even more hilarity.

By contrast Mario played his card hand with a sincere, purposeful poker face and managed skilfully to win each game. He'd been studying English from a text book each day and had joined a weekly English class. He grasped languages easily and also had made time to tutor Rebecca in basic Italian. She snuggled close to him, thrilled to feel the warmth of his naked back, as she surreptitiously inhaled his unique body scent. After the card games, they'd all rested, shaded by the trees and Rebecca reflected on how happy she was. Sandy was the very best girlfriend she could have ever wished for: previously she'd never had the opportunity to have gentile friends. Sandy was funny, loyal and incredibly helpful to push Rebecca to develop her languages. The main common ground they shared was their steadfast love for the two Italians.

After six weeks of dating, the two couples were totally comfortable in each other's company. One Sunday at the beach, the girls had offered information about their families and backgrounds, and then Sandy manoeuvred the conversation towards the boys.

"So, tell us about your families and your villages?"

Neither boy was immediately forthcoming. Then Claudio spoke as he lit up a cigarette. "Both our villages suffered a lot in the last year of the war. Pigna, where I come from, was very militant against the German occupation and Mussolini. Many of our people were killed including my parents. Mario's Mama is like a Mama to me now." The girls' knowledge of the details of the war on the Riviera was limited.

Then Mario spoke.

"In Castel Vittorio there's no work for anyone. It's very difficult and as Mama is alone now, I must support her. That's why we must come across to France to work." He closed the subject. Then he smiled and added. "I have a wonderful cousin called Sylvie in Menton; she and her parents are like family to me. We were thinking of taking you there next weekend. We could all have lunch with her family?" Both girls smiled in agreement.

"I would love to meet someone in your family, Mario!" Rebecca was encouraged. Mario dropped Rebecca off out of sight of the hotel after they'd agreed to catch the train next Sunday to Menton. She had kept out of her Uncle's way as much as possible since the night in the kitchen, and her Aunty had seemed much warmer towards her. Ronnie was her favourite and any spare time they had they'd gossip about the other staff, share confidences and study the magazines the guests left behind, primarily to see what the film stars were wearing.

Aunty oversaw that all the hotel linen was always immaculate. Rebecca was on one of her regular visits to the seamstress with the sheets for mending. She found a short-cut through the old town, as she had become familiar with its alleyways. A few yards ahead of her she captured a glimpse of her Uncle as he turned the corner of the street. At first she stopped to avoid him. Then curiosity got the better of her.

Although she carried a large basket of sheets, she decided to follow him for a bit. In a bid to conceal herself she kept to the shaded side of the lane.

He stopped at a shabby-looking house with a red light in the window. Rebecca had him clearly in her view, a curvaceous woman with badly-bleached blonde hair and heavy makeup, greeted him like a long lost friend; and then he disappeared inside with her. Rebecca waited about five minutes and, when he didn't come out, she continued on her way. She was bursting to get Ronnie on his own so she could update him with the latest gossip. Once they were seated in his room with a cup of tea she dragged the story out to give it more intrigue and finished with "so do you think it is his girlfriend?" Ronnie tut-tutted.

"Becca, you noodle! She's a tart, a prostitute. Men pay her for sex. That's why the red light is on. It's an established signal to say she's open for business." Rebecca's mouth dropped open. "That's disgusting. How revolting! Poor Aunty Liz." "Well, it's preferable he's going there than trying to molest you or some other young girl. They are both consenting adults, so let them get on with it I say."

Twenty-one

Mario confirmed that he'd contacted his Aunt and Uncle in Menton and they had invited the foursome to lunch. "You know Sandy, I'm a little nervous at the thought of meeting some of Mario's family." Rebecca and Sandy chatted over coffee.

"Well at least you're not meeting his mother. Because, from what I gather from Claudio, she's very controlling and pretty fixed on Mario marrying an Italian.

Rebecca nodded in acknowledgement. "Yes, he's more or less told me that. But he's also said he's his own man and will make his own decisions." They both laughed.

"Italian men love making all the decisions – well, they think they make all the decisions; from what I can see, their mothers help them a bit." Sandy said.

She worked as a secretary for a group of Nice-based lawyers. There were both Italian and French lawyers who worked in the practice so her languages had been a great asset to her procuring the position.

"Most of the Italian men I work with are constantly in touch with their mothers. Sometimes I can hear them on the phone or, on the odd occasion when a mother visits the office, I can see these successful, professional men turn into small boys again. I'm lucky with Claudio in a way. He doesn't have a mother so he's happy for me to guide him." Rebecca was surprised at her friend's calculating tone.

The four met up at Nice station for the early train to Menton, as it was too far to travel by scooter, especially if it rained. Rebecca loved to travel by train with Mario as he held her hand and fussed over her. She felt a great sense of self-esteem being loved by such a fine-looking man. They joked and commented about all the beaches that they'd visited together as the train chugged past.

"I'm so excited you will meet my Sylvie, Tesoro!" Mario spoke with fresh excitement in his voice. "I'm already jealous of her. Especially, when you call her 'my Sylvie'!" Rebecca joked.

"Don't be crazy! She's my cousin, but I feel she's my sister. You will love her too."

A short, petite, dark-haired girl with large, almond eyes was waiting on the platform when the train pulled in. Her stance indicated shyness. However, once she spotted the group and Mario had called her name, a sincere smile and open face replaced her previous reticent demeanour. Mario embraced Sylvie and then made the introductions. "This is Sandy. You know Claudio of course and this is the other love-of-my-life, my Rebecca from England." His grin encapsulated his entire face as Sylvie respectfully shook Rebecca's hand.

"I'm very pleased to meet you, Rebecca." Sylvie spoke English almost without any accent. "Mario has talked a lot about you." Rebecca's exchange encouraged a warm smile from Sylvie. During the ten-minute walk from the station to the Reiss Villa Mario proudly pointed out places of interest.

"Mama and I lived with Sylvie and her Mama near the end of the war. I even went to school here for a short time, so I still feel Menton is partly my home as well."

Sylvie loosened up as they walked and added diplomatically to Mario's commentary.

"Your English is so good. I wish my French and Italian were at that stage!" Rebecca praised Sylvie.

"Papa was so strict on me with my education. I'm an only child so I had to be his daughter and the son he never had." Mario chipped in. "My cousin is the cleverest girl in Menton. She was top of the school in all her exams and is going to be a teacher one day."

Sylvie blushed and gave him a shove. "Be quiet Mario! Don't be so … so Italian!" Sandy and Rebecca chuckled, as all the girls exchanged knowing looks. Joseph and Allessia Reiss greeted the four visitors like royalty. "Welcome to our home. Any friends of Mario's are friends of ours!" Joseph spoke English with a delightful French accent.

He was a tall, thin man who carried a look of sorrow about him, but when he smiled Rebecca saw that he shared the same warmth as his daughter. Allessia had a similar sad, slightly-worn-out look. The aroma of lunch cooking and the open fire in the cluttered salon all reminded Rebecca of her home. As she sat down and sipped her aperitif, her eyes rested on the candelabra that stood on the sideboard. Just as she placed her glass down to have a closer look, Joseph had walked in.

"It's a Jewish candelabra Rebecca. It was my grandparent's." Rebecca gently slid her fingers down the cold, polished silver. She bit her top lip, and then took a breath before she spoke. "Yes I know. We have one at home. My parents light it every Friday evening to see in the Sabbath." The conversation had caught Allessia and Sylvie's attention.

"Are both your parents Jewish?" Sylvie enquired.

"Yes my entire family is. They've lived in England for four generations so we're English as well, if you know what I mean."

Allessia had been busy preparing the lunch, but she joined in. "I was born Catholic and Joseph is a French Jew, but we're happy for Sylvie to take what she chooses from both our faiths." "I don't know of many mixed marriages other than that of my cousin in Nice. He married a Christian. But they're miserable," Rebecca added tentatively.

"It isn't an easy decision to make, to marry out of your culture or religion. But we're of the belief any marriage requires hard work. I fell in love with Allessia the first time I saw her in the Menton market and we don't have any regrets do we?" As he spoke Joseph had placed his arm around his wife and kissed the crown of her head.

"No regrets, but I have to tell you Rebecca, it's not for the faint hearted!" she replied, averting her gaze. Then she hastily returned to the lunch preparation.

Lunch was an impressive, gastronomic, delectable, sumptuous Italian feast. They commenced with anti-pasta which consisted of several small dishes of tasty meat and vegetables wrapped in pastry, some salami sausage served with olive chutney, asparagus baked in a crepe-like wrap. The next course was pasta, which Allessia had just finished making fresh that morning. It was accompanied by a walnut sauce, which tasted like nothing Rebecca had ever tried before. They had a break between courses and Sylvie placed a record on the gramophone. It was a collection of Italian songs being played on the mandolin; both boys sang along to the music with animated lively voices.

The main course was roast, milk-fed, baby lamb, not often seen since the War. "Mama's cousin at Pigna managed to get this for us. It's the first time in a year we have had such a treat, you must visit more often." Sylvie revealed her subtle humour.

"Now these potatoes are similar to what we would eat in London. It's the best meal I've tasted since I've been in France Madame Reiss!" Rebecca praised.

"Please girls, not Madame Reiss, call me Allessia; we try not to be too formal in our household." The next course was cheese; served, in French style, before the dessert. There were two types – a soft duo of gorgonzola and mascarpone, Italian specialties, then and a hard compte, for Joseph's taste, a French basic.

"I'm sure my tummy will burst if I put another mouthful in!" Sandy muttered as she heard there was desert yet to come. "This is the Italian way; you will offend if you don't try every course. Anyway we will just take our time, there's no rush," Claudio whispered back to her. It was four by the time they finished lunch and Sylvie invited them to walk around the garden.

"How many guestrooms does your hotel have?" Rebecca enquired. "Well, it's more of a lodging house these days. It was a hotel before the War when my Grandpapa set it up. We can take up to fifteen guests, but Mama and Papa are tired of the work now and I don't want to take it on, so there's talk of them selling it." Once they were beyond the hotel Mario pointed out where the old tree hut was and the secret hiding places; Sylvia teased him as he embellished their childhood adventures. The more the four of them laughed at him the more he performed. "Look it's nearly five; we need to be on that five-thirty train," Sandy tapped her watch.

"I'm so pleased you've visited this part of my life, Tesoro, and you've seen the happy part of my childhood." Mario squeezed Rebecca's hand as they walked back to the villa.

"Was it very sad in your village in Italy?" Rebecca attempted an unobtrusive tone. "Yes. Some things are just too difficult for me to talk about," he snapped, then abruptly dropped her hand and walked briskly ahead.

Twenty-two

The weeks passed by with Mario and Rebecca meeting up most Wednesday evenings on their own and on most Sundays with Sandy and Claudio. But if Sandy's father was out for the day she and Claudio would go to her house and make love. Rebecca and Mario had very limited opportunities and when they did it was in fairly uncomfortable surroundings.

"I have a surprise for you. Can you take a few hours off on Friday at two o'clock to be with me?" Mario asked as they sat in Café Renée enjoying a late-night hot chocolate.

"Well, I'll have to ask Ronnie to help cover for me. But yes, I should be able to. Why, what have you planned?" Mario cheekily conveyed to her his 'naughty' smile.

"It's a surprise, I already told you. But you must put on your best red dress and walk into the Negresco Hotel with the same confidence you had on the first night I met you. Walk straight over to the elevator. Just look straight ahead like you are going to your own room. Go up to the fourth floor and knock on room 415.

Ronnie agreed to cover for Rebecca. "Now Becca, you'll need to put a coat or something over that dress because if you're sprung leaving looking like that, it will look suspicious, mid-week during the day." Ronnie enjoyed nothing better than intrigue. Rebecca made it out of Hotel Samuels, without being spotted by her Uncle; once she was further along the street she threw her coat over her arm. She drew a deep breath as she entered the intimidating foyer of the grand Negresco

Hotel. Then she followed exactly what Mario had said, held her head up high, walked confidently as if she belonged and went directly to the elevator, smiling boldly at the bell boy.

"Fourth floor please!" It seemed to take forever to reach her destination, as it stopped at each floor in between. Once at the fourth floor, she was slightly confused and it took her a moment to work out which way the room numbers ran, but she eventually found number 415 and gave a gentle knock. "Welcome to our suite Tesoro!" Mario was dressed in his black waiter's trousers and a white, open necked shirt. The room was enormous. "Wow! This is the most sensational room I have ever been in Mario! How can you afford this?"

Mario had moved over to a cupboard to put a record on the gramophone. The latest American popular song 'Catch a Falling Star and put it in your pocket' filled the room. "It comes at no charge, except for the champagne, but we must be out by four-thirty. I've arranged it all with my friend, the supervisor for this floor." He pulled Rebecca to him and kissed her full on the lips. They fell onto the bed laughing.

"Now Tesoro we must do this all correctly. Let me pour you some champagne." He had a highly-polished, large, silver champagne-bucket full of ice with Moet & Chandon Champagne, plus two crystal glasses on the bedside table. He over-exaggerated the pouring process. "Champagne, for the most beautiful woman in the world!" They clunked glasses.

"Mario! This is like a dream. I do love you." After a few sips he kissed her again.

"Let's take off our clothes! Soon they sat side by side on the pure crisp, white sheets that enveloped the oversized bed. Mario dipped Rebecca's fingers in the glass of bubbly then slowly licked it off. Rebecca returned the favour as she drizzled some on his soft tummy then licked it, popping her tongue in his belly button. The game escalated when Mario dripped bubbly on her breasts. They hungrily made love which culminated with an intense, mutual climax. "I feel so happy. I wish we could be like this forever," Rebecca spoke with a sigh of contentment. She lay naked, feeling tiny on the huge bed.

"I think we can be happy together, forever," Mario replied as he slipped into the hotel's satin robe. He patted the edge of the bed. "Come sit here". Still naked, with her hair spilling over her tanned shoulders, Rebecca obeyed. He then opened the bedside table drawer and dropped to his knees in front of her. He held a small black, velvet box in his hand.

"Rebecca Samuels, I love you with all my heart. I will never love another and I want you to do me the honour of becoming my wife." He spoke in perfectly rehearsed English. Rebecca's eyes filled with tears. "Why do you cry?" Mario was still on his knees with the ring box opened revealing a delicate solitaire diamond ring.

"Mario, of course I will marry you. I love you so much!" As she sniffed back the tears, she took out the ring and placed it on her finger. "Look, a perfect fit!" They sipped another glass of champagne. Rebecca was silent.

"Becca, I know you're thinking about your parents. I've thought a lot about Mama and what her reaction will be; but I have decided I must live my own life, just like my Papa did. We are us, Mario and Rebecca; we will take it slowly and find a way to work through it." He sounded convinced and mature.

"I'm pleased you've said that, as it's exactly what I was thinking. I know if my parents meet you, they'll love you too. And I have to say that now I've met Sylvie's parents and can see a mixed marriage can work, I'm sure we can achieve the same."

Rebecca leant lovingly on his shoulder as she held her hand out to admire her ring. "You will be my wife, and one day I will have my own restaurant up in my valley in Italy and we will have a house full of children." Mario straightened; his words brimmed with hope.

Consumed with love, they were overcome with passion and made love again.

"Tesoro, you must get up and dressed now. We have fifteen minutes to clear and restore the room. I'll finish here, you walk out just as you walked in and I will see you on Sunday. Let's tell Sandy and Claudio together, over lunch." He held her tight for a moment. She whispered, "I love you so much."

Ronnie had lingered near the door as Rebecca arrived at the hotel. "Quick Becca! Up the back staircase." Aaron is looking for you. I said you had a headache, he thinks you're in your room." Rebecca felt so elated she didn't really care about her Uncle; she floated up to her room. "I want a full report after dinner tonight." Ronnie called after her. Ronnie agreed with Rebecca about keeping the engagement quiet until they had a fool-proof plan.

"I don't like to rain on your parade Becca, but best you prepare for the worst with them. They'll see it differently, he being a gentile and he's foreign to boot."

Rebecca sounded soulful. "Yes I'm not quite sure how to approach it. But in the meantime I just want to enjoy it all. Don't you just love my ring?" She flicked her hand around at Ronnie.

"Ooh! I'm so envious. You're a lucky girl, but he's even a luckier man."

Twenty-three

The tension between Uncle Aaron and his wife had become obvious to all the staff. It made for a very unpleasant atmosphere, and some of the guests had also picked up on it. His drinking seemed to be the root cause of his bad behaviour and Rebecca did all she could to keep out of his way. It had been five weeks since Rebecca and Mario had become engaged. Rebecca had returned from her regular Wednesday evening rendezvous with Mario. She now entered via the back kitchen door to which Aunty had kindly given her a key, and there was usually a light left on.

On this particular evening there was no light on. As she entered the kitchen she struggled to see her way. She fumbled around for the main light switch when she smelt him.

"I know what you're up to, you little slut. I bet you've been out with some boy, acting like a Jewish whore!" Uncle Aaron spat the words out. She rushed blindly to the far door, but his eyes had had more time to adjust to the dark. He grabbed her.

"Uncle, it's late. Please let me go!" He grasped her painfully.

"You're giving it to some boy. After all I've done for you; you can give me some too." He pulled at her blouse; the top three buttons popped off, and exposed her bra. "Help, someone help!" she screamed at the top of her voice, not caring about any guests. "Shut up you slut!" He roughly shoved his hand up her skirt, ripping the skin on her thigh with his fingernails.

"Aaron, get off her!" Aunty Liz had turned on the sink light as she rushed into the kitchen. "Piss off you stupid bitch!" If you gave me what is rightfully mine I wouldn't have to get it from this slut." Aaron appeared totally demented, his eyes were wildly bloodshot, and his speech slovenly slurred. But he still had Rebecca's arm tightly grasped.

"Calm down Aaron. Just let go of Rebecca and we can talk about it." Aunty attempted the soft approach. He released Rebecca and, for a moment, the two women assumed the aggression was over. Then, without any words or warning, he swung his fist at his wife and punched her straight in the face. She screamed as blood poured from her cheek.

"You bastard!" Ronnie yelled, as he crashed into the room pushing Aaron away. Aaron got such a jolt, it unbalanced him; as he began to fall Ronnie angrily grabbed both his hands. "Don't you move, you monster. We're calling the police."

Two of the other staff arrived and stood on either side of Aaron, whom Ronnie had restrained to a chair. At the mention of police he seemed to come to his senses.

"Ronnie, please don't call the police." Aunty stemmed the flow of blood on her cheek with her hanky as she spoke. "Long term it won't do any of us any good if this hotel's reputation suffers because of this stupid man. Let's see if we can deal with it ourselves." Aunty had placed her other arm around Rebecca who still shook as she clutched her ripped blouse.

"Now, now Rebecca, how far did he actually go?" she gently asked, as she noticed the trickle of blood on Rebecca's inner thigh.

"He didn't get that far. The blood is from the scratch of his nails," she whispered, in a muffled distressed voice.

"Well, if you don't want me to call the police, what are

we going to do with your husband? How will you prevent this happening again, with an even worse outcome?" Ronnie fumed.

Aaron had now completely regressed, hanging his head and snivelling. "Ronnie, all I can do is apologise. My husband is an alcoholic and he needs help; I know that's no excuse for his behaviour. I'm going to give him some sleeping tablets, put him to bed and I would ask that you see Rebecca up to her room and stay with her until I can come up myself. You others should go off to bed now and please keep this incident to yourselves." She led her now compliant husband upstairs.

"Come on my Becca. Let me look after you." Ronnie softly wrapped his sweater around her as he walked her to her room. By the time her Aunty appeared, Rebecca had washed herself, removed her ruined blouse and skirt, and sat on her bed in her robe with Ronnie.

"Rebecca, I can only say how truly sorry I am. He's my husband, but it's only pity I feel for him. I'm guessing you'll want to go home, for once your parents find out it won't take long for the news to get around the Jewish community." She sat on the chair, her head in her hands.

Rebecca didn't immediately reply. "She's in shock, Mrs Samuels. It will take some time for her to get through this." Ronnie spoke softly, attempting to offer comfort to both women.

"Aunty, I wasn't ignoring you, and yes I've had a shock, but actually I'm okay; I was just thinking through what to say, and, given the circumstances, I feel I can trust you." She looked directly at her Aunty.

"Of course you can trust me! You can tell me anything in confidence."

Rebecca clutched Ronnie's hand as she spoke. "Well, I'm actually engaged to a wonderful man who lives here in Nice. He's Italian, so I don't want to go home and leave him, just because of Uncle Aaron. But I haven't told my parents yet and I'm still not sure how to broach it with them." Aunty Liz returned Rebecca's direct gaze.

"From my own experience it's a big step marrying out of your own community. But Aaron and I, believe it or not, were very happy in the beginning. Then he became very despondent when we couldn't have children. He started drinking a lot more and now it's totally out of control."

Ronnie smoothed her hand. "There are places he could go to rehabilitate, you know. I had a friend who went to one in Switzerland; he was there for six months. But, as far as I know, he gave up drinking completely."

Aunty Liz slumped further down into the chair. "It's just so exhausting, battling with him. When he's sober and can remember his behaviour, he agrees to accept help. But he's almost never rational any more. I'll see what he has to say tomorrow. Rebecca, I think you should have a few days off."

"Thank you Aunty. I appreciate it, but I'll be better working. It takes my mind off things when I'm busy. But please don't tell Uncle about my engagement." Aunty rose from the chair. "Not a word to anyone!" She pressed her fingers to her lips and offered a weary smile as she left the room.

"Becca, I hear what she says and I feel for her. But it doesn't resolve the big problem of your Uncle's behaviour. It's affecting all the staff. So we'll just have to see what happens after tomorrow," Ronnie diffidently remarked.

"I think I want to sleep now. Thank you for being my friend Ronnie."

No-one laid eyes on Rebecca's Uncle Aaron over the next few days. He stayed confined to his room and her Aunty informed the staff and suppliers he had bad flu. Rebecca decided not to tell Mario, as she felt ashamed by her uncle's behaviour. On Sunday when they'd arranged to meet, it had been chilly enough for Rebecca to wear a cardigan. They sat on a towel on the beach at Villefranche; the sun was high in the sky and Mario had taken off his jacket. "It feels nice to still get some sun. Come on, aren't you too hot Tesoro with that thick English cardigan on?" He attempted to help her take it off.

"Don't touch it." Rebecca snapped. Mario was taken aback. "What's wrong with you? I'm only trying to help." Defencelessly, he stood up. Rebecca hid her face in her hands and let out a sob. "What's wrong Rebecca? What have I done?"

She wrapped her arms around her knees and bit down heavily on her lip. "It's not you Mario. Something happened to me and I don't really want to tell you." She let out another big sob.

He sat back down beside her. "Hush Tesoro! Don't cry. There's nothing you can't tell me; I'm going to be your husband." He lightly stroked her hair and gently touched her lip, willing it away from the grit of her teeth. She responded in a somewhat melodramatic whisper.

"You may not want me for your wife now."

"Rebecca, you must tell me!" He turned directly at her, forcing her to look him in the eye. "It's my arm; I didn't want you to see the bruise!" She slowly pulled her arm out of her sleeve to reveal the injury.

"Who did this to you? I will kill them." Rebecca told him all the details, then pointed out that she needed to stay on good terms with her Aunty and Uncle until such time as they had agreed on how to tell their families about the engagement. "If Father hears all the wrong things he can demand I go home to London. I'm under his jurisdiction until I am twenty-one or married, so I need to tread carefully." Rebecca composed herself.

"Well, why don't we just elope and tell them afterwards?" Mario blurted out.

"I've been thinking of that as well. But it would really humiliate my parents and I'd like to try and gain their blessing first, if I can." They agreed that Rebecca should go home for two weeks holiday to visit her family and tell them face-to-face. She reasoned they'd be so happy to see her that they might be more vulnerable to agreeing. Once that had happened then Mario would tell his Mama.

"I'll go to the travel agent tomorrow after Aunty has paid me." The next morning Rebecca woke up feeling optimistic about her parents. As she took her bath she noticed her breasts were a little sore. On further inspection they also seemed bigger than usual. After she'd dried and dressed she tentatively opened her diary to check when she'd had her last her period. To her horror, she realised it was nearly seven weeks ago. "There must be some mistake!" she cried out loud. She'd always had a twenty-eight day cycle and made note of it in her diary each month. But after triple checking, she could clearly see it was definitely late and over six weeks since she made love with Mario at the hotel.

"Ronnie, please meet me in my room straight after breakfast. It's urgent!" Rebecca whispered to him once all the guests were seated and eating breakfast.

Half an hour later they were in the room with the door closed. "My God Rebecca! Are you sure?" Ronnie's face said it all.

"Well as sure as I can be. What am I going to do?" She was choked with panic. "The first thing you need to do is tell Mario straight away. It's his responsibility as well." Ronnie endeavoured to sound level-headed.

"He has a lunch break at two, so I'll go round to the hotel and see if I can catch him."

Mario had been about to jump on his scooter when he saw Rebecca coming towards him. "What a wonderful surprise Tesoro!"

As she got closer he saw the strained look on her face. "Rebecca what is it? Your bloody uncle! I'll go and kill him for sure this time!" Rebecca reached out her hand to him. "No Mario, it's not Uncle. I'm so sorry to say this, but I think I am pregnant."

He stared at her startled and speechless. "Mario, say something! Please!" He finally stammered Italian words she couldn't understand then added in English "But we used a rubber!" "I think we forgot the second time at the Hotel." She murmured, as she attempted to control her tears.

"I don't know what to say to you Rebecca. I need time to think." His words felt like a sharp slap. Bewildered and pained at his response, she immediately turned; her pride wounded and ran as fast as she could, her tears spilling hysterically. She didn't stop running 'till she arrived at the Hotel.

"Becca wait! What did he say?" Ronnie exclaimed as she rushed past. "Let me in Becca. Please!" Her bedroom door was locked. "Please! Just leave me alone Ronnie, and please tell Aunty I have a headache so won't be working today."

Ronnie called out "bloody Italians!" as he marched off down the corridor. Rebecca's Aunt tapped at the door around eight p. m. "I've left you a sandwich and some milk. I'm ready when you are to talk, if you need me," she called out as she left a tray outside the door.

Rebecca waited a few minutes and then retrieved the tray. She was really hungry and remembered she hadn't even had breakfast. She caught a glimpse of herself in the mirror as she washed her hands. What a mess! Her eyes were puffed and swollen from all the crying. She splashed them with some cold water and decided to write her feelings down in her diary to see if it would help her make any sense of this terrible predicament.

Around ten-fifteen there was a knock at the door. "It's me Becca. You have a visitor. Open the door please." Ronnie called to her.

"Go away! I don't want to see anyone." He rattled the handle. "Open this door now, or I will break it down!" Mario shouted. Reluctantly she opened the door. "I'll leave you two alone," Ronnie muttered.

Mario closed the door and on seeing Rebecca's dishevelled state he lowered his voice. "I'm very sorry for what I said today. I was selfish. I needed time to accept the idea of a bambina. We would be having babies anyway. I am sorry I can't speak better English to explain what is in my heart. Now I've thought about it I'm so happy, and I don't want you to worry. I will look after everything as I am an Italian man!"

"Yes, and we have made a half-Italian baby." She managed some humour. He took both her hands in his. "I love you so much Rebecca. I think we should marry straight away and look for a small studio flat somewhere here in Nice so I can keep working."

She felt calmer as she listened to him. "I'll need some more time to think about it. I still feel strongly about not marrying without my parents' blessing. Please, can we wait a few days then make the decision together?" Mario's frustration was obvious.

"Very well, but I'm going to travel to Castel Vittorio this Sunday to tell my Mama as I have to consider her as well."

"Mario, I know you're angry and I appreciate that you want to do the right thing, but we do have to do this as a joint decision." She kissed his cheek. He took her face softly in his hands and kissed her lips. They fell onto the bed. "What if someone comes in?" Rebecca said half heartily, as she allowed Mario's hands to wander.

"I'm going to lock the door and we will not make a sound Tesoro!

They agreed to meet Wednesday and make an agreement on how to move forward.

Rebecca carried a heavy heart as she walked towards Café Fontaine. How could her life, which had been simple and exciting, have become so complicated?

Mario pulled up on his scooter dressed in his waiter's outfit, just as he had on the first night they met. She still experienced the same rush of excitement each time she saw him.

"Now Mario I don't want you to get upset and I want you to hear me out before you speak please!" She gulped. "I'm not what you would call religious but I am Jewish by birth and it's very important for me not to shame my parents." Her voice faltered. "It's also important you accept I know my parents best and how they will react. I wish to have the baby first without their knowledge and then just arrive home in England with it. It will be a shock, but once they see it,

I'm sure they will soften when they realise there's nothing they can do to reverse the situation. I believe they'll end up agreeing to our marriage, or at least giving it their blessing, probably at arm's length."

"What! You mean not marry first?" he boiled.

"I've seen it happen in our Jewish circle before, girls are sent off somewhere to give birth and their babies are secretly adopted. As I'm under twenty-one, under English law my parents technically have control over my life. You just don't understand how staunch they are with their beliefs. My mother is a bully. I'm thinking we could take a small apartment somewhere out of Nice 'till the baby is born. Then I'll go to England: regardless of their reaction I'll only stay a short time, and then we can marry as soon as I return. At least I'll feel I've done all I can to convince them."

Mario attempted to compose himself before he spoke. "I don't agree! But I don't want to argue. You must understand we can't afford an apartment, maybe we could stretch to a studio room; I need to keep paying for Mama and until I can find work with a higher salary we'll have to be practical."

"What else do you suggest then? I can't stay at the hotel."

He hesitated as he struggled to control his temper. "Let me tell Mama on Sunday and see what she can suggest, she's very good at practical solutions."

Rebecca shrugged. She was emotionally drained and had no desire to argue, but at least she'd almost had his agreement about waiting to marry.

"I don't agree with you, but I love you so I must try and understand your point of view." They sipped their drinks in silence as the café wound down for the evening.

There was a chill in the air and the waiter whistled as

he stacked the battered wooden chairs at the inside tables. Eventually Mario spoke.

"Mama can be difficult, but she is wise about matters in a crisis. I feel sure she'll accept the inevitable and help us. Can we meet on Monday; say around three when I get a break?" Mario was reluctant to take her on the scooter now she was pregnant, so he walked her back to the hotel. Sunday morning dragged by for Rebecca, with Mario away and Sandy spending the day with Claudio: they were now officially engaged. As they were both Catholic it was an easy route for them. Rebecca spent the afternoon up-dating her diary: she wrote down her most private thoughts, treating each page as her confidant.

Uncle had returned to work. He was a lot more subdued than before and it appeared he was off the drink. He hadn't apologised to Rebecca, but she had no expectation of him. Her new set of problems had absorbed all of her focus. Monday found Rebecca and Mario back at the café. This time they sat inside, as the weather had turned, with gusts of cold wind blowing through Nice.

"Mama was angry at first, then, when she thought of a tiny Mario baby just like me, she quietened down. She has quite a good suggestion. She will ask Uncle Joseph and Allessia if you can go and stay with them, and maybe help them in the hotel until you are nearly due, then move up to Castel Vittorio with her for the last couple of months, so she can deliver the baby." Mario hesitated as he watched for Rebecca's reaction.

"Well, I felt very comfortable with the Reiss's so, if they're willing, that would be an agreeable solution. However I am going to have to enlist Auntie's help to deal with Uncle Aaron. I don't trust him." Mario had started to add something, but thought better of it.

"What were you going to say Mario?"

"Nothing, that can't wait." She gave him a prod.

"Come on, no secrets! Tell me! It was something else your Mama said, wasn't it?"

He shifted around a bit in his seat. "Well, I don't entirely agree with her but, she said while you're staying with her you could talk with the Priest and look at converting to Catholicism, which, before you snap at me, I know you don't agree with but you could listen to him anyway, to placate her."

Rebecca felt outraged. "I'm not that difficult! I guess we're both compromising, so I don't think a few words with the Priest will hurt me if it makes you happy. First things first though – I will speak to Aunty as soon as I can get her out of earshot of her husband." That evening the opportunity presented itself. Rebecca was alone in the kitchen with Aunty Liz and she timidly explained her situation and asked if she could help her manage things with regard to Aaron.

"I won't tell you it's not a big shock to hear your predicament. I agree with you about how your father will react and I will speak to Aaron. He won't do it willingly, but I will hold his attack over you as a negotiating point. Mario can post your letters home from Nice each week and collect your parents' ones from me so they won't know that anything is different. However, I must insist you are examined by my doctor to check everything is okay. Don't fret, he's discreet, but you will need to have an idea of your due date for the baby's arrival."

Rebecca hugged her Aunty. "Thank you so much. You're

being so kind to me." She responded with a mutual squeeze. "If I had had a daughter I would have just loved her to be like you. I know we didn't get off to a great start but trust me I'll do all I can to help you."

On the following night Rebecca sat in her room writing in her diary when the door burst open. It was Uncle – his face was beetroot red. "How dare you! You slut! Pregnant! Who do you think you are! Manipulating my wife to cover for you?"

Rebecca was terrified. She slowly backed up.

"My pregnancy happened with my fiancée and we love each other so don't you call me a slut. You're a violent, crazy man, get out of here or I shall scream until all the guests can hear."

He moved closer. "But you don't want me to tell your darling Father do you? So why not give me what I want, then I won't say a word." He leeringly fingered her arm, as he licked his lips. Rebecca couldn't detect any alcohol on his breath so she decided to take a chance.

"Well then, I will tell Aunty and anyone else that will listen about your visits to the lady with the red light shining in her window in the old town, Uncle!" She stood confident as she spoke, and placed emphasis on the word Uncle." He removed his hand and stepped back as he deliberated.

"You win, you bitch! But be out of my hotel within the week and I never want to see you again." He stormed out. Rebecca trembled, as she fell into the chair. The door had re-opened. Rebecca jumped.

"Don't worry it's just me!"

"Ronnie, oh! I thought he'd changed his mind. You must have been close by?"

“I followed him when I spotted him stomping away from Liz. I knew he hadn’t been drinking so you weren’t in immediate danger. I was listening outside the door; if he’d lifted a finger I would’ve been in, in-a-flash. Great negotiating Becca!

Rebecca spoke softly. “I’ll be leaving soon, Ronnie. You’ve been a dear friend to me. We will stay in touch won’t we?”

Ronnie gave a broad grin. “I think you and Mario are just the most romantic couple in all of France. I will visit you in Menton and I expect to be invited to the wedding.”

Twenty-four

The somewhat bohemian view of the world that Joseph and Allessia Reiss embraced overcame any social inhibitions about having an unmarried, pregnant woman living under their roof. They confirmed to Carla Orengo that they would keep Rebecca in their care as long as was needed. During the week that Rebecca spent preparing for the move, she spent most of her time close to her Aunty Liz.

"Aaron has agreed to go to the rehabilitation clinic in Switzerland for three months over the winter period, so I guess that's progress." The two women sat in the small guest salon, as they shared a pot of tea.

"How did you get him to agree to that?" Rebecca quizzed. "I said I'd divorce him on the grounds of adultery if he didn't agree and if he did agree I would stay, forgive him, and do all that I can to make it work for us."

Rebecca raised her eyebrows. "Adultery Aunty?" Aunty took a sip of her tea before she continued. "Yes Rebecca. I know about his visits to the prostitute. I left him to it, as I wasn't prepared to take on the disgusting perversions he was demanding from me. But I'm sure it is all a part of his alcoholism. On a happier note its great the doctor gave you a clean bill of health and very exciting that the baby is due in March."

On the day she left, Claudio, Sandy and Mario arrived to help Rebecca with her suitcases to the train station. Ronnie greeted them at the front door of the hotel. "This is a sad day for me, losing my favourite work-mate."

Rebecca appeared from the kitchen. "Come on Ronnie. You aren't losing me; I'm less than an hour away by train."

Her uncle was nowhere to be seen but as Aunty Liz arrived to greet the group; she held a white envelope. She directed her conversation at Rebecca and Mario who held his arm around his wife-to-be. "This is for you both to help things go smoothly. Don't open it until later, and, if you need anything, please call me." She pressed the envelope into Rebecca's hand. "Aunty thanks for this, and for everything."

Sandy and Claudio waved the happy couple off on the train. Mario was to travel with Rebecca and stay the day with her. "I feel so much better leaving that hotel. Aunty turned out to be wonderful, but the tension and threat of Uncle was too much." Rebecca snuggled in close to Mario. They had a whole compartment to themselves.

"I hate that man, even if he reforms himself. If circumstances had been different, we Italians have a way to deal with men like him." Rebecca was alarmed at Mario's menace. "Let's not dwell on any of it. I just want to look forward not backwards." Rebecca said.

Then suddenly she remembered the unopened envelope in her bag. "Oh my goodness, look Mario, there's five hundred pounds in here. This is a fortune! We can't possibly accept it." She read the note.

"Dear Rebecca and Mario,

I know you will initially feel uncomfortable about accepting this amount of money. That is why I wanted you to open it without me being present. What Aaron did to you was evil and despicable; I can never thank you enough for not getting the police involved. I do know you didn't do it for him, but for me. That is the most wonderful love. We will never have any children and we have plenty of money, so I want you to use this to have the best wedding you can and the best start for your new family.

Much love, Liz Samuels."

Mario spoke first. "Well I still think her husband is a bastard and I would never accept anything from him. But Liz is expressing her love; my mother would do the same if she could." Rebecca placed the money back in her bag and put the letter inside her diary.

"I think we should accept it in the spirit it was given. Maybe we can open a bank account in Menton. We'll need to put it somewhere safe." They chatted and laughed about the various Sundays they'd spent as a foursome and pondered on their future. Mario continually patted Rebecca's tummy, even though it was only a small bump: he spoke to it as if it were a little boy.

"What if it's a girl? I don't want you to be disappointed." He kissed her lips. "If she is as beautiful as you I won't care."

The entire Reiss family greeted them at the station. Joseph packed Rebecca's cases in the trunk and all five just managed to fit into his small Renault car. "This is your room just opposite mine." Sylvie gave Rebecca a tour of the second floor of the villa.

Mario joined them. "That was my room when Mama and I lived here." He pointed to the small room along the hall. "I remember it as the place where I was rescued. I was happy here." Allessia served up one of her special Sunday lunches that continued until just before Mario needed to leave on the five p. m. train. "I know you are safe here Tesoro, with my family, who are your family now. I'll visit every Sunday and phone you every Wednesday. I love you!"

At breakfast the next morning Rebecca instigated the conversation. "Please, can you give me a list of my duties, Allessia? I helped a lot with the elderly wealthy widows at Hotel Samuels."

"You won't get any wealthy widows here!" Allessia informed her. "No widows, just travelling salesmen on a budget, poor bachelors and two displaced soldiers Papa felt sorry for who are still here from the war ten years ago." Sylvie added. "Seriously Rebecca, you're welcome to help with the fowls and the garden, but we are really a lodging house and have our routines and there's not a lot extra to do. We just want you to enjoy your time here. Keep well and get lots of rest; this is a very special baby you are carrying."

The Reiss home resonated with warmth and laughter. Rebecca found it infectious. The days seemed happy with the highlight of the week being Sunday, when Mario visited. She fell into a routine; she fed the fowls in the morning, collected their eggs and prepared the vegetables for the family lunch. Sylvie returned each day around five p. m. from the university in Nice where she was training to be an English teacher. In the evenings the girls chatted in English about all sorts of subjects and had become firm friends.

They often sat in each other's rooms, with Sylvie asking questions about London, which in turn gave Rebecca an opening to ask about Sylvie's family. Her main interest was about Mario's background, his mother, and the Reiss's mixed marriage. Sylvie was less forthcoming, but as time went on she let a few comments slip.

"Sylvie, you don't speak much about your years during

the War here in Menton. Was it a ghastly time?" Rebecca asked.

"I realise that as both my parents are alive it looks as if we survived the War, but that's just not true. I watched my Papa dragged off by the Nazi's and he was interned in a concentration camp from which he barely survived." She paused, and wiped her eyes, before resuming. "Mama had given up all hope when on New Year's Eve he appeared, so badly disfigured with neglect and hunger she didn't recognise him. Strangely, I did. I saw him coming up the road and, although it had been over a year and his appearance was quite altered, I knew it was my father." She paused again.

"Don't go on if it's too upsetting, I shouldn't have pried." Rebecca reached out and touched her hand.

"No I want to tell you. After the initial excitement of having Papa back we had to get on with his rehabilitation. It took two years for his external and internal injuries to heal. He needed new false teeth and his stomach is still sensitive, because of the damage that was inflicted."

"Oh Sylvie I'm so sorry." Rebecca's eyes had filled with tears.

Sylvie touched her knee calmingly before she continued. "Millions of Jews were killed; we are blessed to have him, but although we've all dealt with the physical scars the psychological ones will never go away." They sat in silence for a few minutes then Rebecca spoke.

"My family were safe in England, and although I was aware of the atrocities that happened in Europe I was only ten years old when the War ended and they never speak of it in our household; but it's so real to me now I'm here, so close to where it all happened."

Sylvie made motions to leave. "What happened back then is why we are how we are today. And why it takes something fairly major to offend my parents who are so accepting. Come on that's enough for tonight I have to be up early. Goodnight Becca."

Rebecca had the afternoons to herself and discovered several wonderful public gardens that were free to visit throughout the town. Her favourite walk was along the Promenade to Cap Martin, and around the rocky path at the tip of the Cap. She took her diary and small sketchpad. Because she had so much free time, she'd resurrected her interest in drawing and enjoyed sketching the landscape. She lingered on protracted entries in her diary which included her innermost thoughts and all the details of her exquisite surroundings.

Twenty-five

A month into her stay in Menton Rebecca began to feel very restricted in her clothes which seemed to be getting tighter. Only two weeks previously she'd let the seams out in two of her skirts, but they were snug again around her fast growing tummy. She had assumed her large, loose coat would last her through the pregnancy, but it strained across her bump.

"Allessia, would you mind helping me find some new, larger clothes? I am struggling now to fasten any of the dresses and skirts I have."

Allessia took a keen look at her "Yes you are quite big for your time. It must be a big Italian boy! Why don't we go to the fabric shop and see what they have? Then we could ask Madame Leievre to make you up a couple of dresses and perhaps we can buy a new coat, which you could take in afterwards."

Later that afternoon, after they'd selected several suitable fabrics, they visited Madame Leievre, the local dressmaker, who worked from a studio in the Rue Victor Hugo. She greeted them with extreme French politeness. Madame was thin and statuesque with a prominent hooknose that gave her face a permanent look of disdain.

Allessia introduced Rebecca as her niece-in-law and they exchanged a few rapid sentences in French. Rebecca strained to catch exactly what they said, but could tell, by the dramatic change in expression on Allessia's face that she was not impressed.

"Come Rebecca! Madame Leievre is too busy just now to take on a new client." She clutched Rebecca's arm and, without saying goodbye, they hurriedly left. Once out on the street Allessia exploded in hot Italian. "Mama Mia! That woman! She is a snob and a French cow!" Her face was bright red with anger.

"What did she say?" Rebecca asked.

Allessia briskly switched to English. "I'm sorry to tell you this, but I can't see how lying to you will help. Because you are unmarried and pregnant she feels it would sully her business reputation to sew for you."

Rebecca had felt sullied and offended, but not surprised. She'd experienced some glaring looks in the street but this had been the first time anyone had verbalised direct prejudice at her. "Don't worry! I can buy some clothes. I'm sure they must cater for pregnant women in some of the fashion shops I've passed."

Allessia calmed down. "I know what we'll do, I can actually sew. I just haven't been at my old sewing machine for a few years. Let's buy some patterns and we can make your new dresses together." Allessia linked Rebecca's arm as they walked off in the direction of the shops. The money Rebecca's Aunt had contributed proved to be really useful as the new coat was costly.

As they passed the art supply shop window, Rebecca was fascinated by the display. It was all jumbled, with an easel, piles of sketchpads, boxes of crayons and a graphic poster of the human body, all shrouded in dust as if no one had touched it for years. "Go on in Rebecca! Don't just gaze in the window. I've seen your sketches, they're very good."

"I've been thinking about attempting to use oils, but I can't justify the expense with the baby coming." Rebecca responded, rubbing her belly. Allessia gently pushed her into the shop. It was very pokey and small, and had a musty smell about it.

"Bonjour ladies. What can I do for you today?" The bald-headed proprietor pushed his half-moon spectacles up his nose as he spoke.

"We're looking for a set of oil paints. Nothing too expensive please." Allessia replied, before Rebecca had a chance to use her limited French. "Would I be correct in assuming this would be your first time with oils?"

Rebecca answered in English as Allessia translated. "Well, I used them at school but not very well. It's just that the light is so fantastic here by comparison with England and I'd like to attempt capturing the colour." He gave her a nod, and then rustled around under the desk and brought out what looked like an ancient box of paint tubes.

"These are old stock, but perfectly okay to paint with. And I can let you have them at a good price." The picture on the cover of the box was a bit faded, and the box slightly battered. "Great! We'll take them." Allessia took some francs out of her purse.

Rebecca objected but she wouldn't take no for an answer. The old man wrapped the paint box carefully in brown paper and string. "Good luck young lady! Perhaps you could visit again when you have completed a painting. I would enjoy seeing your progress." He gave Allessia a kind wink as they left.

"You will need something to do once you are up at Castel Vittorio. I'm afraid it will be a bit boring at Carla's house. It's still quite a sad gloomy place. I did suggest we keep you with us 'till your time, but she's insistent she will deliver her grandchild with the local midwife. I have to say the midwife is excellent as she trained in Rome and serves the whole of the valley."

"What do you mean 'It's still a gloomy place'? What happened there to make it gloomy for so long?" Allessia quickened her step "Oh you know, the War and not many young people living up there now." She said.

Once Joseph had over-hauled Allessia's somewhat temperamental sewing machine by cleaning out all the dust and oiling the relevant parts, the two women made up the fabrics. They managed two long-sleeved, very loose dresses.

"I really appreciate your help Allessia, but I'm so fat, I look like a tent with a head on the top in this!" She stood in front of the full-length mirror as Allessia pinned the hem. "I agree. You've become quite large. But, as I said, it is probably a big baby boy. Besides, you are blooming and you look so feminine and beautiful." She attempted to reassure Rebecca.

With her new coat, which covered her and fitted well, Rebecca felt more confident about moving about in public. She had discovered a special place to paint. It was called Parc du Pian, on a hill very near to the Italian border, in Avenue Blasco Ibannez. She could manage the walk up to it at a slow pace. The redundant, ancient olive grove still had some trees that were nearly 700 years old. On Sundays it was popular with the locals, who loved to stroll and picnic there. Rebecca discovered there were over five hundred trees spread on many separate terraces covering about six hectares. She'd found an old stone seat where she could comfortably sit and paint with uninterrupted views of the Mediterranean. Whilst initially anticipating capturing the sea from this viewpoint, it was the trees that continued to distract her. The gnarling and knots in the trunks reminded her of old people who had grown lined and wrinkled with age, but carried their character and stories of their lives within their faces. The trees appeared worn and weary from years of surveying the ocean and shedding copious amounts of fruit. They made perfect subjects for her line drawing.

Rather than be put off by Rebecca's fast growing bump, Mario viewed it as a tribute to his manhood. At every given opportunity he held his hands gently around it. Then, when he felt the baby kick, he announced, "My son will be a great football player!" to anyone who would listen. The highlight of each week was the Sundays she spent with Mario. They usually walked to one of the various public botanical gardens, shared the Sunday meal with the Reiss's or just lay on Rebecca's bed and talked about their future. Mario loved to fantasize about the restaurant he would own one day with Claudio and his eyes glazed over when he spoke of his dream.

"My restaurant will be nestled somewhere up in my valley, we will have seats outside so in the summer the guests can dine al fresco, and in the winter near a roaring fire inside." He picked up her sketchpad. "It looks very clever the way you have put the splash of colour next to the dull grey trees. You do understand of course, when those trees were planted, Menton was a part of Italy. It is only recently, well several hundred years ago, that the French claimed it."

"No, I didn't know that. And if you look carefully at the picture, that splash of colour is meant to be me, in my new blue coat." Next his attention wandered to her diary and he began to turn the pages. "You seem to spend a lot of time writing in this book. What do you write about?" She firmly took it out of his hands. "It's what we call a diary. It's private. But, if you must know, I'm recording the things that are happening in my life just now, mainly for my own sake, but maybe one day our son or daughter or even our grandchildren may read it."

He nodded then added "Husbands and wives shouldn't have secrets Tesoro."

"I agree, but we're not married yet and besides I think there are things you need to tell me about Castel Vittorio?"

He shot her a troubled look. "Who's been talking to you?"

"No-one has actually said anything but I get the feeling there are things I haven't been told?" He hesitated before he answered. "Like your diary, it's private. A part of the past that I'm not just ready yet to remember; once you are up there you'll hear about it all soon enough."

To Rebecca's delight, Ronnie visited one Monday. As a treat he invited her to a brasserie for lunch. Despite a few uncomfortable side-ward glances from fellow diners they engrossed themselves in their own conversation and gossiped like two old women about the hotel and its goings on. Sandy also appeared on several Saturdays and was full of news about her and Claudio's wedding. What she would wear and where they might live.

"Becca I have something special to ask you. Will you be my bridesmaid; you should be all okay again by summer?" Sandy shone with warmth.

"I'd love to. I do hope my body has returned to its original shape by then.

Twenty-six

Carla and Allessia had spoken on the phone and agreed, given Rebecca's size, she couldn't be too far off from the birth. It was decided they would drive her up to Castel Vittorio the following Sunday. It was a crisp, chilly winter's morning as Mario and Rebecca settled in the back seat of Joseph's car. Allessia sat up front with her husband. Sylvie was away, staying in Nice as it was the middle of her end-of-year exams. Rebecca had only travelled into Italy as far as Hanbury Gardens. A sense of foreboding engulfed her as they left the happy Reiss home. Her anxiety rose at the thought of meeting Carla.

"It will be colder when we start to drive up the valley," Mario spoke tenderly. He wrapped the fringed car rug around Rebecca's legs and snuggled in beside her.

After Ventimiglia, when Joseph had turned off to the Nervia Valley, Mario proudly became the tourist guide and imparted details about each village as they passed through. It was the first time Rebecca had seen medieval villages perched on hillsides. Dolce Aqua enchanted her, with its perfect crescent stone bridge set under the backdrop of its Castle ruins.

"This would make a perfect painting, don't you agree Tesoro?" Mario's pleasure was evident as he pointed out the beauty of his home valley. Rebecca quietly nodded and smiled. Mario's commentary had become a faint background hum as she struggled to repress the fear that had invaded her thoughts. As the car climbed upwards through the various hamlets, it felt as if a part of her life had finished. Her thoughts were suspended when the car came to a halt. "We're in Pigna. Let's have a break and give your legs a stretch."

Joseph cheered Rebecca on, as he opened the car door for the couple. "That's your home for the next few weeks." Allessia enthusiastically pointed to the village perched above them. Rebecca was totally captivated. It was beyond her imaginings. The fourteenth century village sat in the mid-morning mist, which had concealed its base. It appeared as if void of any foundations, as if it floated on a sea of cloud. The tall clock-tower shot up in the middle and the surrounding stone houses seemed to lean, in crooked rows, as they graduated up towards it.

Her companions misinterpreted Rebecca's silence. "Don't worry Tesoro. It's not as scary as it looks. It's just the winter mist; Mama will have the house warm," Mario comforted her reassuringly.

"You'll be very welcome Rebecca. Carla is so excited about her first grandchild," Allessia added somewhat unconvincingly, as she attempted to alleviate Rebecca's fear.

"I'm okay. I'm just quite stunned at the magnificence of it all. I can't wait to be up there!" She forced a smile. "All back into the car! The hard climb commences," Joseph called. The car struggled to make any speed up the steep, narrow road. Mario and Allessia exchanged humorous tales of childhood experiences, but both went suddenly silent as they passed the turn off, signed Gordale.

As they neared the village a few old people appeared on the road going about their daily business; Allessia waved out to them; she said their names and made amusing comments about their missing teeth, unshaven faces and fat tummies.

The car finally broke through above the thick mist and Joseph found a suitable place to park at the base of the perched village. Rebecca keenly felt the fresh, sharp air as she opened the car door. It took her a moment to adjust to the temperature and to take in her surroundings. Below her, peeping through the fading mist she surveyed the aerial view of Pigna. The most prominent buildings, that had caught the high sun, were the cemetery crypts, which stood tall and majestic as if they were the supervising guardians of the valley.

Mario and Joseph carried the bags as they walked up the cobbled path into the village square. Rebecca noticed a coldness come over Mario's demeanour as he walked ahead. Allessia took her arm as she strained with the added weight of her body. Her ankles had swollen, but she was determined not to complain and managed to show her interest by asking a few questions as they ascended into the square.

When they reached the water well, the focal point of the square, they paused for Rebecca to rest. The travelling grocer had just arrived with his trays of fresh vegetables and fruit; several of the women were choosing their needs, as he loudly reassured them it was all freshly picked that morning. The women took time out from their food negotiations to scrutinise the new entourage that had graced their square. Greetings were called out to Allessia and Mario, but the sight of Rebecca and her large belly was the primary focus of their attention.

"Come on! Just one more lot of stairs and we'll have you home," Joseph summoned as he stirred Rebecca on. As they passed the Church, Father Antoine greeted them warmly. He looked directly at Rebecca and then spoke to her in clear

English. "Carla has told me all about you, we're happy to have you here. I'm the only English speaking person in the village so I'm hoping that you and I will become friends." He offered Rebecca a firm handshake and then spoke to Mario and Allessi as Joseph slipped in beside her. "Watch him! He's mainly out to convert you," he whispered.

Carla greeted them at her door with kisses, hugs, and a lot of Italian noise. Once they were all inside the small, cosy kitchen, mother and future daughter-in-law appraised each other. Carla was forty years of age, her hair was stark black with just a few grey flecks, and her eyes were shaped just like Mario's but lacked his warmth. She was quite short, but had a straight back. She addressed Rebecca politely in Italian as Mario translated for her.

"I'm very happy you are here. We may both be a little awkward to begin with but I'm sure we'll find a way through it. Mario tells me you've been learning Italian, so I will also try some English. But we can both speak some French, so that's good!"

Rebecca nodded compliantly. "I could understand most of what she said," she told Mario, who seemed pleased the first meeting between his Mama and future wife seemed to go smoothly.

He then showed her around the house, which had originally belonged to his grandparents. It was four stories high but had only two smallish rooms on each level. Carla had selected a room on the second level above the kitchen and living room for Rebecca so she wouldn't need to climb too many stairs. Carla slept at the top of the house; the furniture was all antique, it had been passed down from each generation via both sets of Mario's grandparents. There was only one bathroom and the basic toilet was on the ground floor, just off the kitchen.

Mario sensed Rebecca's concern. "There's nothing I can do about the toilet Tesoro. This house was built in the fourteenth century, and it was only in my grandfather's time we had an inside toilet and sewerage system put in." They joined the rest of the group, who sat around the kitchen table.

"Good, you are here now. Come and sit down. I've prepared some of your favourite pasta, Mario." He gave his Mama a big hug, to which she responded to by stroking his hair. Rebecca was both fascinated and threatened by this tender exchange.

"Mama, I have arranged with the hotel that I will have Mondays off work until the baby is born. So I'll come on my motor scooter each Sunday morning and leave Monday evening or maybe even very early Tuesday. I've assured Rebecca, when her time comes, you'll get a message to Uncle Bartolo, who will then phone the hotel and no matter what, I'll come immediately." Rebecca squeezed his hand. Over lunch Allessia and Carla's chat was mainly about the good times when their parents were alive. Joseph remained silent but when the conversation moved to more sombre things, he skilfully diverted their attention by introducing Sylvie into the equation.

"She'll be qualified next year and will go to a training position in London." Around four p. m. the Reiss's made motions that it was time to go. Rebecca panicked; a shadowy fog of fear overwhelming her.

"Tesoro, please don't cry! I can't leave you like this." Mario held her close, as the baby kicked madly in her belly between them. "Mama, feel this! Your grandson, the footballer, is kicking like crazy!"

Carla warily placed her hand on Rebecca's belly as she glanced at Rebecca's tear-stained face.

"Don't cry! We'll be all right together. Mario needs to work as he will soon be supporting the three of us." After the tearful goodbye, future Mama and Grandmama settled down in front of the fire. Carla's warmth didn't improve. Once Mario had left the house Rebecca sensed the change of mood. However she reasoned to herself that Carla had to deal with a difficult situation. Rebecca considered that had it been her own mother in the same situation, there would have been no allowances.

As the day came to a close, Carla showed Rebecca how to prepare the ancient bath and to close the heavy bedroom shutters. Rebecca had attempted to study her future mother-in-law with a more rational view. But all she could see was desolation and rigidity in Carla's eyes. After supper Rebecca slowly took the few steps to her bedroom that Carla had immaculately prepared with crisp linen sheets, beautifully embroidered pillow-slips and a small vase of fresh flowers. But the gloom overshadowed Carla's arrangements. It hovered around Carla, seeping through the entire house and seemed to cling to the walls like an invisible but disturbing mould. Finally Rebecca fell asleep, only awakening the next morning when she heard the rattle of Carla as she busied herself in the kitchen.

"The midwife will be visiting you this afternoon; she can be abrupt, but she is very qualified at her job," Carla informed Rebecca, as they sat eating breakfast.

"You must tell me what I can do to help you around the

house Carla" They managed to speak a mixture of French and Italian to each other.

"Looking at those swollen ankles, you won't be doing much! You'll need to keep them elevated. Mario tells me you sketch and paint. If we get you up to my room at the top of the house there are some great views I'm sure you would enjoy painting."

As she spoke she pulled up a chair to rest Rebecca's legs on. The midwife was a buxom woman with an intelligent face but a slightly abrupt manner, who appeared very professional as she prodded and felt Rebecca's swollen belly. She spoke a little English which she mixed with Italian and asked several questions about the timing of the pregnancy and Rebecca's weight gain. As she left, Carla accompanied her outside and they chatted out of earshot.

"The midwife is a little concerned at just how big you are for your time, but some babies are just big. Or being your first, you may have the date wrong. Either way, I won't be letting you out of my sight for too long." The gloom of the house seemed to dissipate when Rebecca surveyed the valley from Carla's bedroom window. It was the time of day she enjoyed the most. The view was magnificent, complimented by the tranquillity and the distant bird song, which was such a contrast to London or Nice. She had developed her skills mixing oil colours and experienced a certain sense of satisfaction on completing her first oil painting.

"Look what your fiancée has done! Isn't she so talented?" Carla showed Mario Rebecca's painting on his Sunday visit.

"She is! And she is the love of my life Mama. But I'm concerned; she looks very pale and her legs look so swollen; what does the midwife say?" Mario spoke in a low tone, assuming that Rebecca had dozed off. She felt a little guilty as she strained to eavesdrop. "Well, she is concerned. But we both see no point in telling Rebecca, who needs to stay as calm and relaxed as possible so the baby can reach full term. Mario, this is my grandchild and you must trust me I will do all in my power to ensure his or her safe arrival."

"Mama, my first concern is for Rebecca. I love her more than anything; I love the baby too, but I don't know the baby yet. Rebecca is my best friend; I must be very firm on this point." They finished the conversation as they heard Rebecca on the stairs.

"Sorry, I dropped off! I seem to do a lot of sleeping lately. It must be all this extra weight I'm carrying; it feels like there are about four boys in my belly, all kicking a football about. It's so strong it wakes me up." Mario grasped her hand as she took the last couple of steps into the kitchen.

"Do you feel like a walk Mario? I really need to get out for a bit." She gave him a wink, to indicate she wanted him alone. "Only if you are up to it, Tesoro?" After ten minutes, Rebecca suddenly felt wary, her feet heavy.

"Look, the Church is open. Let's sit inside for a bit until you get your breath." Mario guided her through the high, heavy doors. It was the first time Rebecca had been inside a Catholic Church. Mario said it was reputed to be thirteenth century, though there'd been some debate over the actual date. A musty smell lingered, tinged with a subtle fragrance. Mario explained the smell was a mixture of age and the ancient incense they burned every day during the Mass. He pointed out the different paintings and icons around the walls.

"Like you Jews we are strong in our traditions; just how

much of it is God's hand and how much is the ego of man, I'm not sure?" Rebecca was impressed how articulate he'd become with his command of English, and intrigued to hear him give a balanced view of religion "It's the same for us, a lot of what we do in the Synagogue and a lot of the rituals are just a discipline. But I sometimes think, if there is a God, he wouldn't be as judgemental as all these religions seem to be about other beliefs."

They'd been seated in the Church for about half an hour, when they heard the doors creak. "Oh, I didn't realise anyone was still here. I can come back and lock up later." The Priest had the large iron key in his hand. "No, it's okay. We need to be getting back." Mario kissed the Priest on both cheeks as Rebecca struggled to get up from the narrow Church pew. "I was wondering when it would be suitable to chat with you both about your marriage?" He attempted a humbled diplomatic tone.

"Once the baby is born and Rebecca has told her parents, we will give you a date, Father," Mario retorted. "It's important to both of us that her family will give their blessing and may even attend the ceremony." He then gently ushered Rebecca out of the Church. The Priest gave a half smile and then turned to lock the door.

"It'll be easier for me if you consider studying our faith, but it's your decision. And either way, we are marrying! I don't want you pushed into anything." Rebecca was reassured by Mario's words as he tenderly steered her back to the house.

Carla wouldn't allow Mario to sleep with Rebecca, so he slept on the sofa in the salon. That evening Rebecca had been in such discomfort, sleep had been impossible. She had lit the small lamp at her bedside to update her diary when she heard the cry. It sounded distressed and desperate. It was Mario.

"No, no stop the gunfire! please don't be dead, wake up! Papa wake up!" She understood every word. She moved as fast as she could, but was hampered by her weight. Carla had already reached him. She held her son's head in her hands and gently stroked his sweat-drenched hair. Rebecca watched unnoticed. Mario appeared to be in a type of delirious nightmare and it was apparent Carla had dealt with the scenario before. "Hush my Darling; it's all right now. Papa and the others are in heaven. We will soon have another Orengo here to carry on the family. Hush my son."

Mario rose as dawn broke as it would take him two hours to return to Nice. He sneaked into Rebecca's room to give her a kiss goodbye. "Are you alright Mario? I heard you having a bad dream during the night?" He looked a little taken back.

"Oh it happens sometimes. I'm okay now. I'll tell you about it on my next visit I promise, I need to rush now." He lovingly kissed her and quickly left.

Rebecca had become less and less mobile, and the days until Mario arrived seemed to drag by. Carla tried her best to entertain her, but it was limited, because of the language barrier. Rebecca vented a lot of her frustration in her diary. The pages were full of her feelings, her guilt, and her hopes. The midwife had visited again and her concern was obvious.

"You must stay on bed-rest now, only get up to use the toilet and for no other reason. If you have any pain at all you must tell Carla; this is very important!"

It had been two days since the midwife's visit, and one day until Mario's next visit, when Rebecca felt the first pain.

"Carla, Carla! Come quickly! I have a bad pain in my back!" she yelled as loud as she could. Carla rushed to her room.

"I'll call the neighbour to ring the midwife, and Mario at the hotel." Carla dashed out of the room. "Let's get you into a loose nightdress and change the sheets." Rebecca's sheets were saturated.

"I thought there would be a break in the pain – that's what the baby book said!" There was no respite. Rebecca screamed.

"The midwife will be here soon. Breathe deeply!" Carla's words were the last words Rebecca heard.

Twenty-seven

She could see twilight. It seemed to go on forever, a hazy, half-light; muffled sounds, almost familiar. Rebecca strained to hear them; she felt she needed to respond but she couldn't quite understand what they asked. Momentarily she had felt soothing strokes on her arm before she fell back into oblivion.

"Rebecca, Rebecca! Tesoro, you must try and wake up now, your daughter needs you, I need you." She recognised the voice and struggled to open her mouth to respond. At first the words didn't come, then, a soft hand dampened her mouth with a wet cloth.

"Mario?" The first word came out.

"Oh, my Rebecca! You're waking up. Try harder!" She opened her eyes and the haze lifted.

"Mario, where am I?"

"You're in the hospital, in Ventimiglia. We have a beautiful baby girl!" It slowly came back to her.

"How did I get here? How long have I been asleep?"

A tall man appeared in the room. "Hello Rebecca. I am Doctor Graziane. You have been a very sick young lady, but I think you will mend." His English was clear,

"Don't tire her Mario; she will need a lot of rest." The doctor abruptly left and Carla stood at the door with a white bundle in her arms. Rebecca managed to focus on it as she heard the first cry.

"Is that my baby?" She laboured to lift her arms out.

"Mama, bring her here!" Mario took the bundle, pulled

back the blanket from her face and laid it next to Rebecca. The baby immediately ceased crying. Her tiny head was covered in thick black hair and her eyes looked far too big for her small face.

"Oh! She's so dainty and so beautiful." Rebecca was overcome with emotion.

"She's our precious daughter. We haven't named her yet. We were waiting for you." Mario joined mother and baby on the bed. Carla had tactfully left the room.

"Can we call her Sarah? That was my grandmother's name; she can have an Italian second name." Little Sarah grabbed onto her mother's finger.

"Yes. She is now officially Sarah Carla Orengo. Our very own, precious daughter."

It took several days before Rebecca was able to leave her bed; her milk had come on, so she was able to breast feed at least four times a day, while at other times, Sarah took the bottle. Mario returned to work part-time and Carla attentively helped nurse Rebecca herself. "The Doctor has said, because of the caesarean, you must restrict yourself to this room and your bathroom; there's a high risk of infection otherwise." At first Rebecca didn't question this, as she was so tired she welcomed Carla's help. However after ten days she was well on her way to recovery, her suture line had almost healed and she decided to leave her room to collect Sarah herself from the nursery.

"Where are you going? You really must stay in your room!" Carla intercepted her in the hallway, sounding angry.

"I'm nearly all healed now, I need to get out of that room, I'm going crazy. It's dawned on me today I haven't seen anyone else since I've been here. I thought maybe I could see the nursery and chat with some of the other mothers." Carla appeared agitated.

"Rebecca, I don't think you understand. This isn't a maternity hospital, it's a general hospital, so there are many sick people in here, and you're still easily open to infection." Rebecca stood her ground in the hallway. "But, I was sure I could hear more than one baby crying!"

A nurse had stood behind Carla, observing the exchange. Carla's face had reddened but she ignored the nurse, as she attempted to guide Rebecca back into her room. "Yes, some of the visitors bring their children with them. Come; let's get you a cup of tea. It's nearly Sarah's feed time." Rebecca complied and returned to her room.

"I feel almost like a prisoner in here Mario. Your Mama hardly lets me breath; she's in and out all day long and I've only seen the doctor once, and I never get to speak to any nurses," Rebecca told Mario.

He shifted uncomfortably on his seat. "The doctor is based in San Remo and only visits every other day. You're not really sick now so I guess the other very sick patients take preference, he knows Mama is looking after you and her care is best." He blushed as he spoke and avoided eye contact.

"Also the Reiss', Sandy, Claudio or Ronnie haven't been to visit. And they all promised they would!" Mario looked down at his feet. "The doctor said it was best you didn't have any visitors other than Mama and me, so as not to tire you."

Rebecca was irritated. "Well I'll visit Sandy when I get to Nice. I think I'll leave for London next week, so would you be able to book my train and ferry tickets. You can use some of Auntie's money to pay for them?"

Mario nodded and promptly went for the door. "I'll check Sarah is awake and bring her in." When he arrived back with little Sarah, he relaxed as he watched Rebecca put the baby to her breast.

"I'll make your travel bookings Tesoro. Please just do as Mama says, it's only for a few more days." Rebecca could only express her apprehensions through writing in her diary, and she continued to pour her heart out on the pages.

"I'm feeling so lonely, even though Mario or his Mama is always here. Sarah is beautiful! All I could wish for. But it's as if something is missing, I guess it is my own family. My mother should be with me; I also read in the baby book that sometimes mothers get the 'baby blues' after giving birth. But both Mario's and Carla's behaviour seems altered in some way. I just can't put my finger on it; well it may be just my hormones. But it feels strange, not really seeing anyone else in all the time I've been here. I also noticed the nurse in the corridor giving me an odd look before Carla shooed me back into my room."

She closed the diary when Carla appeared with Sarah for another feed. The atmosphere between the two women had become frosty. It was agreed. Joseph would come and collect Rebecca and Sarah in his car, and Mario would travel with them to Nice. The new family of three would then spend a night with Sandy and her father, before Rebecca and Sarah left for London the following day.

Mario had brought all the baby clothes and Rebecca's suitcase to the hospital.

She had busied herself with packing, when she was distracted by Mario's raised voice. She discretely moved as close to her open door so as she could hear what he was saying. He was along the hallway. Carla was arguing with him, but Rebecca couldn't quite distinguish the words as they spoke in rapid Italian. Mario sounded incensed as he raged at his Mama. Carla's response sounded equally heated. Rebecca was hesitant to step out, and, before she could, she heard a third voice butting in. Tactfully she popped her head around the corner of the door and saw a mature, uniformed nurse. Rebecca assumed she had been the matron. She appeared to placate them, and then she spotted Rebecca, and let Carla and Mario know she was there. Rebecca darted back into her room. Mario was right behind her.

"Sorry Tesoro. Mama is being difficult about Sarah leaving and I guess we just both got a little over-heated."

Rebecca wanted to believe him. "It sounded more important than a family spat. I've never heard you two speaking like that before." Mario flushed with shame; looked away and said nothing.

"Never mind, let's just be happy for the short time we have just now. I'm sure everything will be okay. When I return from London we'll have the rest of our lives together." Rebecca's generous reconciliatory words seem to work their magic as Mario composed himself and furnished her with a smile.

"I'll go and check if Joseph has arrived yet."

Carla handed her granddaughter over to Rebecca. She appeared to be over her outburst, but she showed no emotion. "Be careful on your journey and hurry back!" Carla tautly kissed both Rebecca's cheeks. As they left the hospital, Rebecca experienced an unexplained sense of loss. She thought she was going crazy, for only half an hour before, she couldn't wait to get away. Joseph chatted about Sylvie, who was away in Marseilles sitting her exams. But he seemed distant to Rebecca and puzzlingly avoided any conversation about her new baby.

They arrived at Sandy's house late afternoon. "Goodbye

Rebecca. Remember, you can phone us any time if things don't work out quite how you hope. We're all here to support you." Joseph's wrinkled eyes were tear-filled and his words barely audible as he hugged and said goodbye.

"Rebecca, Rebecca! I'm so pleased to see you. Let me see your daughter." Sandy took Sarah in her arms. "Oh she is just beautiful! I can see half of each of you in her." They moved into the salon and after some small talk Sandy steered the conversation onto her wedding plans. Mario took the opportunity to escape to the kitchen and joined Sandy's father for a pastis.

"The wedding is on July 5th so that should give you time to be back. You're still going to be my bridesmaid aren't you?"

"Wild horses wouldn't keep me from being here, regardless of whether Mother and Father have agreed to my own wedding. But I'm sure they will have by then!"

Rebecca sounded uneasy. "I have to tell you, I'm nervous, I think initially they'll explode, but once I place Sarah in their arms I feel confident they'll love her and give my marriage their blessing. I am sure they won't want it in London; being abroad should suit Mother."

Sandy's Papa had agreed that Mario could stay the night, so parents and baby were all happily cocooned in the spare room. It was the first proper privacy they'd had for months. "Your figure has all returned now Tesoro. And you look even more beautiful than before!" Mario whispered as he touched Rebecca's face.

"Yes I feel almost normal again. I don't know why I was so big, as Sarah is just a normal sized baby".

Mario dropped his hand. "I think the doctor said it was excess fluid." His face reddened a little.

"Are you embarrassed to talk about it?" Rebecca stroked his back. "The worst is over now. We will all have a wonderful life.

When I come back you will have found a small apartment, and we three will be together." She leaned forward to kiss him.

"Are you sure it's okay Tesoro?" She kissed him again, more forcibly. "Yes I'm sure. Sarah is sound asleep and I want you Mario. You're mine." After a brief hesitation, he responded zealously and they made love with Renéwed passion.

They were woken early the next morning by their daughter, who screamed loudly from her carrycot on the floor beside them. Mario quickly handed her to Rebecca. As she fed her daughter, Mario opened a small box, took out a gold heart-shaped locket and carefully fastened it around baby Sarah's neck.

"I love you so much Rebecca. Please promise me, even if your parents won't agree, you will still come back. This locket is my special gift to our daughter."

"Mario, you and Sarah are my life. Of-course I'll come back, regardless. But I'm sure they will love Sarah as soon as they see her. I'm now thinking, what's the worst they can do?" The noise level at the train station had been deafening, as they both fought to be heard. Sandy had said her goodbyes on the platform. Mario had assisted them onto the train and helped to settle his precious little family into the compartment.

"Goodbye Tesoro. Please write to me and phone Sandy as we agreed as soon as you have your parents' answer. I will love you forever." The departure whistle had blown so loudly that he didn't clearly catch Rebecca's reply. He jumped off the train just in time, as the steam spat and hissed. Guilt and sadness racked his heart as he watched the train shunt out of the station. He wished he hadn't agreed with his mother's actions. The tears spilled uncontrollably down his face as he made the sign of the cross and offered up a silent prayer for their safety and ultimately for their forgiveness.

Twenty-eight

"You will not take my baby from me, I don't care if I've humiliated you, I'm leaving. I'll be back for one last time, to collect my case after I've bought my train ticket." Rebecca left the door of her parent's house ajar as she stormed out. She held her daughter tight. She'd wrapped her in a warm blanket with a woolly hat and booties on. A cold wind blew up the high street, as she headed towards the travel agent. "Little one we will be away from here soon and back happy and safe with your Daddy."

Little Sarah gurgled and gave her mother a big smile. Rebecca was so engrossed and delighted at her daughter's first smile she didn't see the truck as she stepped out on the pedestrian crossing.

PART THREE
SARAH

London, 2009

Twenty-nine

Sarah Anderson walked briskly across Hyde Park towards High Street Kensington. The early crocuses of the season popped up their heads in anticipation of a sunny day. The stubby pastel buds fondly reminded Sarah of her dear husband Simon and the fitness walks they took along this route. On those excursions, their mobiles were banned. He'd be totally hers. She had always felt reassured by their ordinary chatter about simple things, and his witty observations, aimed at dog owner's and 'look alike' dogs.

Their family life had been required to fit in with Simon's professional commitment. That had been their agreement from the onset of their marriage. When Simon died, after twenty-eight years of marriage, she'd lost the plot. But over the past six months she'd found the motivation to move on.

Sarah's GP had been very perceptive when he'd recommended Barbara. As she stepped up her pace, Sarah mulled over the conversation that had triggered the change. She recalled her best friend Robyn's words.

"For goodness sake Sarah, stop trying to deal with all this by yourself. You're middle aged, menopausal, grieved and vulnerable. You have lots of friends, and several avenues of support open to you. Use them!" Sarah who stood at 5feet 2 inches had managed kept her slim size 8 figure. Her large, chocolate brown eyes contrasted attractively to her highlighted blonde bob hair style and thanks to her late husband's insurance policy she retained a modern stylish wardrobe.

She had arrived at 25 Fairfax Place, on time. The sign it on the stucco, pillar-fronted Georgian building read 'Mrs Barbara Jones. Counsellor' and an arrow pointed to the basement. Barbara greeted her like an old friend and offered her a cup of tea. Over the past six months, Sarah had grown fond of this homely, comfortable room with its two rather worn sofas and three large, welcoming arm chairs covered in various miss-matched floral designs. The two walls featured floor to ceiling bookshelves which bulged with a diverse array of hard-covered reference books and tatty paperbacks. The counsellor matched the furniture; she was short, comfortable with wispy grey hair and exhibited a preference for floral dresses. Sarah finally felt she'd progressed with these sessions. Her constant, exaggerated anxiety attacks had dissipated and she no longer felt entirely invisible.

"So tell me all?" Barbara gently asked once they had sunk down, tea cups in hand in facing arm chairs. "Well, maybe there is life after death, so to speak. I found my adoption file; it was just as my parents had always told me. All the information was there, for when I was ready. I'm sure they hadn't imagined I'd be 55 years old."

Barbara shared an encouraging smile, and waited for her to continue. "Then the children, ah, well! That didn't go quite as planned as my big mouth brother blurted it all out at the wrong moment. But, it was all rescued in the end and went down better than I'd anticipated."

Sarah placed her tea cup on the side table and sunk back in her chair. "I didn't tell them about my sessions with Mr Patel, I feel a bit silly about my visits to him now, I'd prefer to keep that to myself." Barbara diplomatically ignored the reference to the psychic Indian gentleman.

"So, you have a birth parent name to commence your search?"

"Yes, well just my father, his name is Mario Orengo .It appears, according to the certificate in the file that my mother is dead, but both Hugh and my son Nick – with their lawyer hats on – feel that as it's not the original certificate, we can't assume it's entirely accurate."

Barbara leaned forward and engaged her counsellor voice. "So how do you feel knowing your birth mother probably died all that time ago, possibly just after you were born?"

"In a way I feel better knowing she didn't desert me, I keep dwelling on why my father wouldn't have wanted me, or possibly why my grandparents wouldn't either, especially if their daughter had died."

Sarah gave a little sigh, rubbed her hands and pressed them to her face. "So what will be your next move?"

"My daughter Florence has offered to assist me with the search for my father or his family as he would be well in his seventies by now, if he's alive. She's much better with Google and the internet than I am." They both sipped their tea and Sarah nibbled on the digestive biscuit Barbara had placed on her saucer. "I've also started the ball rolling on my move to the Riviera. The long term desire Simon and I had to retire there is still something I'd now like for myself .Also my passion to paint will be a purposeful way to spend my time. I've found a local agent to handle the rental of my London house and I've engaged a French agent to help me find a suitable apartment in a town called Menton, about 30 minutes from Nice.

"Has the 'missing' feeling and anxiety attacks abated since your new decisions?"

“Sort of.” Sarah replied hesitantly. Noticing the tell-tale hand rubbing signs, Barbara softened. “I must reiterate, this is a process that will take time, I agree with you the initial grief at the loss of your husband has somewhat abated. I do still firmly believe from all our chats, the loss feeling stems from the repression and shame of your adoption. This search will be difficult, not just logistically, but emotionally as well.”

Sarah opened her mouth to reply, and then stopped herself. “Go on Sarah, what were you about to say?”

“No you’ll think I’m even crazier than you did when I told you about Mr Patel!”

“That’s what this process is all about, your voicing the preoccupations you hold in your head. My view of Indian mystics is irrelevant”

Sarah gave an exaggerated swallow. “You know you previously asked me when my sense of something missing began. Well I didn’t really remember ’till the other day when Hugh teased me about it. I had an imaginary friend when I was very small, she looked just like me and I shared everything with her. She even wore a gold heart-shaped locket just like the one I had. Soon after I started school and had real friends she just faded away. But strangely I remember being so happy with her around.”

Barbara gave Sarah one of her supportive smiles. “I can’t tell you how common it is for children to have imaginary friends; in my view it’s normal, especially in only children or children much younger than their siblings. It may have been connected with some suppressed effect of your adoption, but I’m sure it’s not something you need to dwell on.”

They chatted, until the designated hour was up. “Goodbye Barbara, thanks so much for everything.”

"It's been my pleasure and please keep me posted on your progress."

Once up on the street she turned her mobile on and immediately a text appeared from Florence. "Are you free for a coffee?" Working free-lance had its advantages. Sarah jumped on a bus heading in the direction of the Fulham Broadway.

"Hi Mum! Sorry, I just have to dash to the corner-shop, I'm out of milk. The stuff in the fridge is off! Have you got a couple of quid I can borrow, save me going to the cash machine as well?" Sarah smiled and handed her daughter a ten pound note. She was proud of what Florence had done with her tiny flat, in a good area. It was one bedroom, an open-plan kitchen, minimal décor, stark white, as befitting a graphic artist. Her drawing board and computer were set up on the only table in the room, which she concealed in a cupboard when she entertained. One end of the table had been laid on some art deco styled table mats with two coffee cups and a sugar bowl.

Florence rushed back full of more apologies. She was dressed casually, immaculately coordinated in denim jeans, a navy Benetton sweater and white plimsolls. Her thick black hair was tied tight in a ponytail. "Sorry again Mum! Because I don't have milk in my coffee I guess it just sits there too long. I know you really don't like yours without milk. I'm so glad you could come over, I've heaps to talk to you about".

Sarah had already boiled the kettle. Her daughter carefully measured the fresh coffee into the Danish designed coffee-pot. "I'll just put the change in your purse Mum." As she opened the purse a piece of A4 paper fell out. Florence immediately picked it up. Under the heading of 'Sarah's List of Goals' she read:

1: Look into relocating to the Riviera.

2: Pursue your hobby of painting more seriously

3: Commence research into who my birth parents were.

"Well Mum I'd known about the first two, but the 'birth parents'? This has been a bit of a shock." Sarah mentally counted to ten.

"Now if we're going to work together on the 'search' as you offered the other evening, you'll have to get over the blame. Making me feel guilty won't help anybody, will it?"

Sarah looked defiantly at her daughter. Watery tears appeared in Flo's eyes. "Sorry Mum, it's just all still fresh." Sarah pulled her daughter close and hugged her.

"Yes for me too, after so many years of denial, but hey it's a new adventure!"

They sat face-to-face on the corner of the table, coffees in hand.

"I took the liberty of looking on line how to commence searching for your birth parents. I found an informative site, but our challenge is your age, as they didn't promote open adoptions in 1955 and electronic records only go back so far."

As she spoke Flo pulled her laptop over and booted it into life. "The letter from the adoption agency is the starting point." Sarah leant over to see what her daughter was tapping into Google. "When I took a closer look at the file Mum, I saw the name Cohen & Co as the adoption agency, so I'm guessing that's Jewish?"

"Yes, I had the same thought and it makes sense as my grandmother, well that is Mums' Mum was Jewish. Although we were sent to Christian schools Mum was always Jewish in her heart." The Google search pulled up many Cohen &

Co's, but all seemed to sell something commercially; none was in the adoption business. She then tapped in Jewish Adoption Agencies and there was only one London based, called Norwood.

Next they Googled Mario Orengo. Responses popped up from all over the world, but they narrowed it to the UK and Europe. The most predominant place the Orengo name appeared was in Italy. When they went into Wikipedia, it informed them the Orengo name was originally Northern Italian from the Liguria area. Flo glanced at her watch. "My God is that the time?"

"I have to be with a client in half an hour. Sorry I have to go Mum, just when it was getting interesting." She quickly closed her laptop and pulled her makeup purse out of her handbag.

"Don't worry Darling, you've pointed me in the right direction. I'll do some follow on from home and update you tomorrow." They parted on the Broadway, Sarah waited for the no 14 bus and Flo hurriedly waved a cab down.

Thirty

As Sarah unlocked her front door the land line shrilled out. "Oh Hello Nick, I just got in."

"Look Mum", said her son, "I know you're doing this search thing with Flo, and I understand as she has much more time than me, but I've had a few thoughts on it and wondered if I could swing by this evening and go through what's in that file with you?"

Sarah beamed. "Nothing would make me happier! And I'll have your favourite meal ready; say around 7.30?" Sarah cherished any opportunity to have Nick to herself. Once she'd lovingly prepared his favourite childhood meal of bangers and mash she sat down in the sitting room beside her computer .This room was such a contrast to Florence's. It was cluttered with books and magazines, an easel stood begging in the corner with a half-finished painting. Soft blue flocked wall paper was exposed in a few spaces where there was a gap between the gallery of paintings that adorned the walls.

With the adoption file beside her, she timidly typed in Liguria, Italy. Up popped an option for Google Maps and she could clearly see where to type Liguria in. To her amazement the map of Italy appeared with the area being directly located beside the French border.

"Hi Mum, it's me!" Nick sung out as he opened the door with his own key.

"Great now you're here I'll dish up and we can chat over the meal." Half way through supper Sarah felt the time was right to approach the delicate subject.

"How are things progressing with the diabetes treatment?"

Nick placed his knife and fork down. "It's okay mum, you don't need to pussyfoot around me, I don't blame you and it's not terminal!" His voice was reassuring. "The nurse I'm working with at the diabetes clinic feels I'm more or less sorted with the injections, I do them all myself now, no probs. She and I chat a lot and she has told me lots of people develop diabetes with no family history, so don't beat yourself up."

A sense of relief swept over Sarah. "So Mum, just to change the subject, why Menton? I remember our childhood holidays there, but it's not the most chic place on the Riviera."

"Well your father and I often used to fantasise a bit about what we'd do when you two left home and we retired. We liked the fact that Menton isn't really on the Brit radar. I haven't read a lot about it in the travel sections of the papers; they all talk about St Tropez, Cap Ferret and Cannes. My inspiration is to live a French village lifestyle but be close to civilisation if I want it, and Menton is only 30 minutes from Nice airport."

Nick leant across and patted his mother's hand. "I'll miss coming here, for it will always be my real home. You know sometimes I can practically smell Dad's presence." They were still sipping the red wine when Nick wandered over and rubbed the mouse on his mother's computer. "Google maps .I'm impressed Mum you are moving forward, a step up from e mails!"

"Yes, I was watching Flo today and it's all quite logical isn't it? Coincidently, where I'm planning to move to is right on the French-Italian border and the first area or borough, I guess it's called, is across the border is Liguria, where the name Orengo originated."

Nick held the tatty green worn file and turned to the first page as he spoke. "Now Mum, don't make presumptions,

I have to agree it looks like this Orengo chap was, or is, Italian. However your first name is Jewish along with the fact of a Jewish Adoption Agency. So you have to work through this logically if you want to find the truth, and not be lead purely by emotions or any romantic notion Flo may have about her heritage."

Sarah fondly watched as her son studied each of the six pages of the adoption file. He was a tall handsome man just like his father, with his nut brown hair cut short and preppy. Just like Josh out of 'The West Wing' Flo had kidded. He executed the same diligent, exacting manner with every task he set upon. Flo ribbed him that this was a case of too much 'legal 'and not enough fun.

"Mum, I definitely think this birth certificate is dodgy or has been massively tampered with. Firstly it's so faded in places that I believe it's a photocopy – besides it looks like some of the print has been tampered with. You can't technically register a birth without saying the place of birth, also writing in 'deceased' without writing in the actual name of the deceased. I feel the facts of your birth mother were being deliberately concealed for some reason."

Sarah sighed. "So how do we verify any of this? We couldn't find any record of Cohen & Co Adoption Agency. There's only one Jewish Adoption Agency in London, called Norwood." He typed Norwood in and was directed to a web page of the same name.

"Look here it is! Established in 1949, in London by a Martha Norwood. The agency specialises in adoptions of Jewish children, for Jewish parents. So my advice is to set up an appointment with a senior member of staff and see if they can enlighten you about Cohen & Co."

Sarah wrote down the phone number and email address from the screen. "But what about Mario Orengo, what's your advice on this?"

"A colleague at my office assisted a client in his birth parent search and gave me a few pointers. You need to assume this Orengo chap's age is within a ten year radius – then do a UK search for him. Then if nothing shows up do a European search, and yes, like you, my instincts tell me he may be Italian."

Sarah wrung her hands then pressed them to her face. "Now Mum don't get stressed, we will do all we can to help." He gently rubbed her back.

"One minute I'm confident about it all, and then I can't seem to see how I can possibly do all this." She dropped her head onto his shoulder. "Well my colleague worked with an adoption search specialist, so if you are prepared to pay, this chap's full time job is helping adoptees and birth parents to find each other."

Sarah straightened. "The money's not a problem; I think this is something your father would have wanted me to do".

"Ok I'll email you the specialist's details tomorrow, I'd better get on now, but Mum, will you be okay?" Sarah faced her son and then affectionately squeezed his hand.

"I know I've been a bit of an emotional wreck in the past few years, Son, but losing both my parents so close together, then your father, I guess it all just overwhelmed me, I'm so sorry if you feel I neglected you."

He smiled soothingly. "No Mum, it's a lot for anyone all that loss, I'm just glad as a family we can all do something to help resolve this 'missing' feeling you've banged on about for years. I'm sure your counsellor is right, once you know where you originally came from it'll fill in the missing pieces."

"Goodnight, I love you."

Thirty-one

Sarah's hand trembled as she dialled the number. "Norwood. Good morning hold the line please!" A monotone voice greeted her, followed by a rude click as classical music whooshed into her ear. It seemed like an eternity before the faceless voice returned.

"I'd like to make an appointment to speak to a senior member of your staff please?" A brisk voice responded. "What's it concerning please?"

"I'm researching information about a Jewish Adoption Agency that has most likely closed now, which was operational in around 1955/56."The voice made an "ahh" sound before she replied.

"Well the only person who may have any information that far back would be our founder's daughter, Mrs Miriam Norwood. She's retired now but if you emailed all the details to us we can print it out and pass it on to her."

"Wouldn't it be quicker to give me her phone number? Does she live in London?" Sarah grew braver. "No, I'm sorry Madame we don't operate that way; besides she's 83 and we just can't hand out her phone number to anyone."

Sarah conceded, and wrote down the email address. Four days later Sarah received an early morning call. "I do hope I haven't called too early, I seem to wake up with the birds – it must be my age. Oh! Sorry I didn't even introduce myself; I'm Miriam Norwood, Martha Norwood's daughter from Norwood Adoption Agency."

Her voice sounded soft and fragile. "Hello Mrs Norwood,

thank you so much for calling me."

"You sound surprised? Don't let that frosty receptionist put you off, she knows she'd be in big trouble if she didn't pass on all my correspondence and these new-fangled emails." The old lady paused as if to catch her breath.

"Now dear have you a pen? Good, then write down my address and come for tea tomorrow at three. It's much better for an old girl like me to talk face to face than on the phone." Sarah scribbled down the address and reassured her she'd see her tomorrow.

Then she dialled Flo's number. "Mum, that's great news: I wonder what she has to say. Perhaps we won't need that expensive adoption consultant after all? Shall I come with you?"

"I much appreciate your help and your enthusiasm, but I think I should see Mrs Norwood and the consultant the first time on my own."

"Oh all right." Sarah ignored the disappointment in Flo's voice. "I'll keep you posted, love you."

Sarah spent the rest of the day organising her reconnaissance trip to Nice and Menton. She planned to stay in Nice with her old friends, Mary and Peter Pinter. The rental agency she'd contacted had informed her they had three properties for her to view in Menton. Later she'd spent an hour in Waitrose looking for a couple of delicious options for the dinner she'd arranged for her friend Robyn. She felt somewhat apprehensive as she dwelt on how her best friend would react to her news.

"Darling you look fabulous, gosh has it been a month already –so much happens in a month doesn't it?" Robyn overflowed with enthusiasm, as she handed Sarah the bottle of wine. "Oh do let's get the top off this, I'm parched!"

Robyn's best feature was her long slim legs and she crossed them to their best advantage as she perched on the stool. They chatted as Sarah added the final touches to their meal. Robyn was hypoactive and had a no nonsense personality. She wore her hair in a feathery pixie cut which was expensively highlighted by their shared hairdresser.

"That was delicious my Darling, now you've gone very quiet, I realise I haven't stopped rabbiting on! Though, I must say your face seems more relaxed somehow, as if that dark cloud has been lifted. Is it the counselling sessions, or Mr Patel?"

Sarah wrung her hands together and then pressed them to her face "What is it Sarah?"

Robyn reached out and touched her friend.

"I feel so guilty I haven't told you this before, but I felt the children had the right to know first and that's been hard."

'Tell me what?" Sarah squirmed in her chair. Robyn had withdrawn her arm and sat upright as she stared at her to continue.

"I was adopted."

"What! You're joking! How could you have never told me? I've been your best friend for thirty years!"

Sarah stood up. "It's all been difficult for me, I'm sorry I didn't mean to hurt or exclude you. Other than my adopted family and Simon, I have told no one. I felt so ashamed."

"Sarah Anderson, I've listened for years about all your anxieties and this 'missing feeling' you've apparently suffered with, long before your parents and Simon died. However, you omitted to tell me you were adopted, bloody hell Sarah it would be sodding bloody obvious something was 'missing' if you were adopted!"

She stormed off to the loo. Sarah frantically rang her hands together. By the time Robyn returned to the sitting room they'd both calmed down. "Okay I'm over it now, let's talk totally honestly this time, did you tell Mr Patel this important fact?"

"No, because I figured if he was as good as you said he was, mystically, seeing all with his gifted ways, then he'd see it. You and Barbara are the only ones I've told about my visits to Mr Patel, so I would prefer that stays between us, please!"

They both sat back down at the table as Sarah topped up their wine. "So just out of interest did Mr Patel tell you anything significant?"

"He only talked hypotheticals really. Then he asked me to bring him an object that I'd had since childhood. The only possession that accompanied me when I was adopted was a small gold locket, so I gave him that to do the 'reading'. He closed his eyes as he touched it, and after a few minutes said he could see a dark haired deaf woman. That's the only definite thing he told me. Sorry Robyn, I'm afraid I just couldn't take him seriously. He could have found out from the internet or you, for that matter that I trained as a teacher to the deaf."

Robyn attempted to curb her irritation. "For your information I didn't tell him anything. He's been hailed as a great mystic in certain circles for a very long time – besides he's so old I bet he can't even use the internet."

Sarah ignored her friend's tone. "So, if you want me to tell all, let me speak!" She paused and Robyn nodded. "The children are helping me with a search for my birth father and I'm also employing a specialist consultant whom I meet for the first time next week. From now on, dear friend! I'll keep you in the loop; am I forgiven?"

Robyn leaned across and tapped her hand. "I'm sorry too; I do love you so much, Sarah 'whoever you really are'. Now show me what clothes you're throwing out before you move, and what I can squeeze into?" As they sorted and laughed their way through the bags of discarded clothes, Sarah updated her on the details of the adoption file, her next day visit to Mrs Norwood and her preliminary trip to France.

Thirty-two

Sarah carefully blow-dried her hair and then selected a demure black pencil skirt and a caramel coloured cashmere sweater. Her nerves almost got the better of her, but she pulled herself together as her phone buzzed a text to inform her that the cab was outside. Miriam Norwood's house looked impressive with a very neat, well-kept front garden. The elderly woman greeted her at the door. Miriam had bright, intelligent eyes that put Sarah immediately at ease as she was ushered into a traditionally-decorated sitting room. A very senior housekeeper brought a pot of tea and Miriam poured as she opened the conversation.

"So your email said you are searching for details of your birth parents and you believe your mother was Jewish?"

"Well, I am assuming that as the documentation I have refers to a Jewish adoption agency called Cohen & Co. My information also suggests my birth-mother is dead."

Miriam took a brief thoughtful pause. "Jewish people were as sensitive and affected by these situations back in the 1950's as any others. Illegitimacy was a huge embarrassment all round, especially if it was a mixed race or religious union. So all sorts of denial and cover-up went on to save face, mainly to conceal the facts from ever coming out."

Sarah squirmed in her seat. "Are their many Italian Jews? Perhaps both my parents were Jewish and possibly when my mother died my father couldn't cope."

Miriam spoke frankly. "It would have been very unusual circumstances for a Jewish/English or Italian family to give up a child from a marriage. If one partner had died they would nearly always be brought up in the extended family. However there were very few Jewish Adoption Agencies in London in the nineteen-fifties. I knew Cohen & Co well, but it closed down in the early seventies. You have left it quite late in your life to search. Have you just discovered you were adopted?"

Miriam listened attentively as Sarah told her the abridged version of her adoption. "I can appreciate your situation; I have spent my whole working life dealing with adopted children, adoptive parents and birth parents. It's a complex road when we go back as far as 1955.It's all easier now, as there's not the same stigma attached. Birth parents and adopted children have the option to leave the 'door open', so to speak if either wants to make contact later in life."

She took a little rest before she continued. "I'm in a position to contact the daughter of the late owner of Cohen & Co, she's 89 but very spritely. We're often at the same weddings and Bar Mitzvah. If you wish, I'll ask her if they kept any records for that time period."

Sarah wrote down the dates, and her birth-father's name. "Don't forget also to put your adoptive parent's names and their address at the time of the adoption, if you know what it was." Sarah handed her the details.

"Give me at least two weeks to see what I can discover for you. If I haven't contacted you by then, feel free to phone me." She handed Sarah an old fashioned, inscribed calling card.

During the taxi ride home Sarah's mind wandered. She recalled a girl at her school who it was rumoured was pregnant at sixteen. The girl had left school abruptly, which was followed by a lot of gossip and speculation. For the first time Sarah tried to visualise her birth-mother as a real person. She tried to imagine what she might have looked like, and what disgrace she may have suffered. Her thoughts were interrupted when the cab stopped. "A penny for your thoughts and ten quid for the ride, thanks."

Thirty-three

Sarah was pleased she'd chosen to wear her skinny jeans and boots to the meeting with the adoption consultant. His office was modern and informal. "Hello Mrs Anderson, I'm Eric Watson, please come in and take a chair."

"Please call me Sarah." Eric appeared to have a perpetual smile, which was a great asset because his face featured a rather large hook nose, on which he placed his thick black framed spectacles. His hair appeared to sit in an untidy fashion on his head, but his designer jeans and smart shirt rescued his overall quirky appearance. He ushered her into an up-to-the-minute office, furnished with Philippe Stark designer transparent chairs and a large black leather topped-desk. An entire wall was devoted to photos of various people whom Sarah assumed were parents and children who'd been reunited. Fulfilment and warmth radiated from the frames.

Sarah handed him her file, and briefed him about her conversation with Miriam Norwood about Cohen & Co. "Well I think I can help you, my suggestion is, once you get the information back on any Cohen & Co files, you pass them to me and then I should be able to make a start. I'm not a time waster so if I think it's too much of a challenge, because of the lack of information and the elapsed time span, I'll tell you."

He spoke with assurance. "Thank you. I'm off to France for a few days so I'm sure I'll have something for you by the time I get back; I'll be in touch." As she stepped out into Holborn, Sarah felt a fresh sense of hope.

Thirty-four

At Gatwick airport Sarah just had enough time to purchase a new, slim line, digital camera before her flight was called. Mary and Peter greeted her at Nice airport with the genuine enthusiasm that only comes from very old friends. Once they'd arrived at the house and had settled on their terrace with its magnificent sea view, Sarah repeated her story of the adoption and shared her aspirations for the future. Peter eyes lit up. "It would be great if you're living in Menton; we often cross the border to our favourite Italian restaurant up in Pigna, which is only about a forty minute drive from Menton."

"I have appointments to view some rental properties tomorrow morning so perhaps you could accompany me. Then afterwards I'll buy you lunch at this favourite restaurant?" The next morning as the three of them drove off in Peter's large comfy Citroen. Sarah was infected with excitement. The journey only took only thirty-five minutes, via the motorway. They easily found the real estate office. The slim, blue-eyed agent introduced herself as Martine. Her English was limited, so Sarah was grateful for Mary and Peter's fluent French. After they'd viewed all three apartments Sarah's good mood had abated. The apartments all had odd furniture, were pokey and didn't meet up to her expectation.

"I'm sorry Martine, but I think I'd prefer an older property with more character, if you possibly have anything else you can show me?"

"If it is unfurnished would that be okay?" Martine

attempted her English. "I think if it was exactly right, I'd be happy to furnish it." Martine assured Sarah she'd sort out some more properties to view before she left France. They exchanged mobile numbers and then Peter drove out of Menton along the coast in the direction of Italy. After crossing the border, he navigated his way through the very busy seaside town of Ventimiglia.

They'd turned left into the Nervia valley when Sarah started to feel queasy. She feverishly wrung her hands as a huge wave of anxiety engulfed her. Then her body shuddered as if someone had walked on her grave. "Drat! Just when I was getting all this under control," she almost spoke out loud, but she considered it better to keep quiet and hope it would pass. She had managed to gain some composure as they passed through several more small hamlets. Then for no apparent reason another wave of angst flooded over her as they approached the hill village of Pigna.

Mary, who couldn't see Sarah from the front seat, obliviously chatted on, as she conveyed historic details of the area. "This is a fourteenth century village that suffered a lot of damage during the war. There is a wonderful B&B up the hill, where I have often thought I'd like to spend an evening." Sarah murmured a reply and took in some small breaths in an attempt to calm herself. They passed through Pigna and then turned into the driveway to the restaurant which was situated just up the road above the Terme Spa Hotel. Sarah had to steady herself as she opened the car door. Mary then saw her distress and immediately went to her aid.

"Are you okay? You look as white as a sheet."

"Yes, don't worry. Just give me a few minutes, a bit of car sickness. Sorry!" Sarah attempted to stand up straight and take in a little more air. Then she forced a smile and momentarily sat down on an outdoor seat under some nearby trees.

"There's no hurry, your colour's coming back. We'll go in just when you're ready," Peter comforted.

It only took a few minutes for Sarah to regain her composure, after which they moved inside and studied the enticing menu. "Claudio just came out of the kitchen; he must have what you've got Sarah. He went as white as a sheet and ran back in." Peter looked puzzled.

Sarah sat with her back to the kitchen, facing the view of the valley. "We don't usually see you on a week day Signor Pinter!" An older waitress eventually came out to greet them. "Where's Mario today?" Peter made small talk as she took their order.

"Mario comes in late on a Monday and young Claudio is not feeling well so I'll look after you today." She hastily took their order, dispensed with any small chat, and made a hurried retreat to the kitchen. "I guess Mario is a common Italian name?" Sarah commented.

"About as common as Brown or Smith is back home. All a bit strange today, Claudio taking ill just as we arrived. Never mind you'll love the food; it's all seasonal. Mario has had this place forever and Claudio is his godson – they're as thick as thieves," Mary replied.

The pasta and the lamb tasted wonderful but there was no way Sarah could eat dessert. She excused herself whilst the others tucked into their pannacotta. She wandered outside, where the light had a strong glare so she put on the rolled up Panama hat she had brought in her bag and shielded her eyes with her sunglasses.

A gentle mountain mist floated lightly about but was punctuated with enough sun to allow a clear view. Sarah lined up her new camera, which was so easy, with modern technology – all the work was done for her .As she turned to shoot the view up the hill behind her she couldn't quite believe what she saw. Sarah rubbed her eyes to make sure it was real. Precariously perched on the steep hill loomed a dramatic medieval village. Because of the mist, it appeared to be floating in the sky. An exceptionally tall tower in the middle gave it the appearance of a Castle. The sight of the village was so unexpected.

"Buongiorno Signora. You like my village? I see it every day and still love to look at it." An old man on an equally old motor scooter had parked just near her. He wore a bright blue helmet and dark goggles. His delivery of English was charming. "I'd love to paint it," she replied.

"I wondered when you'd spot it. Isn't it marvellous?" Mary interrupted their exchange. The old man wasn't perturbed as he strolled off in the direction of the restaurant still wearing his helmet.

"It's called Castel Vittorio and they say it is actually thirteenth century. There are only a few people living up there now, not like the villages lower down which have healthy populations," Mary continued.

"It's a profound visual delight; the architecture looks almost magical." Sarah poetically remarked as she took several more shots of the 'floating village'.

"Next time we come, we'll make time to visit up there, but Peter needs to be back by five p.m. so I think we'd better crack on." Mary's historic commentary continued on the journey down the valley and she shared some of the stories she'd heard about the Nazi occupation during the war.

At breakfast the next morning Sarah received a call from Martine who had three more apartments for her to view. She caught the train from Nice. Despite yesterday's lapse, she was encouraged. The sea shone with such purity, Sarah felt overwhelmed with a compelling urge to paint. The light on the Riviera was so much more conducive to paint than the perpetual overcast skies of London.

Martine greeted her at the station and the first apartment they viewed was definitely old, but the furniture was ugly and uncomfortable. After Sarah's rejection of the second apartment, Martine's frustration was obvious. As they walked towards the sea front she warned Sarah the last one she had to show her was unfurnished, had no elevator, but a great location. Soon they'd arrived in Square Victoria, a cul-de-sac off the promenade. They entered the front doors of a building called Maison Manera.

Sarah was immediately impressed as she looked above at the ceiling which was fully decorated with slightly-faded fresco paintings. Martine picked up on Sarah's new interest and pointed out the marble staircase and wrought iron banisters, all original from the late nineteenth century when Queen Victoria visited as a young Princess. As they reached the second floor, a man passed them on the stairs. He warmly greeted Martine who in turn introduced him to Sarah as Jean-Pierre. He smiled, and then quickly apologised that he was in a rush as he was late for a patient.

"Jean Pierre is a doctor here, a very important man. Very beautiful, or how you say handsome, do you think?" Sarah smiled at Martine's English and agreed. "Yes very handsome."

It took two big keys to unlock the apartment. They

stepped first into a long hallway and Martine rushed ahead to open the pale blue, antiquated shutters. As the light poured into the main salon, Sarah felt exhilarated. The front of the apartment looked out through a few roadside trees to the beach beyond. At the rear of this room the back doors opened on to a small terrace that huddled, dilapidated close to the hillside. It was an awful mess outside, but Sarah easily envisaged how she could give it new life. The apartment ceilings were at least fifteen feet high, attractively set off with plaster cornicing. In the salon and the main bedroom the ceilings featured elaborate, tired frescos that included cherub angels, fleur-de-lys and a coat of arms.

Martine had observed the transformation of Sarah's face. "This style is what we French call belle époque." She then added, "If you like this one, it is good for you, but not so much for me, as it is a very little price!" Sarah took this on board as she considered the extra challenge of an unfurnished apartment. After one more look out at the beach view through the floor to ceiling windows, she offered Martine fifty euros less a month than the stated price.

Sarah enthusiastically boarded the flight home to London, with a camera full of shots to show Robyn and the children, and a new home. The next couple of weeks flew by as she sorted out the London house. She'd engaged an estate agent to rent out it out, deciding to leave it partly furnished, having selected a few key pieces to have shipped over to France. It had been three weeks since her visit with Miriam Norwood, when Sarah answered her mobile to the old woman's distinct voice.

"Hello Sarah, I haven't been able to discover a lot but I do have something that may help. Perhaps you would like to call at my home again. I do dislike talking on the phone." Sarah readily agreed. "Great I'll see you tomorrow, at ten a. m."

The old lady had the tea pot waiting on the table and appeared quite upbeat as they sat down. "I met with Sandra Francis; she's the daughter of the original Cohen of the agency. She's seventy-five now. Her parents were motivated to set up the agency straight after the war in 1945 to help a lot of displaced Jewish children. Then it carried on from there. Sandra worked in the agency until she was about twenty-five and had her first child. They kept meticulous records, as a lot of European families came in search of their children long after the war was over.

"Although the agency closed down a long time ago the records are stored in Sandra's basement. Her son has encouraged her to have them all put in electronic storage but it's all a bit beyond Sandra at her age. I told her your story and she agreed to have a look though. The only thing recorded is what you've already seen – that your mother passed away when you were put up for adoption. Your father was listed as an Italian living in Italy named Mario Orengo – all of this you know."

As Miriam paused, Sarah chipped in. "No I didn't know he was Italian, I just assumed it."

"Ah! Well, I now have what we believe is the original birth certificate that yours was copied from, and the birthplace can be seen through the blackening out event though it's faded over time." She handed her a yellowed piece of paper. As Sarah fingered it, she smelt the musty odour of 55 years of concealment. "But who put me up for adoption if it wasn't my father?"

"I anticipated that may be your next question. This is

where it all gets a little hazy. The notes said the grandparents brought you in, but their names have been blacked out on the file. Someone went to a lot of trouble to conceal your mother's family identity. I can only surmise from this that they were well known in the London Jewish community at the time and ashamed of a child from a mixed union, but also in shock at losing their daughter." Miriam paused as she allowed Sarah to digest the information.

"My advice is to pursue the search for your birth father, as what is clear to me is, as his name wasn't originally withheld, the entire situation may have been out of his control." Sarah's chest seared with a blanket of pain. Sorrow overwhelmed her as she clutched her clenched fist to her chest. The pain was replaced by tears that tumbled out in loud uncontrollable sobs. Miriam sat close with solace, handed her a box of tissues, and then gently pressed her hand. "Have a sip of some sweet tea, dear".

"It feels very odd experiencing such emotional grief for a mother that I never knew. I feel so sad her parents were so ashamed," Sarah had finally managed to speak.

Miriam replied, "Based on my experience with adoption, I can tell you 'nature is as strong as nurture'. The grief has to manifest itself sometime. A lot of adoptees would probably have started their searches earlier in their lives, and youth deals with things differently, but then there are no rules."

Miriam's reassurance rallied Sarah. "I really appreciate your help, I am sorry I'm so upset."

"Before you leave Sarah, would you indulge an old lady by permitting me to say something personal to you?" Sarah managed a smile as she nodded.

"I am truly sorry that a Jewish family was ashamed of

their granddaughter, for whatever reason we'll probably never know. The Jewish race is as ancient as time itself and we believe the religion is passed down through the mother. So in the eyes of the Jewish faith you have a born right to be Jewish, something I believe is worth being proud of. Tuck this information away in your heart somewhere and when you're strong enough to deal with it, bring it out and consider it. You have children to pass it on to, if you choose to do so. This is how we preserve our faith and our beliefs."

Miriam's aged voice never faltered. Before Sarah left, Miriam embraced her and secured a promise that she would keep her updated on her final discovery.

Eric Watson had agreed to meet with her the following day. "This is good stuff Sarah, I feel more confident knowing we have a name, a country and a date. Providing you can agree to my fee I feel sure I can progress this search. You'll need to give me a month, at the outside."

"Great, the only thing is I'm moving to France but I'll be all geared up with the internet and this thing called Skype my daughter has told me I must have, so I'm sure we can speak electronically?"

Eric grinned as he adjusted his spectacles. "Absolutely, that's the way it's all done, I'm usually able to do all the searching electronically, as you put it. So flick me an email, as soon as you have your French email address."

Thirty-five

Easyjet charged Sarah for 20kilo's of overweight luggage, but she didn't care – this was her new life. Robyn had driven her and Flo to Gatwick and as she left for the departure gates, Flo burst into tears. "Oh Mum I'll miss you, I feel like I'm orphaned." Sarah put her free arm around her melodramatic daughter.

Robyn had interjected before Sarah could speak. "For God's sake Flo you're nearly 26 years old; get a grip, Nice is less than two hours away."

Then Sarah quietly added. "Yes Darling, you can come and stay any time and I'll be back often, like I said. Let me give it twelve months and then I'll review my situation."

Flo's crocodile tears receded. "Sorry Mum, It's just for a moment I wished it was me leaving, not you!"

Sarah had chosen silently to slide into her new life, rather than have any fanfare or well-meaning assistance. She'd contact Mary and Peter once she was settled in her new apartment. The driver held a large neatly printed sign with 'Madame Anderson' written on it. Sarah experienced goose bumps as the well groomed, dark skinned man with a peak cap attentively accompanied her through the arrival lounge to his large comfortable Mercedes. The motorway signs for La Turbie and Monaco flashed past and Sarah's heart raced with expectation as they exited via the sign for Menton. The big car only just squeezed into the Square Victoria cull de sac. When they had pulled up directly in front of Maison Manera, Martine was waiting.

"Bonjour Madame Anderson, Bievenue."

"Martine, please call me Sarah."

Martine could see how the driver struggled as he lifted the heavy cases from the boot; but she wasted no time as she firmly requested that he carry them up to the second floor. "That's a bit much to ask, Martine; I can take them if I do it one at a time."

"He will be okay: it's his job, just give him a tip."

Martine walked her to the apartment door. "If there is anything you need to know please call me."

Sarah was relieved to see the fridge and bed she'd ordered had been delivered. As she wandered through the apartment she threw open the worn paint-chipped shutters and marvelled at how the rooms came to life when the sun danced in. After she'd made up the bed with linen, she'd lugged in her overweight case and turned her attention to immediate necessities.

Martine had mentioned if she walked up one flight of stairs, the door on the landing would take her onto the upper street through Menton old town. The short walk took her along the 14th century dark cobbled lane, lined with historic houses. Sarah observed by the rows of door buzzers that they'd all been converted into apartments. Along the lane after a few metres, a space allowed the sunlight to shine down. At this point several sets of sweeping stairs lead up to a proud and majestic Basilica. It lorded over the old town like a dominant father with its giant doors and distinctive steeple. Sarah's medieval journey was disturbed, as the lane morphed into a more modern, bustling street.

She'd found a mini market where she was seduced by a delectable array of interesting packets and fresh looking produce. Just as she had finally sorted out how to go into the heavy door back into the apartment building, a hand picked up the grocery bag beside her. "Bonjour Madame, please let me help you?"

Startled, Sarah turned to face the handsome neighbour. "Thank you, but I'll be able to manage." She blushed. "Allow me to introduce myself, I'm Jean-Pierre but everyone calls me JP." He extended his hand. His touch ignited a sensation that had been long forgotten and her hand trembled with anticipation as she responded to his handshake.

As he carried the heavy bag of groceries, he negotiated the stairs walking directly beside her. She didn't speak, but fumbled embarrassingly for her key. "This is my place."

"I leeve directly across the hall; let me carry these to your cuisine." He'd used the French word for kitchen, and as she opened the door, he followed her in. "I'm Sarah Anderson, I'm sorry for being rude. I just arrived today so I guess I must be a little jet lagged forgetting my manners, I'm afraid my French isn't very good; I'm hoping to improve it while I'm here."

"Seera, what a très jolie or how you say what a veery beautiful name." He dropped the 'H's and extended his 'E' sounds when he spoke English.

"I'm sorry I can't offer you a drink as you can see I'm not quite organised yet."

In a bid to avoid his gaze, she started to remove the groceries out of the bag. "I am so worried, what will you eat for your dinner? I will be back at 7 and a alf to take you next door for pizza. Okay?" Sarah was about to object, but he'd already left the room. She took a quick shower, and then rummaged through her cases to find a suitably casual, but stunning something to put on. She settled on a pair of good fitting denim jeans and her favourite white shirt.

At precisely 7.30 pm the doorbell rang. It was obvious JP had freshened up too. He smelt delicious. He'd dressed in denim jeans accompanied by a flatteringly fitted pale blue shirt and he'd stylishly draped a matching blue cashmere sweater around his shoulders.

"Seera! You look revived. The pizzeria just next door is always good. We go there." Sarah experienced another rush of chemistry as he spoke her name. They walked out through the main front doors of their building to the pizzeria. He imparted a brief history lesson on Queen Victoria's visit in 1870 and details of the monument in front of the square. They were shown to an intimate table at the rear of the pizzeria. The close proximity gave Sarah the opportunity to study JP at close range without blushing. He was only marginally taller than her, with wonderful thick 'pepper and salt' coloured hair. His clear blue eyes were framed with rimless modern glasses, and sat on an aquiline nose. She enjoyed the way his mouth dropped a little, favouring the right side as he spoke.

Due to the limited language their conversation was quite direct. JP had freely shared that he was divorced with no children and practised as a GP in a surgery just along from his apartment. Sarah held back and offered very limited information about herself, other than that she was widowed with two grown-up children. Once they'd arrived back at her door he pecked each of her cheeks and said a polite goodnight.

With no bed pillow, Sarah stuffed a soft jumper in a pillow case. She'd left the window shutters open, so the street lights illuminated the frescos on the ceiling. Sleep soon came with a warm content smile. The following day the removal van from

London arrived at around two p.m., so by late afternoon, all Sarah's belongings were in the appropriate rooms. Although she relished the spacious atmosphere the partially empty rooms created, she definitely needed more drawers for her clothes.

She'd seen the shop the day before, so re traced her previous walk. The shop sign read 'Patrick's Antiquities'. Although its entrance was narrow, once inside it was a treasure trove of antiques and a lot of interesting junk.

"Bonjour Madame!" Sarah was greeted by a small smiling man.

"Bonjour Monsieur!"

"Ah Anglais!"

"Oui, Monsieur. But I'm not a tourist; I am living in Menton and looking for a few pieces of furniture for my apartment. I'm interested in the chest of drawers you have in the window. May I take a closer look?" He led her through to the rear of the window display area. The marble topped chest of drawers was just what she needed. "I will deliver for you, no charge Madame," the small man enthusiastically added.

"I can offer you three hundred euros, as that's my entire budget," Sarah negotiated. After some huffing and puffing, the owner finally agreed. An hour later the owner and his wife struggled up the stairs three separate times with the heavy set of drawers which broke down into several parts. As they enjoyed a cold beer with Sarah, they introduced themselves as Patrick and Vera. "Excuse me Madame, but are you living here full time or just for holidays?" Vera spoke excellent English.

"I hope perhaps for a couple of years, at least. I'm hoping to improve my painting skills. Also I'm intending to learn French. You don't happen to know anyone locally who teaches do you?"

"Yes, I know an older lady. If you call into the shop sometime I'll find you her phone number." After Sarah had cleaned out the chest of drawers and filled them with her folded clothes she filled the large old style bath. She was immersed in bubbles and slathered in a mask when the doorbell chimed.

"Who is it?" She called out through the door.

"It's me, JP. I am just checking on you, if that is the correct English?" Sarah jumped up onto the tiled floor.

"I'm sorry JP, I'm just out of the bath, so I can't invite you in." She'd thrown on her white towelling dressing gown, managed to wipe the mask off and had her wet hair wrapped in a towel as she peeped around the door.

He gave her a distracted, lustful glance. "No, I am sorry for disturbing you. Perhaps we could go together to a concert at the Menton Palace on Samedi?" Sarah reddened and hesitated.

"Ah, could I let you know perhaps over the next couple of days, I've got a lot on with setting up the apartment." His eyes fell flat, but he maintained his smile.

"OK, you call me?" He handed her his business card. Just as she'd closed the door her mobile rang.

"Hi girlfriend!" greeted Robyn. "Just calling to see all is okay." Sarah updated her in on all the current activities of setting up the apartment, then, near the end of the conversation, mentioned the offer of the date on Saturday. "It's probably not a date really! He's perhaps just being friendly to his new neighbour. I think he's younger than me," her confidence faltered as she spoke.

"He's a bloody Frenchman Sarah! I've never heard of them being neighbourly, more like horny! You're a free agent, go out and enjoy yourself. Flirt a little."

"I don't know, I'm not over Simon really and besides I'm not sure I can even remember how to flirt."

Thirty-six

Sarah was busy unpacking the boxes that had arrived from London and had opened the front window to let in some air when she heard her name called from below.

"Seera I come up?" It was JP. She rushed to the bathroom, brushed her hair and quickly applied some lip gloss. He'd rung the doorbell before she could change her clothes. "It's been two days; maybe I missed your call?"

JP spoke with a 'little boy lost' tone. "No, I've, um, been busy." Sarah faltered, but she didn't usher him in. He stood his ground, his foot firmly inside her door. "I bought two tickets anyway just in case." He raised his eyebrows, smiled and moved a step closer.

"Oh alright! I accept, thank you."

"See you at seven p. m. Samedi." As he opened the door to his apartment across the hall he turned and offered Sarah a warm winning smile. "Smarmy bugger, what the hell am I going to do now?" she muttered as she closed her door. It was Friday by the time Sarah was able to return to the antique shop. Vera wrote down the French teacher's name and number on the back of a business card and Sarah popped it in her bag.

The next morning she'd begun to display signs similar to a silly young school girl. There were clothes strewn all over her bed and shoes all over the floor. "I bet that's Robyn," she said out loud when she heard her mobile.

"Oh hello Flo! I thought you were Robyn."

"No Mum it's me. I haven't spoken to you for a couple of days, so thought I better check in. I guess you're a bit lonely."

"No, not lonely. I've so much to do and the computer people are coming on Monday to set me up with everything, so I'll be able to email you from next week. She omitted any mention of her date.

By seven p. m, and several changes of clothes, Sarah had settled on a simple black dress with short sleeves to cover her aged upper arms. The hem sat on the knee, but the neck line gave a slight hint of encouraging cleavage, as that part seem to be still holding up. She'd rushed off to the shops and had treated herself to a pair of sheer black stay-up stockings with lacy tops. Her hair had been professionally blow-dried at the local salon and she assured her makeup was expertly applied.

Sarah had just sprayed on her Guerlain fragrance when she heard the door chime. JP was exactly on time. He looked handsome in a navy sports jacket, beige chinos and a fresh white shirt. "Bonsoir Sarah! You look maqnifique and smell delicious," his French words sounded so sexy.

The concert was classical and restrained, but relief came with a bonus, for once it was over JP informed her he'd planned a late supper at a very special restaurant. It was called Les Deux Frères, and sat perched in Roquebrune village up above Monaco. His manners were perfection; he'd helped her into his smart Alpha Romeo car. Sarah had felt quite giddy as he drove fast around the windy uphill road. However she recovered quickly when she'd seen how stunning the restaurant was.

"Bonsoir, Doctor Jacobs. What a beautiful evening it is, and it's wonderful to see you again," greeted the Maître d'. They'd been seated outside on the terrace, with a perfect view over Monaco and Cap Martin. Once their glasses of champagne had been served and they'd exchanged a few niceties. Sarah questioned JP.

"Is Jacobs an unusual name for a Frenchman? Are you Jewish, JP?" He looked surprised. "Yes, is that a problem?" Sarah swiftly rectified her obvious mistake. "I'm half Jewish myself. Well, full I guess, as it was my mother who was Jewish."

"Well I think your Jewish half is wonderful," his manner was restored. "What is the other half?" Sarah cleared her throat. "Italian, actually."

He wasn't fazed. "You should feel right at home being both Jewish and Italian. You can have a foot on either side of the border. It's a pity you don't speak either language yet, and my English is not so good."

"I'm sorry. It's me who should be trying harder with my French. I intend to start lessons as soon as I can. I've possibly found a teacher to contact on Monday." After the second glass of champagne Sarah had relaxed, managing the same poker face as JP as he subtly rubbed her leg with his shoeless foot under the table.

"You are a very beautiful woman Sarah, I am so happy you are living near me."The bubbles had enabled her curiosity "How old are you JP?" He smiled. "I am forty-nine, a little older than you". She was embarrassed, and the alcohol content had encouraged her colour. She excused herself to visit the loo. On route, he discreetly patted her bum.

Once in the loo she splashed herself on the back of the neck and wrists with cold water as she attempted to reduce the redness. After desert, JP moved close and whispered, "Let's have coffee back at your place." Sarah attempted some basic French conversation during the drive back and they were both still laughing at her pronunciation, when they arrived at her door.

JP, sensed her unease and took control. "You go and put that coffee machine on and I will be back in five petite minutes." Sarah did as instructed, then rushed to the bathroom for a freshen-up and a quick squirt of her fragrance. JP returned with a heavy looking carry bag, from which he took out several candles which he lit and placed around the room, then asked where her CD player was.

"I don't think I'm ready for any of this JP. Can't we be just friends for a while longer?" She continued making the coffee and he didn't answer her, but as he'd found the CD player on the bench he put in his CD and took a bottle of lemon coloured liquid out of the bag. "This is a Menton speciality called Limoncello. Although an Italian name, the lemons are from Menton."

They'd finished their coffee's and stood eye-to-eye in the kitchen, as they sipped the Limoncello, Barry White's silky, guttural voice sang 'Just the Way you Are' from the CD player. "You are a very beautiful, calm woman Sarah," he tenderly whispered as he stroked her hair "I didn't answer your question, because why on earth would we want to be just friends? We are grown up, free spirits who desire each other."

Sarah was lost for words. He spoke the truth. Then he gently led her up the hall to the bedroom which he'd illuminated with twenty more of the small T light candles. Sarah stood seductively mesmerised by the flickering light.

"It's been a long time for me JP. I'm not sure I'll know what to do," Sarah quietly resisted. He looked at her directly with his lopsided smile. "Don't you worry about anything, I know what to do." Eagerly he pressed his slightly open mouth onto hers. Sarah tasted a hint of garlic and lemons, as they flopped on to the bed. JP removed her shoes, and then skilfully unzipped her dress. As she stood up it promptly slipped to the floor. A moment of inhibition quickly passed.

"Leave those on". He murmured as he ran his hands down her 'stay up' stockings. "Your body is so beautiful, Ma Cherie!" His words rasped with a sense of urgency as Barry White sung 'I'm gonna Love you Just a Little More Babe'. Sarah welcomed his touch, closed her eyes and gave herself up to him with abandon. A moment of inhibition quickly passed. He efficiently unhooked her bra, slipped off her panties and then stroked the moist aching mound between her legs. She closed her eyes and encouraged his entry to her sacred place. Her voice gave an involuntary moan as his hard member took her to the point of supreme, erotic ecstasy.

They fell asleep in each other's arms.

Sarah awoke slightly confused with a thumping headache and no JP beside her. As she managed to sit up, he appeared at the door with a tray laden with coffee and croissants. "Bonjour, Ma Cherie! You look even more beautiful in the morning." He wore a fresh shirt and jeans. "I have a dreadful headache," she attempted to smile.

"That will be the Limoncello – always does it until you get used to it." He offered her a sympathetic glance. She shyly stood up and pulled on her long white cotton nightdress. "I'll be back in a minute." Once in the bathroom, she downed a couple of aspirin, then quickly cleaned her teeth and brushed her hair.

"Sarah, please don't feel awkward, we're not children. I may have rushed things a little, but I am sincere. I can't believe I have found someone so beautiful, so close to me." His heavy accented words were a little mixed, but he sounded so desirable.

"I'm very happy JP, I just feel a little naïve, not having been with another man for some time". Her colour rose.

"I don't know what this 'naïve' word means but what I like is you have no aggression, you just feel calm. French women seem to be so demanding and your independence is very attractive." They'd finished the croissants and coffee and sat propped up on the bed. "How is your headache, Ma Cherie?" JP had his arm around her as he affectionately nibbled her ear.

Sarah smiled. "That nibbling is certainly helping."

The entire day seemed to disappear – it was the longest Sarah had ever spent in bed. She finally kissed JP goodbye only after promising to see him on Tuesday evening. Sarah woke early Monday morning with the sun flooding through the window. She allowed herself the indulgence of basking in thoughts of her young French lover. Had she taken it too fast? Was it what she needed right now?

Then her mind focused on the morning's task. The English-speaking IT consultant was due at nine. "Bonjour, I am Jill from Computers Plus," the young, slightly overweight girl announced when Sarah opened the door. After an hour Jill had the internet connected as well as Skype and the new recorded voice message for her landline. Sarah's next task was to book her French lessons.

Thirty-seven

"Bonjour Madamee Dubot, my name is Sarah Anderson and you were recommended to me as a French teacher. Would you be available to help me?" A sweet sing-song voice replied, "I am retired now but if you wish to have a fairly informal programme I may be able to help. I charge nineteen euros an hour so maybe you could come for an hour first and we can see how we get on?" Sarah readily agreed.

Madame Dubot said she would email her the address and expect her Wednesday afternoon at two p. m. Sarah's next task was to email all her family and friends to announce she was on-line and had a landline.

When she opened her hot mail account after the long absence, there was a deluge of mail, but her eagerness was short lived as she read the email headed 'Progress Report' from Eric Watson. He'd commenced a search of Italian Church records for baptisms, but to no avail. So his next step had been to do searches of hospital births on that date, but as many of the hospitals had not yet computerised their files, it had been a laborious task, but he would be back in touch as soon as he'd completed the search.

On Tuesday evening, JP had invited her to his apartment for supper. It lacked the old world charm of her place. "My father bought this place sixty-four years ago, just after the war. He was a doctor. All of us children were born and brought up here. The décor was updated in 1970 but you can see it needs to be done again. Since my divorce, I've been living here alone." They ate their supper out on his large balcony which had a perfect vista out to sea and across to the border.

"JP, I need to buy a car, something I've never done before. Would you have the time to help me go through the process?"

"It would be my pleasure!" he said. "You should buy French and something small and economical as these small streets are no good for a large car." He'd then proceeded to bore Sarah throughout the meal on the merits of French cars.

After the third glass of wine, JP's attention had shifted as his hand rested on Sarah's knee. Once he'd cleared away the plates, he pulled his chair closer to her and softly kissed her neck. Sarah gave a small involuntary shiver. Coffee was put on hold as he guided her eagerly to his bedroom. The intensity of their love making carried them both away. She'd met with substantial resistance when she attempted to leave. JP finally smiled with acceptance after she'd agreed to spend Saturday with him looking for a suitable car.

Sarah had printed out Madame Dubot's instructions and allowed herself half an hour's walk. She wore her signatory rather battered Panama and large sunglasses the sun was so much stronger than in London and she was intent on doing all she could to preserve her complexion. She found the shabby but charming villa up a slight incline behind the town. It was painted a pale pink with local blue coloured shutters, all of which appeared to have lacked paint for many years. The heavy wrought iron gate creaked when she pushed it open.

As she made her way up the path, she was greeted with the heady scents of overgrown fragrant flowers and plants, the perfume of the jasmine mingled with a bouquet of rosemary and roses. The potpourri pathway was serenaded by various wind chimes made of shells, tuneful pipes and drift wood that hung under the eve of the villa. Madame Dubot sat in an old, white-cane chair with a large, straw sun-hat sheltering her face from the sun.

"Bonjour! You must be Madame Anderson?" She stood up to greet Sarah. Madamee Dubot was as short as Sarah and dressed in a floral gypsy type skirt, a loose blouse with wavy grey hair brushed behind her ears. "Please call me Sarah, if you are comfortable with that. I guess we English are not quite as formal as the French."

They both removed their sunglasses. As her eyes settled on Sarah's face she let out a small gasp, then reached to steady herself by clutching the back of the chair. "Are you all right Madame?" Sarah rushed forward to assist her.

Madame managed to straighten, and then seemed to pull herself together. "I'm so sorry Madame Anderson, I sometimes have these spells when I arise suddenly," she took a small breath then added "It's my age I think." Then she forced a smile.

"Please call me Sarah. I've brought the French books I've been learning from, but I'm sure you'll have some recommendations for me." The older woman took a few more moments to compose herself, then talked through her suggestions for the French lessons. By the end of the hour, Madame seemed completely steady and relaxed. "How long to you intend to be in Menton, Sarah?" She stared curiously into Sarah's eyes.

"Well hopefully two years. My intention is to paint as well as learn a new language. I was recently widowed, so this is my new beginning." Sarah sensed the genuine warmth of Madame's smile. "Ah yes, new beginnings. I think we should all have one every decade and now I am in my seventy-fourth year, I too am enjoying new experiences. Until next week then Sarah. Au revoir!"

Thirty-eight

All her paints, easel and drawing pads were strewn around the living room when JP, walked in. He kissed Sarah full on her lips. "What is this? My beautiful woman is a painter?" He flicked through her sketch pad. "I would rather you didn't do that JP, my painting is personal to me. Besides, I'm going to be working from photos that I intend to take with my new camera."

He put down the pad with an exaggerated look of hurt. "So when you have your new car, we can go together to take photos, yes?" Sarah mused, for a grown man, and a respected doctor, in many aspects he was quite like a boy. "I enjoy your company, but some things; to begin with anyway, I need to do on my own. You go to work as a doctor and I hope to go to work as a painter."

Buying a car was a whole new experience for Sarah and she was grateful for JP's help. She'd chosen a small, but efficient, Renault. JP had filled in all the appropriate forms and organised the insurance. All she had to do was the bank transfer of the funds on Monday – then she could drive it straight out of the showroom.

"Where do you want to drive to take your photographs, Ma Cherie?" JP probed. "I want to explore across the border. I've seen some picturesque medieval villages up in the valley behind Ventimiglia, which look a lot less commercial and inhabited than the French ones and the stone work appeals to me." JP listened with a fresh ear. By Wednesday Sarah was ready for her first drive out. She'd had a few practice runs around the town and felt confident enough to venture further.

She'd checked her map, but had good recall of the previous trip to Pigna. She intended to drive up beyond Pigna to the 'floating' village of Castel Vittorio. Once through Ventimiglia she was relieved to be off the busy main road as she drove with comfort up the quiet valley. She pulled the car in near the restaurant in Pigna where she and JP had lunch, so she could get the best view of the village.

It was a clear day with no mist. Much more of the base of the village was revealed and she could see clearly just how steep the drive up would be. As she cautiously descended the hill road a wave of anxiety flooded over her. She tried to ignore the sweat forming on her brow as she drove at snail's pace and focused wholly on the road ahead.

When she'd finally arrived at the village base, she managed to pull in to a compact parking space, then turned off the engine and took a few deep breathes. There were very few late model cars, mostly dated motor scooters and a couple of old trucks. Sarah's anxiety had gradually dispelled as she became curious about the relatively modern monument she'd spied at the entrance street up into the village. She walked over to photograph it but was immediately distracted as her eyes moved up the cobbled street into the ancient village. She took a few quick shots to look at later.

She was decked out as a typical English woman with her usual Panama hat and sunglasses as well as sensible walking trainers. Several locals had given her a prolonged second glance, fascinated, as there were very few tourists who visited mid-week. She navigated the narrow lane heading towards the high bell tower which appeared to be the village's most prominent piece of architecture; she'd made a mental note of a small restaurant along the way. On route towards the bell tower Sarah arrived at the village square. This didn't disappoint. It was all the stone work, arches and angles, as well as a water well that was probably used for washing clothes in years gone by.

"Buongiorno Signora! Welcome to our village." Sarah turned to see a small nun with a big smile on her face. "Hello Sister! I do hope I'm not intruding. I would just like to take a few photos so I can paint from them later." Sarah replied. "I am Sister Mary. We are a very small population up here now, and decreasing I am afraid, so we welcome visitors. I live down in Ventimiglia, but come up twice a week to check on the old ones and teach the children their catechism. I studied in England many years ago and love to practice my English."

Sarah removed her sunglasses so as not to appear rude. The nun stared intently at her. "My, you do remind me of someone Senora, what is your name?" she queried. "My name is Sarah Anderson. I'm from London, but now living down in Menton."

The Holy lady then abruptly finished the conversation, wished her a good day and walked off in the direction of the Church.

Sarah was briefly bemused by the Nun's fast retreat, before she proceeded to photograph the water well and other aspects of the square. She continued up the stairs to the right of the square where the ancient heavy Church doors directly faced the tall bell tower. One of the doors to the Church was slightly ajar so Sarah quietly slipped inside. It was a first for her; she'd never seen anything quite so old, untouched and authentic. Nothing had been modernised and a musty odour seemed to reaffirm its age. She decided against taking photos, as it might show disrespect to the sanctity of such a holy-feeling place.

Suddenly, another wave of perspiration swept over her. She needed to sit down. The Church pew was narrow and uncomfortable. Perhaps I'm getting a virus? She forced herself to stand up and made her way back to the car. As she hurriedly crossed the cobbled square, she caught sight of a woman sitting at an easel, painting. The woman had her back to Sarah; but she just managed to capture a peek of some vibrant colours on the painting the woman was working on.

"Drat if I didn't feel so ill, I could have gone over and perhaps chatted with her," she mumbled to herself and scurried off. Once at the car she'd slowly sipped her water bottle, when her mobile phone rung. "Hi Mum, just checking in on you and seeing if you've driven the new car very far yet," said a cheery Florence.

"Hello Darling! I'm up at the village in Italy; I showed you the photos of, but I'm not feeling well at the moment. I just want to get the car down the valley and return home. I'm sure it's just a virus or something, but it all came on very suddenly." Sarah had recovered slightly once she had had a drink.

"Okay Mum. You're a worry. Please call me as soon as you get home. Love you." Sarah drove slowly down the hill. The only vehicle she passed on its way up was a solitary motor scooter, travelling even slower than her. She recognised the rider's bright blue helmet, which was a good thing as it made it easier for her to see him on the narrow, tricky road.

Once back in Menton, she seemed to be back to normal. Sarah made herself a strong coffee and then phoned her daughter. "Hi, it's me checking in. I'm back safe and sound and I'm not at all sure what came over me up there – it may have been the altitude, as it's fairly high up."

"Are you sure it wasn't a hot flush Mum?" Flo kidded. "No dear! You know I passed all that stage a few years ago, smarty pants!" They chatted on for some time. The she plugged her camera memory into her computer to look at what she'd shot. Her computer screen was a twenty-four inch one, so it had clarity for her painting. The shot of the water well was the one she was most drawn to, and she decided there was no time like the present to start her painting.

A few hours later, the chimes of door-bell disturbed her. "Bonsoir, Ma Cherie!" A tired looking JP walked in. "I have had a sad day. I lost a patient this morning. I know it is a part of my work, but I always feel so frustrated I couldn't do any more."

Sarah sensed he needed to talk. She poured him a large glass of red wine and they sat quietly together as she stroked his hand. She said, "Shall I make you some light supper? I have some salmon and salad if you like." JP responded with a smile. As she prepared the meal, he proceeded to tell her the sad story about his patient, the type of cancer and the ramifications on the patient's family.

Once he'd finished deliberating, JP's attention was drawn to her easel and the computer screen. "I can see you are very good, not just because you are my woman but because it looks just like the photo." Sarah experienced a rush of affection as she listened to his pronounced accent and dropped 'h's.

"I am your woman, am I?" she countered, with a mocking tone.

"Well what do you English say if you are not a wife?"

"I will allow you to call me your girlfriend, as it makes me feel young." JP misinterpreted the laughter in her voice as an opportunity to make love. "Sorry JP, not tonight. I'm keen to keep painting. I think you should go to your apartment tonight."

He wore a look of rejection as he reluctantly left. Sarah quickly cleared away the dishes and returned to her easel.

She felt quite manic, but inspired to work until she finished the painting. The main subject, the water well, was set under an archway. It didn't allow much light so Sarah mixed up diverse blues on her palette to give it a more surreal appearance. She finally fell into bed at three a.m. The alarm woke her at eight a.m. As she scrutinised her work in the light of day she could see room for improvement, but felt an essence of gratification at having completed it.

Thirty-nine

As she walked through Menton-old-town on her way to her French lesson, Sarah comfortably reflected how well she'd adjusted to her new environment.

"Bonjour Sarah!" Madame Dubot greeted her. She sat at an outdoor table. "I hope you are happy to work outside, it is more pleasant out here in the shade." The wafts of fragrance from the lush garden added to the lazy summer ambiance Madame had created under the large leafy tree.

They proceeded to chat in somewhat limited French with Madame correcting Sarah like a young schoolgirl. "I can hear you've been practising, and your accent is quite good for an English woman." Madame meant this as a compliment. For some unexplained reason Sarah blurted out. "Well actually, I'm not entirely English!"

"Really! Where are your parents from originally?" Madame enquired. "My birth-father was Italian and, as far as I know, my mother was English. I was adopted as a baby and you're the first person, other than close family, to whom I have told this. I'm in the process of researching them."

Madame removed her glasses, rubbed her eyes and leant forward, intrigued. "How interesting! How do you research your birth parents?"

"I've employed a specialist consultant to assist me in the search. In Italy when you have to go back fifty-five years it isn't easy. I'm also becoming more proficient with the computer. I'm learning how to use the internet, it's the best tool, and my children are assisting me."

"So what are your children's names?"

"Florence and Nicholas but they are usually called Flo and Nick." Sarah felt she'd said enough. As she stood to leave Madame stood close to her and affectionately pressed her wrinkled hand to Sarah's wrist. "I've really enjoyed our chat and good luck in your search Sarah. See you next week."

Once back at the apartment, when she'd turned her computer on, the first email she opened was from Eric Watson.

"Dear Sarah, I've had a breakthrough with my research. I've been through all the hospital birth records in northern Italy, as that's where it appears most Orengo families have lived. A baby was born the same week as you were. She may be of interest to us, as she was called Rebecca Orengo. The hospital is now closed – it was in the town called Ventimiglia. The birth records for that hospital are now kept in the records department at the maternity hospital in San Remo, further along the coast. Rebecca Orengo was born there on the 30th May 1955, which is a day before your UK birth certificate shows you were born. It stood out to me, as Rebecca certainly wasn't a name commonly used in Italy back then. Italians were normally traditional and nearly always used family names for the children. The mother is listed as Rebecca as well, family name, Orengo, and the father as Mario. As you are living nearby perhaps you could find someone to assist you locally to track down any Mario Orengos? Or, if you wish, I could come for a few days and we could look together. I will wait to hear from you.

Kind Regards
Eric Watson"

Sarah could hardly breathe. She felt trapped in her seat. It was as if someone had shot her with a stun gun. It felt all too close and too fast. The sense of shock was followed by a wave of perspiration. She forced herself from the chair to get a drink of cold water. She grappled to compose herself, when she was startled by the phone ringing.

"Hi Mum, I thought I'd just see how you are."

Sarah was thrown. "I've just read an email from Eric. I haven't yet had time to take it all in."

"What do you mean, what did he say?" Florence rushed her words. "Calm down Florence! I just have to take it at my pace. It appears that a baby girl was born on the day before the date of my UK birth certificate. The Italian records show she was born with a different first name and the parents registered as Mario and Rebecca Orengo. It was in a hospital quite near here, just across the border, which has now closed down. I am trying to stay calm as the first name is different and it may just be a coincidence."

"So what will you do now Mum? Shall I come over for a few days and we could look together?"

"Thank you Darling, but please give me some time to digest it and to think it through." Sarah needed to recover. She assured Flo she'd phone her back within a few days. To Sarah's relief, JP had late surgery that evening so she knew she'd be alone. In a bid to distract her thoughts, she turned her attention to her painting. As she pondered as to what she might paint next, she flicked into her picture file on the computer to take a closer look at the photos of Castel Vittorio.

She viewed her first shot of the modern monument and could see a list of names engraved – it looked like a war memorial. The names of the fallen were a blur. So she steered the enlarging arrow to see if she could read any. The picture enlarged on the list, and as it self-focused she could clearly read the names. Amongst the thirty or so names at least eight Orengo's were listed. The date of their deaths was November 1943. Transfixed, she scrolled down the list and read the name of a two-year-old boy and a seventy-five-year-old woman. Why on earth would they have all been killed?

The sight of her recurring new family name threw Sarah's fragility into emotional overdrive. She poured herself a large glass of wine. Then tiredness overcame her and she embraced it as a welcome escape and fell into her bed.

Sarah's first thoughts the following morning were of the monument. Once she'd made a coffee, she booted the computer into life and hit Google. She put in the date and name of the village. Up came a few paragraphs of murders by the Nazis throughout the Nervia valley, including Castel Vittorio and Pigna, all within a week of each other. When the doorbell rang she was reluctant to answer, but reasoned she may as well tell JP sooner rather than later.

"Bonjour, Ma Cherie, I have brought the breakfast croissants. I missed you last evening." JP was upbeat as he lovingly kissed her, then he noticed her face. "Ma Cherie, you look like you didn't sleep very well, are you okay?"

"JP, I've been very upset. It is all quite personal and I want to tell you, but let's wait until tonight as I know you will need to be at the surgery soon.

"No, my first patient is at ten and you are much more important. Tell me all." Sarah took her time. She poured them both a coffee, and JP listened patiently as she spoke. She laid bare her whole journey, including the anxiety attacks, the adoption, the search and where she was at now. He listened, fascinated.

"Well, Ma Cherie, I think it sounds too much of a coincidence that a baby was born with those details a day before you think you were born. I am sure details were lost in translation during the change of countries and the adoption process. You should pursue this Orengo man, he may still be alive and if you meet him I am sure he will tell you your true story; if not, perhaps his relatives know something."

JP expounded like a professional. Sarah felt salvaged, kissed him and invited him for a home-cooked English meal that evening. Over dinner, Sarah began the conversation. "I've decided to invite Florence over to stay, as she can take some days off in two weeks' time and by then, we will hopefully have some more information to continue the search."

JP gave an aggrieved glance. "Will I be invited to help you as well?"

"Of course, but just let me take this at my speed, JP." She gently brushed his cheek with her lips.

"I'm thinking tomorrow I would like to visit this romantic Italian village with you, as I have lived so near all my life and never visited. Perhaps we can have lunch at the local restaurant, and I can see this water well you have painted." JP had reverted back to his romantically-inclined self.

"Okay, but you can drive, as it's a very tricky road."

Forty

They rose early next morning to the voluminous peel of the Basilica bells heralding a Saturday of weddings. JP had packed a chill bag with bottled water and honey melon. He carried his rather large, out-of-date camera. "We may wish to stop along the way; I always like to be prepared". His car was meticulously clean and tidy. As they drove, they chatted through the facts about Sarah's birth parents. There was definitely no hospital in Ventimiglia anymore, but JP remembered as a boy his surgeon-father being called there to emergencies.

They stopped at Dolce Aqua where JP walked Sarah to the famous stone arched bridge, and asked a passer-by to take their photo. "Your Italian sounds very fluent!" Sarah commented as they returned to the car, arm in arm.

"Growing up in Menton, we always seemed to be switching from one language to the other, I am sure it's the same in most border towns." As they neared Pigna, Sarah began to feel quite ill. JP noted that her colour had drained and he pulled the car over.

"Ma Cherie, what is wrong, is it your head?" He gently took her pulse. "Your heart is beating very quickly. What is making you so anxious?"

Sarah felt self-conscious. "I'm so sorry. I'm sure it will pass. It's happened before; perhaps it's car-sickness or the altitude. I have no control of it, and previously it's just passed best we keep driving." They'd pulled in close to the spot near the restaurant Sarah had eaten at with her friends

Mary and Peter. Castel Vittorio was in full view, looming above them in the morning sun. JP drove slowly and safely up the last incline and Sarah forced a smile to reassure him she was okay.

Once they'd parked they stepped over to the side of the road and looked out across the valley. "Breathe in this wonderful air, Ma Cherie, and we will just take our walk slowly. Your colour is returning; you have no need to be anxious and you have your very own doctor with you." His smile was full of mischief and Sarah was comfortable enough after her episode to move on.

They stood for a while and read the names on the monument – Sarah counted the eight Orengo's out of the thirty people and spoke each name out loud from the list. Then they slowly, reflectively, meandered up the narrow, uneven lane into the village.

"This square is not exactly beautiful, but I can see why you want to paint it. The lack of people gives off a sense of despair. Our French medieval villages around Menton have been commercialised, but this one feels like it is still in its past," JP commented, as they passed two older, grey-haired ladies dressed in black, with head scarves, who studied them inquisitively.

"I didn't see any other tourists on my last visit so I guess we are a bit of a novelty for them, but I did see a woman painting and thought it would be great to have a chat with her, assuming that she's a local". Sarah led him up to the Church, which was unfortunately locked, so they walked behind the bell tower where many of the houses appeared almost derelict.

She spotted a 'for-sale' sign, so she climbed the few

entrance stairs to have a closer look. It was obviously empty and the front door was slightly ajar. She removed her sunglasses and peered in, and was confronted with an unexpected scene. She could see an old, rusty iron bedstead, with a faded, ticking mattress, a trunk open with several partially-burned, leather-covered books and two wooden balloon-backed chairs.

"JP, come and see! This is as if time has stood still. The décor looks as if it is from at least the 'forties." She quickly took a few photos.

"Ma Cherie, I feel as if we are intruding. Let's go on." They progressed along to the next gloomy street, and then there was some respite. An obviously occupied house stood bravely between two decaying neighbouring houses. It flaunted a carefully restored façade, which was enhanced by colourful geraniums that were lovingly potted in its window boxes and fresh white net curtains that hung immaculately in the windows. The windows sat comfortably on either side of an ornate green painted door. They took a break on the outdoor seat that had been placed conveniently near the door.

There was a shuffling noise inside followed by raised voices, the second voice giving out distinct grunting sounds. Sarah stood up. "That sounds like a deaf person." A fresh surge of cold perspiration swept through her entire body.

"Yes I think you are right. The other person is telling her to quieten down. Let's go and have some lunch Sarah, you seem to be clammy again. Perhaps you are getting the flu." JP swiftly moved her on and they returned back the way they came.

"That voice troubled me, JP. It's been a long time since I had anything to do with deaf people. My first job when I finished university was as a teacher to the deaf. I do hope whoever it is has not been stuck up here and been deprived of the help that's available."

"It's perhaps remote, but it is the twenty-first century, Ma Cherie, and the Italians adore their children, so I hardly think he or she would have missed out. I just think we had been looking at that derelict house and then hearing a voice without seeing the person, has exaggerated the situation." He encouragingly took her arm, as he led her towards the restaurant.

"Ciao, welcome!" the owner enthusiastically greeted them. He was an older man with a craggy, lined face, and a thick snatch of wiry grey hair. He limped slightly, as he ushered them to a table with a magnificent view of the valley. Sarah removed her sunglasses and, as she endeavoured to decipher the menu, she noticed that JP was looking keenly at someone or something behind her. She turned around to see what had caught his attention, assuming it would be a beautiful Italian woman.

It took a moment for her to register. He'd focussed on a painting hanging on the wall. "Sacré bleu! Sarah, this is almost exactly the same painting as yours. I didn't know you had been here before?" He'd stood up to take a closer look. It was exactly the same scene as the one Sarah had painted, but this one had what looked like the image of a small girl standing by the water well .It had been framed in rather an amateur fashion. Sarah gaped, fixated, beside him.

"I've never been in here before and I've never previously seen that painting. I can't believe someone could paint so precisely the same as me, even with the extra blues and in oils. How weird! This feels surreal to me, like I am a part of a Stephen King movie." At this point the owner approached them.

"Who painted this picture Signor?" JP questioned in his best Italian. The owner gave Sarah a second look, and then paused before he responded. "A lady from this village. I'm happy to display them as they brighten up the place". He then pressed them to order, before rapidly retreating to the kitchen.

"JP, I'm not sure what we just ordered, but I think I've lost my appetite." Sarah was disturbed with this latest coincidence. She agitatedly sipped a glass of water. "You must calm down, Ma Cherie. Have a little pasta and a glass of wine. This painting is just a coincidence; it cannot hurt you, and there will be an explanation."

They ate their meal in silence. Sarah finally spoke. "My mind is spinning with the family-name of my birth-father and the fact that I may have been born less than a few miles from here, and now this painting business. I wonder if the woman I saw the other day painted it. I really do feel unwell – I think I'd rather just go home now, please."

Once they'd arrived back down on the coast Sarah appeared to have re-gained control of herself. Relieved, JP prudently remained silent for the rest of the drive home. On arrival at her apartment, Sarah gave JP a kiss. "Thanks for today JP, and for being so understanding. You probably think I'm totally neurotic. I'm sorry that you have become involved. I just need to be on my own tonight and make a decision as to where I go next with the search."

He held her hands inside the hallway. "I don't think you are neurotic, I was affected seeing that painting. On top of that, you have been through a lot. For what it's worth, my instincts think something good will come of it all. Also, I want to be involved. " His fingers lightly caressed her face.

"Please answer one thing, when you were upset you said

you felt like you were in a Stephen King movie. What does that mean?" Sarah gave a thankful chuckle. "Surely you know who he is. His speciality is writing science-fiction in seemingly normal situations. That's how I feel, as if something supernatural is happening to me." She gave him a gentle push in the direction of the open door.

"Please, may I see you tomorrow evening, Ma Cherie? You may need my professional services." He flashed her one of his compelling, familiar smiles.

She melted. "I have a late French lesson with Madame Dubot, so let's say seven-thirty."

Forty-one

Sarah had spent most of her day going over all the information she had about Mario Orengo. Her mind was still in turmoil when she arrived at Madame Dubot's villa. "Bonjour Sarah, comment ça va?" Madame insisted only French was spoken at these sessions, but when she observed the drastic change in Sarah's usually happy demeanour she reverted to English.

"Can I make you a tea or coffee? You look like you may have had too much heat?" Sarah graciously accepted some tea. "I'm sorry Madame, I've been having a difficult time with myself, but thought coming for my lesson would help distract me. Perhaps I should leave it and come another time?"

"Sometimes Sarah, it's good to talk to someone removed from a situation. I am here and have nothing else to do, so if you feel comfortable I'm a very good listener" Madame relaxed back in her chair. Sarah cleared her throat. She told Madame most of it. She began with her mental state, her anxiety attacks, and the missing feeling she'd always had. Then she moved on to the adoption search details. As she spoke, the realisation dawned on her that it all may be tied somehow with her visits to Castel Vittorio. Madame listened intently.

When Sarah had recalled the part where she'd seen the identical painting in the restaurant Madame raised her hand. "Sarah, please excuse me a minute, I need to use the bathroom." As the old woman had turned to walk inside, she held her hands to her eyes. Ten minutes later she returned, wearing her sunglasses and carrying a jug of fresh iced-tea. "I'm sorry Madame; I shouldn't be boring you with all this. I'll have my tea and leave you in peace."

"Sarah, you are not boring me; quite the contrary. I think it's safe to say we are friends now, so stay to chat some more, and now please call me Sylvie, as Madame is so formal." Feeling at ease Sarah continued.

"The really weird thing is up in the village on the same visit JP and I heard this woman talking loudly from inside a house. I couldn't understand the words but I knew from my experience with speech therapy that she was deaf. I felt a crazy urge to go in and see if I could assist her in some way with her speech. In fact, knowing now as much as I do about my birth-father and where I am sure I was born, there are most likely relatives of mine all over the area."

Sarah felt slightly disadvantaged not being able to see Madame's eyes behind the dark sunglasses. The old lady seemed to struggle with her response. "I think everything you are experiencing must be normal for someone just discovering where they originally come from. There is no getting away from our birthright. You may well be the baby who was born in Ventimiglia all that time ago; the records may not be entirely accurate. If I was in your situation, I would go back up the Nervia valley to Pigna and Castel Vittorio and start asking about Mario Orengo. From what you have told me it seems like a good starting place."

Sarah felt a surge of reassurance. "Thank you Madame, I mean Sylvie, I feel so much better talking this out with you. I'm so pleased we're friends." The two women walked together towards the gate. "Sarah, I'm sure it wouldn't do any harm to knock on the door of that house where you heard the deaf woman. She may welcome some support. Italian women are always friendly no matter how foreign you are. Also, why not go back to the restaurant as well and press the owner to introduce you to the person who painted the picture?"

Sylvie then surprisingly embraced Sarah, who was a little puzzled when she noticed the older woman's teary eyes. On her way home, Sarah bought some fresh salad vegetables at the small market stall. The stall owner recognised her as a regular and attempted his English as he handed her a bunch of free parsley with a cheeky wink. She had only been in the door a few minutes when JP arrived.

"Sorry Darling, I haven't got the meal quite ready yet. I was a long time with Sylvie. She was so welcoming; I really feel I have a new friend in her." Sarah gave him a peck on the cheek. "I am so glad. You seem much calmer, Ma Cherie, but who exactly is this Sylvie?" Sarah detected a hint of envy.

"Oh, don't be threatened. She is Madame Dubot, my French teacher. Now we are friendly she asked me to call her Sylvie."

"I didn't realise it was that Sylvie! I think she was Sylvie Reiss before she married. She was an old friend of my fathers and is a very educated lady. She was divorced from the Marseilles man she married and it made much gossip with my parents' friends at the time. She must be quite old now."

Sarah served the salad with cold meats and some hot baby-potatoes and gave the rosé to JP to open. "Is this an English tradition, cold meat, at supper time?" Sarah glared back at him. "No, it's not. It's an easy, tasty meal because

I've been in a rush. And, quite frankly, if you don't like it you can go home and cook your own."

His eye's widened. "I was only making a joke, Ma Cherie. Please don't be angry! Anything from your hands I will eat – please forgive me."

Sarah's landline rang before she was able to retort. "Hi Mum, it's me, you sounded quite stressed last time we spoke. Are you okay?"

"Hello Darling Florence. Yes I'm a lot better now. I'm just coming to terms with all this information about Mario Orengo. I feel sure I was the baby born in Ventimiglia that Eric Watson has identified. So my next step is to somehow start making enquiries in Ventimiglia and the villages up the valley. I 'll probably need a translator of some sort."

"Mum, I really would like to come and do this with you. It's very important to me as well. I'll look at some flights. Do you know anyone who can translate?" Sarah saw this as her opportunity to come clean about JP.

"Yes, I have a new friend who speaks Italian. Actually I think it's a good idea for you to come over. I'm missing you and also would like you to meet my friend, he's become rather special." There was a mute pause on the end of the phone.

"What do you mean? A man! My God Mum, Dad isn't even cold in his grave yet! You can't be seeing someone, surely." Sarah placated her daughter. "We'll talk about it when you are here, face-to-face. I'm your Mother first and foremost. However I'm not going to live my life like a nun." Florence said a curt goodbye.

Sarah had completely forgotten about JP. He'd eaten all his meal, like a good school boy and sat waiting for reconciliation. "Sorry JP, I forgot you were there. I needed to talk with my daughter, she's coming to visit."

"Will she not approve of me?"

"It's not you personally; it would be any man. However, she'll get used to the idea eventually and I'm sure once she meets you she will love you as much as I do, cooked or cold meals and all."

Feeling guilty for her previous outburst, she gave him a seductive smile, as she leant over to kiss him. He receptively prolonged the kiss, then steered her off to the bedroom where he tenderly made love to her with the skill and passion that became pleasurably strengthened each time.

The next morning Sarah had received a somewhat condescending email from Florence saying that she may have been a bit over-reactive about the 'new man' on the phone. She'd be willing to meet him when she arrived in Menton. Florence hadn't wasted any time calling her brother as the next email was from Nicholas who used phrases such as "I hope he is financially independent" and "be very wary of foreign French men."

Sarah giggled as she typed her response in a joint email to both children. She advised them of JP's name, his divorced status and his profession, knowing that a doctor sat up there with a lawyer in their book. She did, however, omit to mention his age.

The next email waiting in her 'in' box was from Eric Watson. He'd attached a scanned copy of Rebecca Orengo's hospital birth certificate. Sarah opened it and hit print without looking at it on her screen. She made herself a coffee before sitting down to study it. Although it was written in Italian, the name was clear for her to read on the old-style document – Rebecca Orengo'. It sent a small shiver through her as she spoke both names out loud. So, if this was her birth certificate, was her real first name Rebecca and had her English mother been married to her Italian father? But why would they have split up? She continued to gaze at the document when the doorbell interrupted her thoughts.

"Bonjour, Ma Cherie. I had a patient cancel so thought I would have my lunch with you. I have brought us both a piece of courgette tort. We can eat it cold, it's delicious." JP took the document out of her hand and proceeded to read it, translating it out loud into English. "I appreciate your help JP, but I can read all the relevant details. My current challenge is just how to progress."

He selected his words carefully. "I heard you tell Florence you had a friend to translate. I don't want to impose, and my Italian is not that great, but please consider me? I am your lover and I want to be involved."

Sarah scrutinised him lovingly. "Of course, that's what I meant when I spoke to her. I thought immediately of you. Although, you may want to reconsider, she will be a bit difficult to begin with; she is after all her mother's daughter."

Despite her raised anxiety Sarah's week passed quickly. She busied herself preparing the second bedroom for Florence, who would be her very first official house guest. After a struggle with her limited French, she managed to order and have a bed and mattress delivered from the local furniture shop.

In her favourite antique shop she'd found another perfect marble-topped chest of drawers. The marble was a little cracked, but it worked with the era of the apartment. The owners Patrick and Vera delivered the chest of drawers along with an interesting turquoise vase Sarah had picked out. She offered them a drink and then took the opportunity to thank them for the introduction to Sylvie.

"Ah, so you call her Sylvie!" Vera replied, with a certain tone to her voice. "She must like you very much as, being an ex-school mistress, she is usually quite formal and we would only dear to address her as Madame." Sensitive to small town gossip, Sarah kept her response to a minimum. "Yes I think I can confidently say we have become good friends."

The new bed was made up charmingly with a classic French blue-and-white bedspread. It worked well with the coordinated blue scatter cushions and the chest of drawers, with their dark wood-polished finish and ornamental brass keys. As a final touch, she sat the turquoise vase on the marble top with a mind to fill it with roses.

No sooner had Sarah completed the new bedroom, when JP arrived. In his typically French manner, he surveyed the new décor. "I think possibly the walls are a little bare, perhaps a painting should go just here." He pointed to the wall behind the bed. "Thank you JP, I will bear that in mind, but actually I like the minimalism of it with bare walls and the focus on the view."

He gave a snort, which Sarah ignored and then they moved to the salon to share a bottle of wine. "JP, I just want to talk a little about Florence arriving to visit. This will be a first for both of us, as well as for Florence. You don't have children, so it may be a little more difficult for you to deal with it. My daughter has only ever known me with her father, so to begin with, I think it best if we are a little discreet with open signs of affection, until she is used to the situation."

She took a large sip of her wine, in expectation of a barrage of French indignation. "Ma Cherie, I am not a child. You do not have to spell things out. I may not have had children but I do work closely with people every day, so naturally I have thought this through and you have my word, I will act in a suitable manner." His delivery was spoken with a pleasant sense of wisdom and finality.

"Now that is all said, let's eat at the pizza place. Perhaps I can still hold your hand and enjoy our last night of freedom together, for a while at least."

Forty-two

Sarah rose at 7a.m. and arrived at the market by 7.30.a.m. to buy her roses and fresh vegetables for the evening's special meal with her daughter. She'd managed to push her recent apprehensions to the background whilst she immersed her attention in lovingly arranging the peony roses. Back at the apartment she'd scrutinised the spare bedroom. She'd taken JP's comment on board and held up her water well painting against the blank wall to see if it would work with the blue of the bedspread. A hot flush swept over her, again. She took it as some kind of 'sign', and laid the painting on the bed. In a bid to cool down, she sat on the bedside chair. As she examined the painting, she deliberated how precise she'd been about choosing the extra colour, mainly strong blues, to make the water well appear less gloomy. It was spooky how similar her painting and the one in the restaurant were.

Then she attempted to compartmentalise her anxiety and rationalise how someone else could have painted the same subject in exactly the same way. Curiosity had replaced her angst and she decided that she must go back up to the village as soon as possible to question the restaurant owner and find out exactly who had painted the picture.

Sarah glanced at her watch, suddenly realising that time had slipped away on her. Hurriedly she refreshed her makeup, eager to arrive at the airport in good time to meet Florence's plane. As her daughter stepped out of the arrival hall, Sarah studied her with pride. She looked so smart in her white jeans and navy and white striped t-shirt. All perfectly styled for the Riviera; even her plimsolls were the exact shade of navy with white edging, and pristine clean.

Mother and daughter embraced with joyous eyes. "Mum you're looking so tanned and beautiful. I guess this new man must be doing something right," she chatted as they sped up the motorway.

"Yes Darling, he's done most things right so far. I haven't been the easiest person to be around with my emotions all over the place. However I really need to concentrate driving on this motorway, as the big trucks scare the hell out of me, so let's save the emotional conversation for once we're at the apartment."

Flo continued to chat. "I'm most impressed with how clever you are with driving on the right and parking in this narrow street, it's like you have a whole new set of skills Mum!"

"I now have a whole new life, so I guess the new skills follow. I do hope you like my apartment, there's not much modern in it." Sarah contemplated her daughter's contrasting taste as she'd pulled up directly outside Maison Manera. "Wow Mum, this building is glorious! I love the frescos, the staircase, everything! It reeks of atmosphere."

Flo made no immediate comment as they entered the apartment. She walked through into every room, taking in all the detail, while Sarah went to the kitchen. "Mum, I can see a whole new part of you in this apartment. It feels so 'you' if that makes sense. Not my family home with you, Nick and Dad, but a 'Sarah' place. I'm so proud of you."

Sarah hugged her daughter. "Do you mean to hang that painting that's on my bed?"

"Sorry Darling, I rushed out and forgot to remove it. I had

thought about hanging it but, knowing you probably prefer the minimal touch, I think I will just leave the walls bare, what do you think?" They'd moved through to the bedroom.

"It must be one of the first paintings you have painted in your new life, so I'd love it anyway. But I think somehow it would be better positioned in the hall." She carried the painting there and held it up. "Just here, would be great Mum. Have you any picture hooks? Let's do it straight away."

Sarah scrabbled around to find the hammer and a picture hook. Flo's trained eyes seem to know exactly where the painting should hang. "You are absolutely right Flo. It is actually my first and only painting so far."

"When do I get to meet this JP who has stolen my mother's heart?"

"I thought tonight, just you and I would have supper together and JP could join us for coffee afterwards, if that suits you? Either that, or, I can hold off until tomorrow if you want." Then she softly added, "He only lives across the hall."

Florence's eyes opened wide "Mum how bad is that! Or should I say, how convenient!"

Mother and daughter enjoyed a two-course meal. The starter was the fresh pasta Sarah had purchased at the market sprinkled with local fungi, Florence's favourite vegetable. Next, a veal chop, cooked with a little butter and fresh sage, and salad, all washed down with wonderful red wine from the Italian village of Dolce Aqua.

"These tomatoes have to be the best I've ever tasted. The Italians really have the edge on tomatoes and red wine," Florence commented as she poured herself a second large glass.

"Actually, the village that wine is from is in the area

where I think I was born. I thought we might discuss with JP what timing would suit him to assist us with our search. I think we're probably best to start at the Mairie in Ventimiglia – that's similar to the local town hall and local council. They should have the names of rate payers in the area."

This was the first time the birth parent search has been mentioned and Florence treaded cautiously with her reply. "Sounds fine with me Mum, Just whatever you think's best. My role is to support you and of course I am very keen to see why I have this love for all things Italian."

The doorbell chimed on the dot of nine p. m. and a well groomed, fragranced JP walked in, holding two bunches of lilacs. "Florence, meet Jean-Pierre, known as JP. JP, meet the light-of-my-life, my daughter Florence." Sarah introduced them with a mocking, formal style as they both studied each other inquisitively.

"I am pleased to meet the beautiful daughter, of my beautiful friend. May I present you both with these fragrant lilacs from the garden of one of my grateful patients?" He offered over the flowers and bowed a little, as he carried on the mock formality.

Florence graciously accepted her posy. "I'm very pleased to meet you JP." Sarah looked on; impressed that her sceptical daughter was taken with JP's charm. Leaving them to chat, she moved into the kitchen to make the coffee.

They agreed to visit the town hall in Ventimiglia on Friday morning, as it was closed on weekends. As mother and daughter walked JP to the door, he acknowledged the painting's new home. "I see you have come to terms with the painting, Ma Cherie. It looks like it belongs there, the perfect spot."

Sarah shifted the conversation along. "Good night JP." She planted a rather chaste kiss on his cheek. Bon nuit to both of you!" As Florence walked back up the hall he grabbed Sarah and kissed her swiftly on the lips. "Don't kiss me like I am your brother, Ma Cherie. I am your lover," he whispered, then promptly scooted out the door.

"Mum, what did JP mean about coming to terms with the painting?" Florence casually asked, as they sipped a Limoncello. The wine and the night cap had lowered Sarah's guard. "I wasn't sure it was the right thing to do, to burden you with all my issues. I feel I'm your mother first and foremost and I don't want you to feel all the anxieties I have need be a burden you as well." She spoke with resolve in her tone.

"Mum, I'm an adult. It doesn't really stress me. It's more that I'm concerned. What's with the painting?" Florence listened raptly as Sarah retold the entire story about her visits to Castel Vittorio and the identical painting. "Perhaps the person who painted it is connected to you – a cousin or something?"

Sarah opened up. "Yes that's what's been passing through my mind. I feel compelled to return to that village. I can't articulate the exact sentiment, but something my new friend Sylvie said has stuck in my mind."

Florence quizzed her mother. "Who's Sylvie?"

"Sylvie Dubot is my French teacher who has now become more of a friend. She's a good listener and seems to have taken to me. She must be about seventy-five, but she's as sharp-as-a-tack. Her advice was that I should just go back up to the village and ask the direct question about who painted the other painting. Also perhaps offer to help the deaf person I heard. Italian sign-language is the same as American, but quite different to British. I studied the three different versions when I did my training. Sylvie also advised me that Italians are very receptive and friendly. I think Sylvie is perhaps Jewish as JP said her maiden name was Reiss. She was apparently a friend of JP's father."

Tiredness had washed over Sarah. "Come on Flo, time for your Mum to go to bed. This night cap has hit the spot!" The next day the two women shopped and Sarah introduced her daughter to the delights of Menton. In the late afternoon, both were footsore and hot. They choose a shady spot to sit in one of the outdoor bars in the town square and ordered two glasses of chilled rosé.

"I would never do this on my own, I almost feel guilty doing it now, but it's special having my only daughter to visit." Just as Sarah spoke, she spotted Sylvie across the square dressed in a bright blue gypsy-type long skirt, a white shirt and carrying a large basket. She waved out to her to catch her attention.

"Sylvie, this is my daughter Florence." Florence immediately stood up and put her hand forward. For a moment Sylvie appeared to be lost for words. "Bonjour Florence, I am pleased to meet you." Her eyes were riveted on Florence's face.

"Hello, I am pleased to meet you too. Mum was telling me last night how nice it is for her to have made a local friend." There was another long pause as Sylvie stood, speechless; surveying Florence with a penetrative stare.

"Are you alright Sylvie?" Sarah asked gently.

"I must apologise. It's just that Florence bears an uncanny resemblance to someone I knew many years ago and, for just a moment, I drifted back."

She started to hurry off. Sarah followed. "Sylvie, just before you go a quick update. We commence our search tomorrow at Ventimiglia and after that I am definitely going to return with Florence to Castel Vittorio."

Sylvie acknowledged this with a wave as she briskly walked up the street. "That was a little strange don't you think Mum?" Florence commented.

"No, not for her. She' a little eccentric, but I have to say she was looking at you as if she'd seen a ghost."

"According to an article I read in the Daily Mail recently, we apparently all have a doppelganger." Flo added. "She must have been a beauty."

Early the next morning JP sent a text to say he was downstairs waiting at his car. "He's groomed to perfection, but then he is French!" Florence remarked discreetly to her mother, and then directly complimented JP on how pleasant his after-shave was. Sarah felt acutely aware of Flo in the back seat, knowing she'd be interpreting every glance between herself and JP.

Within fifteen minutes they'd arrived in the rather ugly town of Ventimiglia. However, the town hall was an attractive building, located on the main street. It didn't open 'till nine o'clock so they went off in search of a coffee. Sarah and JP sat in relative silence, slightly lost in their own thoughts. Florence was clearly excited. Sarah voiced what the other two were thinking, "I'm sure that after all this time Mario has passed away."

JP responded, "Well I have been thinking about it. On that birth-certificate for Rebecca Orengo it gave the father's date-of-birth from which I calculated he was twenty years old in nineteen-fifty-five, which would make him seventy-five now, which, by today's standards, isn't that old."

Sarah added, "Yes, I guess Sylvie is in her early seventies and she certainly seems to have a few years left in her." The Church bells chimed on the hour. It was nine o'clock. They walked back to the town hall where the large doors had been opened. JP confidently spoke with the receptionist who sent them through to the equivalent of the English council-tax department.

The clerk in charge appeared less responsive as JP explained their request. They agreed, where possible, not to mention it was an adoption search. The line they used was 'trying to find a distant relative'. He informed JP he wasn't sure it was legal to give out property owner names. JP grew agitated, but Florence gently tapped his arm and beckoned him to back off.

"I appreciate your frustration but let's just leave him for a bit –there may be more than one way to skin a cat." Sarah followed the other two out onto the street.

"What does this mean about cats?" JP was still uptight. Both women laughed. "Sorry JP, Flo just means we need to be a bit devious to get the information."

Sarah brushed his hand. "Ah, I see like we should bribe him?"

"Well it's not exactly what I had in mind, I thought I might go back in on my own with a little less testosterone than you exhibited and see what I can extract. What do you think Mum?"

"Worth a try, we'll wait for you on that bench!" Sarah pointed to a seat under the shade of a road side tree.

Flo refreshed her lipstick and walked back in. "You two are speaking words that are too difficult for me, but I won't get upset!" JP said.

"It's been a full twenty minutes; perhaps I should go and see what she's up too?" JP queried, just at the same time as Flo appeared from the building. "Mission almost accomplished."

As she spoke Flo did up her top button. "What happened?"

"Keep calm Mum, I basically chatted him up in my best pigeon Italian, and after I agreed to meet him for lunch on Monday, he agreed to print out and bring me the list of Orengo's on the electoral role for this area and the Orengo's who also are home owners and pay rates. So I need to be back here at 12.30 on Monday to fulfil my side of the bargain."

A wave of disappointment flooded over Sarah as they drove back to Menton. JP had offered to take Monday off work and to book into the B&B in the old Pigna village, so whichever way the search took them they could have an enjoyable evening and meal up near Castel Vittorio.

Forty-three

On Monday Sarah and JP sat for two hours in the café opposite the restaurant where Flo was with the man from the council office. Sarah's anxiety level had almost reached a fever pitch when her daughter finally appeared clutching two pieces of A4 paper. Flo sat down and all three of them peered at the lists. JP scrutinised the perspiration and raised colour on Sarah's brow.

Sarah clutched her hands tightly on her handbag, whilst JP gently rubbed her shoulder. There were three M. Orengo's listed as tax paying property owners. Only two matched with any M. Orengo's on the electoral list.

"There are no personal details other than the address listed," JP commented. Florence took out her smart phone and entered the first address. JP and Sarah looked on intrigued. She Google-mapped all three addresses. The first one was in Bordighera, which is the next town after Ventimiglia. There were two in Pigna.

"None, in Castel Vittorio?" Sarah finally spoke.

"Let's start with Bordighera first, then drive up to Pigna," JP suggested. The drive to the next small town along the coast was only five kilometres and after they'd asked a couple of people for directions, their search led them to a modern apartment.

The door was opened by a young woman of about thirty, who held a small baby. After she had listened intently to JP, she responded in very good English, "My husband is Marco Orengo, but he is only thirty-one, so not the man you are looking for. He has a few distant cousins, who live in the Nervia Valley, I think one is called Mario but he would be perhaps forty-five." They thanked her.

As they walked back to the car, Sarah's optimism wavered. "There's still one more Orengo whose age we don't know and, in addition, if this younger Mario is up in Pigna he may be able to give us some information," Florence spoke encouragingly to her mother.

The drive up the Nervia valley seemed to take for ever. Sarah was familiar with all the villages en route and, despite her nervousness, gave Florence a brief commentary as they passed by. JP added his comments here and there about the historical facts. Once they were in sight of Pigna JP recognised all the signs in Sarah. The wringing of hands, the pallor of her face and a few beads of perspiration gathered her on brow. He supportively patted her knee.

Florence's Google map showed they should take the sharp left turn up the steep cobbled road to the old part of Pigna. Once parked, the sun was setting and they needed to ask for directions, as the lanes dated back as far as the 13th century and had few street signs – and the ones they could see were almost illegible.

"I suggest we check in to the B & B and continue our visit in the morning, what do you say ladies?" Flo readily agreed and Sarah had reluctantly nodded. "Come on Mum, it's no use trying to find street numbers and names in the dark – besides this Casa Rosa looks wonderful."

JP knocked at the door and a beautiful local woman called Marisa ushered them to their rooms. Marisa and JP exchanged a few sentences in Italian, then he'd translated to the ladies that Marisa would prepare them a meal for seven p.m.

"I'm going to freshen up then have a poke around the village so I'll see you in the dining room later," Flo called out as she shut her bedroom door.

Sarah had just checked out the quirky bathroom and was in the process of refreshing her makeup when JP opened her door. "I hate the thought of you so near. Ma Cherie, when I can't sleep in your bed. Perhaps we could enjoy a petite early evening delight before your daughter returns?"

He reached for her hands and gently kissed her fingertips. "JP, Flo could walk in at any moment!"

"No she couldn't I just watched her leave from my window, let me make you feel wonderful."

They were the only guests staying in the remote guesthouse. Marisa served them a delicious meal of fresh pasta followed by poached figs in filo. The dining room windows looked back from Pigna up across the valley to Castel Vittorio. With no street lights between the two villages, once the sun had set, Castel Vittorio's nightlights began to dance like tiny doors in heaven.

"Come on Mum you're just playing with your food, at least try the desert; it's delicious." Flo had finished every scrap of the pasta on her plate.

"My hearts not in it, I keep thinking about my father and maybe that he's eating his dinner somewhere close by." She wiped her eyes with the cloth napkin and then continued to speak.

"It's always been like this for me, as if I'm physically in a place, like with my parents at home, and at school, then in our family home together. But my mind wanders and I have no control over it. When I'm awake and often when I dream, I'm puzzlingly trying to grasp something or someone, I just can't quite reach or see. It's a sense that always frustrates me; it's repetitive and insistent and it's what made me question my own lucidity."

Sarah had placed the napkin on the table and nervously rung her hands as she gazed across the valley at the twinkling fairy lights of the floating village. "It's been worse than ever lately, I just want something or someone revealed to give me some respite."

"Tomorrow is a new day, let's all have an early night and commence fresh in the morning." United in their concern, JP affectionately squeezed Sarah's hand, as Flo leant over and supportively kissed her mother's cheek.

Immediately after breakfast and armed with vague directions from Marisa, they headed upwards from the Casa Rosa. But after a half an hour they still couldn't locate the street name. A weather-beaten older man, who had keenly observed their activity, offered to walk them to the address they'd written down. Along the way he quizzed JP as to the reason for their visit, but JP feigned a lack of Italian.

After snaking their way through more of the narrow streets they arrived at a grassy square and spotted the number of the house they were looking for. They thanked the older gent, assuming he'd leave, but he sat himself down on a near-by stone wall as if to watch for any action. JP knocked at the door. A protracted minute passed before an attractive dark haired woman of about forty appeared at the door. JP addressed her very politely and questioned if her husband was Mario Orengo, and if he might be at home. She informed them that her husband's name was Massimo Orengo and he was away at work. When JP asked if Mario was perhaps his father, she advised that his father was Massimo too, and that he'd passed away.

Florence stepped in once again and first apologised for her lack of Italian and then, with JP's assistance, pressed her to see if maybe she knew of another Mario Orengo elsewhere in the village. The woman replied too rapidly for Florence to catch, but JP was able to translate.

"She says there's a very old man called Mario who owns the restaurant across the valley, just by the Spa hotel before you drive further up the hill to Castel Vittorio. He's a very distant relative."

The old man who'd accompanied them rose from his seat on the wall and followed them as they walked briskly back down to the car. He slipped into the phone box beside the car park and then proceeded to make a local call. Sarah paid him no more attention, but Florence mused to herself that not everyone had a home phone or mobile like in London.

"That must be the restaurant I went to with my friends Mary and Peter, but I don't remember any old man working there." Sarah practically jogged to the car. It was only a short distance to the Terme restaurant situated just across the valley, up above the river. There were several customers seated at the tables as the three of them walked in, Florence and JP standing on either side of Sarah. She'd vaguely recognised the waiter from her previous visit.

Florence was first to speak. "Is Mario Orengo here please?" Her voice was taut.

"Bonjorno Señora! You have just missed him. He needed to leave, to deal with a sudden family matter; can I show you to a table?" It was JP's turn. "No thank you. We actually wished to speak with Mario. When will he be back?"

"Mario lives just up the hill in Castel Vittorio. If you are going up there ask anybody, they all know his house." The muscles in Sarah's jaw tightened, her heart pulsated. She couldn't move fast enough. JP had taken time to thank the waiter as the two women scurried out at top speed for the car.

"I am driving as fast as I safely can, Ma Cherie" JP replied to Sarah's demand to drive faster. She was momentarily distracted as they passed a rather slow motor scooter on the way up. The bright blue helmet prompted her memory of the first time she drove up there. Within minutes they'd parked at the base of the village.

"We will ask the first person we see for directions to his house. Just try and be as calm as you can Mum!" Sarah looked silently straight ahead as Flo and JP scrambled to keep up with her. The local restaurant owner stood outside his premises having a cigarette. He gestured up towards the square as he delivered a few instructions. JP didn't bother to translate.

"Follow me". They followed the route JP and Sarah had taken on the previous visit. JP paused several times to look at the numbers on the houses and they eventually arrived outside the house where they'd heard the deaf person.

"Is this it JP?" Sarah demanded. He nodded. She trembled. The other two stood back apprehensively, as they faced the green door. They all heard the distorted, raised voice of the deaf person through the open window.

Sarah inhaled and then she stepped forward to knock. As she lifted her hand to the door, the man on the scooter sidled up alongside them, carrying his blue helmet. Sarah ignored him and knocked hesitantly at the door.

As the door opened, the man with the blue helmet stepped forward. The elderly woman who had opened the door stared at Sarah and then gasped as her eyes rested on Flo. She was gently pushed aside by another woman who stood directly behind her.

Sarah focused on the second woman. A spasm of pain enveloped her body. She was transfixed. The woman who stood before her was a carbon-copy of her own self. She differed slightly as she had black hair that was flecked with grey. Sarah's eyes swept down the body of the doppelganger in fascination – she was a little heavier, but exactly the same height, exactly the same eyes and mouth.

The doppelganger returned the same intent gaze. Florence was equally mesmerised and slipped her arm inside her mother's. No one had spoken. Then the man with the helmet tenderly took Sarah's hand. She turned to face him.

"Sarah, I am Mario Orengo, your father. This is your twin sister. We call her Rebecca in memory of your late mother. She is deaf, so has some trouble speaking. I am at an advantage as we were expecting your visit for some days now. My cousin Sylvie told me of your search. I decided you would find me in your own time."

As the old man spoke in understandable English, the tears ran down his lined, rugged face. Sarah turned back from the face of her father to the face of her sister.

She could hear her heart beating; it ascended with the mixed emotion of profound joy, and the discovery of lost love.

"It all makes sense now. You are a painter aren't you Rebecca?" She spoke clearly; she looked directly at her twin so she could read her lips.

Rebecca couldn't understand the actual words, but gave the older woman an indication to speak for her.

"She saw you through the window on your previous visit with the man. But I wouldn't allow her to approach you until her father was here and we could explain everything to her." The woman spoke perfect English.

The sisters simultaneously embraced; Sarah stroked Rebecca's hand as she spoke. "All my life something has been missing and I didn't understand what it was. I am still a little confused, but I feel the darkness has gone. I feel strangely complete now being next to you."

She turned to Florence, "This is your niece Florence." The older lady translated everything Sarah said in Italian, as her twin intently read her lips.

Florence was speechless as she reached out and simultaneously took her mother's and her new Auntie's hands. As she connected between the two of them her heart soared, first with amazement, then with a whole new sense of love.

JP and Mario stood close by transfixed by the highly charged emotional scene. A group of local onlookers had gathered.

"Let's go inside." Mario took control. He ushered them all into the house. They found seats in the small living room. The walls were decorated with aged pencil sketches and bright familiar oil paintings.

Sarah scrutinised her father. "You must have so many questions Sarah. I am old but I'll be around long enough to answer them all." He then turned his attention to Florence.

"You are the exact image of your grandmother. My cousin Sylvie warned me it was like having my Rebecca back with us when she was eighteen years old. I loved your grandmother with all my heart."

Sarah then asked the obvious question. "Why were we split up?"

Mario let out a long sad sigh. "It is a long story. Something I've felt guilty about my whole life. Your Mama and I were engaged, when she became pregnant and we were so in love. I was twenty when you were born and back then, an Italian Mama had the final say in most things – and my Mama was no exception. She would have never tolerated me marrying a Jewish girl in normal circumstances, especially when the girl was already pregnant, but we had lost all the men in our family during the war except me, and Mama wanted the baby to be brought up here, no matter what.

Your mother went into labour early. I had no idea she was having twins. It was so dangerous. She was unconscious for two days and the delivery was performed by caesarean in Ventimiglia by the local doctor. My Mama had agreed with Rebecca's plan to return to London with the baby to break the news to her parents and gain their blessing for our marriage. However when there were twins Mama convinced me to conceal one of them from her just in case something happened and you both never returned.

She also convinced and manipulated all of the relevant hospital staff. She gained their sympathy as she'd lost most of her extended family in the war, so they agreed to go along with it. In the end she bullied me to agree as well. I reasoned Rebecca would forgive me when she returned and that she wouldn't cope travelling with two babies anyway. So your mother left Italy with you, never knowing she had another daughter."

There was silence in the room as they all digested this tragic statement. Mario opened a draw in the dresser and took out a worn looking leather-covered journal. Sarah sat directly next to her sister who had not let go of her hand; they smiled simultaneously as they noticed their identical wrists and the same crooked small right finger.

The older woman took up the story. "I am Sandy. Your mother and I were best friends. I married Mario's best friend, Claudio who passed away ten years ago. I live up here now and assist where I can. When your mother never returned as planned and never phoned me, Mario paid for me to travel to London and see what had happened. None of us had much money at that time. We had your English grandparents' address. I wasn't well received and they only spoke to me on the doorstep. They told me that Rebecca had been killed in a road accident; she was hit by a truck when she was out purchasing her travel tickets to return".

Sarah pushed her hands to her face. Rebecca placed her hand on her sister's knee. Sarah straightened as she attempted to compose herself.

"Sorry Sandy, please go on".

"Without giving an explanation, your mother's parents told me the baby had been adopted and there was no changing that. It was obvious they both grieved for their daughter, but your grandmother in particular was humiliated by her illegitimate granddaughter. When I returned, Mario was devastated."

Mario wiped his eyes with his hanky, and cleared his throat. "I was young and immature. Once again, I listened to my Mama, who convinced me the baby would be better off where she was. Back then, an Italian in London searching for an illegitimate baby would have been a difficult task and I was already under extreme financial pressure to provide for the baby I had."

Then Mario lovingly handed Sarah his hanky. The sombre mood of the room changed as Sarah loudly blew her nose. It triggered a fond giggle from Sandy and knowing looks from Rebecca and Mario.

"A family trait I'm afraid." Mario's cracked face gave a joyous smile.

"Was Rebecca born deaf?" Sarah gently probed.

"I think so. We discovered it when she was eighteen months old. On hindsight I was over-protective of her, but she was all I had to cling on to".

Sandy beckoned Florence to follow her into the kitchen and they returned with a large jug of fresh lemonade and a tray of glasses.

Mario continued to talk. "Never a day has gone by when I haven't thought of your Mother, my beautiful Rebecca, or you. I have suffered terrible guilt. I pray that you will be able to forgive me and that, through your redemption, we can all move forward together? The only generous gesture your English grandmother made was to give Sandy Rebecca's diary. She tells her own story so well .It expresses perfectly the love we had. Here take it, it's yours."

Epilogue

Sarah eventually married JP, and embraced Menton as her permanent home. She regularly visited her new found family and with Sandy's assistance, she skilfully and patiently taught her twin international sign language. Rebecca's new ability to communicate was her liberation. She walked with more confidence, lost weight, learnt to drive, and one of her first requests to her sister was to ask if she could take her to the Menton hairdresser.

There was much laughter in the local hair salon as the two women morphed even closer in appearance with Rebecca's matching hair style.

During the winter, Sarah would spend an evening a week at Castel Vittorio. Nestled by the open fire, Sandy and Mario watched and listened with tearful pleasure as Sarah articulately read and signed her mother's story to her sister, bringing it all to life from her well documented diary.

The deceit could never be reversed, the stolen time would never be retrieved, but the sister's lives opened out together like young sunflowers that had discovered their first burst of sun. Their roots had always been their infallible bond. Reunited, Sarah had found her missing piece and Rebecca had been given her voice.